FROM THE ENDOWMENT FUND

ROSEBUDS

Recent Titles by Margaret Mayhew from Severn House

OLD SOLDIERS NEVER DIE
OUR YANKS
THE PATHFINDER

ROSEBUDS

Margaret Mayhew

This first world edition published in Great Britain 2004 by
SEVERN HOUSE PUBLISHERS LTD of
9–15 High Street, Sutton, Surrey SM1 1DF.
This first world edition published in the USA 2004 by
SEVERN HOUSE PUBLISHERS INC of
595 Madison Avenue, New York, N.Y. 10022.

British Library Cataloguing in Publication Data

Mayhew, Margaret
    Rosebuds
    1.   Female friendship - Fiction
    2.   London (England) - Social life and customs - 20th century - Fiction
    I.   Title
    823.9'14 [F]

    ISBN 0-7278-6077-1

Typeset by Palimpsest Book Production Ltd.,
Polmont, Stirlingshire, Scotland.
Printed and bound in Great Britain by
MPG Books Ltd., Bodmin, Cornwall.

For my daughters, Ella and Tilly, so they can read about those times

And for my sister, Mary, who remembers them

Prologue

1947

The tide was going out. It had left behind ridges of wet sand like corrugated cardboard that felt bumpy beneath her bare feet as she walked down to the water's edge. She did a hop, skip and jump over some clumps of glistening, smelly seaweed and picked up a long brown ribbon, squeezing the slimy bobbles between her fingers. When they were all popped she paddled about a bit in the shallows. Because this was the last day of her first ever seaside holiday, she was trying hard to store it all up in her mind for when they went back to Surrey and she was sent away to boarding school.

Actually, she'd been to the seaside once before, but that hadn't counted as a proper holiday. They'd only gone to Brighton for the day, by train. The war had still been on and she hadn't been able to go near the sea – just look at it through a lot of rusty barbed wire put all along the beach to stop the Germans invading and people treading on mines. But the war was over now and so there was no more barbed wire or mines, and this was Cornwall, not Sussex, and so far away that it was almost like going abroad, which she'd never done. They'd stayed for three whole weeks at the Tregenna guest house at the top of the cliffs, right above the beach. The dining room had a big picture window, so she could watch the sea while she ate, and it was never dull and flat and grey like it had been that day at Brighton, but deep, glittery blue. And it wasn't the boring old English Channel, but the Atlantic, leading to the New World. She could picture explorers like Sir Francis Drake and Sir Walter Raleigh sailing off far beyond that misty horizon to discover other lands. The cove below the guest house had proper sand, not pebbles like Brighton, and spooky dark caves in the cliffs where smugglers had hidden their casks of wine and brandy in the olden days. One of her Enid Blyton adventure books was all about them, and she could easily make believe that they still came there at night with their lanterns and cutlasses, rowing in on muffled oars.

At high tide, on rough days, she'd watched the waves crashing on to the rocks at the foot of the cliffs, sending white spume flying high into the air while the water below swirled around furiously. At low tide the rocks held still pools like aquariums, with anemones, seaweed, little crabs and fish. Cornwall was tons better than Brighton.

She shut her eyes for a moment and breathed in the salty smell of the sea in a big gasp, trying to store that up as well, but she decided that smells were much harder to remember properly than things you could see or hear. Your mind didn't have a nose, like it had an eye or an ear. You couldn't really smell bacon frying, for instance, unless it actually *was*. So after a few deep breaths she gave up and opened her eyes again. The sun was making the surface of the water shimmer and sparkle prettily. She watched the waves curling over as they rode fast towards her, and she gazed into their glassy ramparts until, one after another, they collapsed into frothy bubbles that turned into a sudsy scum, like old washing-tub water, by the time they'd reached her feet. When the water all ran back again it sucked hard at the sand beneath her heels as though it wanted to drag her with it.

Out past the breaking waves a seagull was floating about, vanishing into the wave troughs and then bobbing up again like a rubber duck. Beyond it, a fishing boat chugged along in the direction of the harbour beyond the point. She could hear its engine making popping noises and see the men moving about on the deck. More seagulls were following the boat, flying along behind its stern like attendants, and weaving about with their lovely mewing cries. She watched the boat go out of sight, past the headland, and then turned back towards the beach. She could see Humphrey climbing over the rocks by the cliff, carrying his fishing net and bucket, and decided to go and have a last look at the pools there so that she could remember them properly too.

He was crouching beside the biggest one and put a finger to his lips as she scrambled towards him. 'Don't make any noise. I think there's a jolly big crab down there. I saw something huge move by the ledge just now.'

She knelt down carefully on the opposite side of the rock pool and stared into its mysterious, frondy depths – half fascinated, half repelled. You never knew what weird creatures the tide might leave behind – like that disgusting jellyfish they'd found one day, stranded on the sand, a slimy, slithery blob, like half-cooked egg white. They knew the pool was pretty deep because Humphrey had climbed down into it once and the water had almost come up to his waist, so all sorts of things might be hiding among the seaweed and under that ledge on one side. There were lots of tiny fish darting about near the surface, and limpets and anemones stuck all over the sides. The anemones were like pink flowers but she knew that they ate things.

Her plaits were dangling in the way and she flicked them back over her shoulders. '*I* can't see anything,' she said.

Humphrey kept his eyes fixed on the pool. 'He's in there somewhere. I know he is. He looked enormous!'

He would wait patiently for ages – hours, if necessary. Her brother liked patient things, like birdwatching, which she secretly thought boring, and collecting stamps and sticking them all in order in albums which was awfully fiddly. Perhaps when she was two years older she'd like those sort of things better – but then he'd be fifteen and probably doing something else, so she'd never really catch up.

The barnacles were hurting her knees and she shifted back on to her haunches. She was getting bored already and amused herself for a while by trying to pull limpets off the rock beside her. They were always too quick. You could move them a tiny bit and then they clung on too hard. Even Humphrey couldn't ever manage to surprise them. She looked down into the rock pool again and poked the tip of her forefinger gingerly into the mouth of an anemone. The pink tendrils bunched up greedily round it at once. If her finger hadn't been attached to her hand it would have been swallowed up. She pulled it out and poked it into another one.

'Don't keep doing that.' Humphrey was frowning at her. 'You'll go and scare the crab. You can't stay unless you're going to keep still and be quiet.'

'Flora! *Flora!*'

She turned her head. Her mother was calling and beckoning from where she sat in the shade, her back against a rock.

'Go on,' Humphrey said. 'She wants you.'

She trailed across the sand. It was always something. Do your homework. Eat up your supper. Turn off the wireless. Brush your teeth. Wash your hands. Go to bed. Get up . . .

At first she'd been quite excited about going to boarding school because she'd been reading *First Term at Mallory Towers*. Then Humphrey had told her it wasn't really a bit like that. They didn't have midnight feasts all the time and she'd be bossed about even more than at home. So now she was dreading it, and the nearer it got, the more she dreaded it. One week and three days left, that was all.

Her mother was holding out her hat – the one she hated with the silly floppy brim.

'Put this on, darling. The sun's very hot. I don't want you getting sunstroke.'

'*Must* I?'

'Yes, if you're going to stay out in it. Otherwise come and sit in the shade.'

She flopped down on to the sand. 'I'll stay for a *bit*.'

Her mother always fussed so much about whether she was too hot or too cold and things like that. She fussed over Humphrey, too, but he never seemed to take much notice. He wandered about wearing and doing more or less what he liked when he was home for the holidays. *And* he was allowed to stay up late and listen to the nine o'clock news and grown-up programmes on the wireless.

'What's Humphrey doing, darling?'

'Trying to catch a crab. He thinks there's a big one in that

4

pool, but I couldn't see anything.' Flora dug one foot into the sand and wriggled her toes. The sand was very dry and powdery above the high-water line, like it must be in a desert. She dug some more and uncovered a Sharp's toffee wrapper.

'Mummy, why do I have to go to boarding school?'

It was a question she had asked before and she always got more or less the same answer.

'Because it's best for you, Flora. And your father wanted you to have a good education.'

'How do you know he did?'

'Because we talked about it when you were born. He believed very strongly that girls should have just as good an education as boys.'

She buried the toffee paper again with her big toe, thrusting it down out of sight. 'I wish I could remember him properly, but I can't.'

'You were only six when he was killed, darling, and he was home so little during the war.'

'Was he awfully brave?' She had asked this question before, too, and the answer was always the same as well.

'Very brave indeed.'

He must have been, she supposed, to have flown a huge great bomber in the dark all the way to Germany and back while the enemy tried their hardest to shoot him down. He'd been given a medal for it because he'd done it lots of times – until one night he hadn't come back because the Germans had hit him . . . She hated to think about that, to imagine what it might have been like when his bomber fell down out of the sky.

She rolled over on her front and trickled sand through her fingers. 'I still don't see why I can't stay where I am at day school. I can speak some French, you know. *Je m'appelle Flora. J'ai onze ans. J'ai un frère qui s'appelle Humphrey. Il a treize ans. Je suis, tu es, il est, nous sommes, vous êtes, ils sont.* I can do the future and the imperfect too. We were going to do the perfect next term.'

'You'll do French at Beechlawn, too. And all sorts of other subjects.'

'What sort of ones?'

'Oh . . . Chemistry, physics, biology, Latin . . .'

'Latin! Yuk! Humphrey does that. But he's brilliant, isn't he? He's always winning prizes on speech days. I thought we were poor, though, and that's why he went to Christ's Hospital because you don't have to pay for him there. How can we afford for me to go to your old school?'

'We don't have to pay the full fees. They sometimes give special rates to daughters of old girls, and when you did that entrance exam so well they decided to give them to you. Only I shouldn't talk about that to the other girls at Beechlawn, if I were you.'

This was something quite new. Flora stopped playing with the sand and looked up. 'Why not?'

Her mother's head was turned away towards the sea. 'Well, I think it's best to be the same as everyone else when you live in a community like a boarding school. That's all.'

She digested this unsatisfactory answer slowly. The importance of being the same as everybody else had never occurred to her before.

'You mean the other girls'll look down on me if they find out we're poor?'

'No, of course not. I'm just saying it's better not to talk about it. Keep it to yourself.'

That *is* what she means, though, Flora thought. And she minds that we're poor. I don't think I mind very much, except I wish I could have a pony and that we could have summer holidays like this one every year. And I'd like a new bike, instead of Humphrey's old one. And a new paintbox. I can't think of anything else especially.

Humphrey was walking across the sand towards them, his fishing net over one shoulder and the bucket in his other hand. He was carrying it very carefully, so he must have caught something. She wondered if he minded about them being poor. He'd never said so and the other boys at Christ's Hospital probably would be too, so it wouldn't matter there. At home, she didn't think he cared about their having very old carpets and curtains and saggy chairs, or about wearing jumble-sale clothes and making do all the time. Anyway, his rich godfather gave him the things he really wanted, like a bigger bike and a microscope. If he wasn't out birdwatching with Daddy's old field glasses, he was arranging his stamp collection, or looking through the microscope at dead flies and things. And he spent hours and hours doing school work in the holidays, shut up in his bedroom with his nose in books and wearing the wire-framed spectacles that made him look a terrible swot. He had once told her that he wanted to be a surgeon when he grew up and so he'd have to pass a lot of exams. She didn't understand how he could possibly want to be anything so awful – cutting up people, with blood spurting everywhere – but his eyes had shone behind the spectacles when he'd talked about it.

He was looking terribly pleased now as he walked towards them, so he must have caught the crab. He set the bucket down gently on the sand.

'I got him! He wasn't quite so big as I thought, but he's still a jolly good size.'

Her mother leaned over and peered into the bucket. 'Poor thing. Doesn't he mind being in there?'

'Oh, I won't keep him long. I'll put him back in a mo. He'll be able to go off when the tide comes in again, if he wants.'

That was the nicest thing about Humphrey, Flora thought. He was very kind. And especially kind to animals. He didn't even kill the flies for his microscope but found them dead on windowsills. When he was a surgeon he'd probably be kind to all his patients, too – not like the grumpy old man who'd taken her tonsils out last year and told her to stop making such a fuss afterwards. She stood up to see the crab. It was sitting at the bottom of the bucket, waving its claws and legs about very slowly, as though it was trying to climb up the sides. It wasn't nearly as big as she'd imagined – only the size of a small saucer – but a lot larger than the little ones they usually saw in the pools.

Humphrey pointed out the interesting bits to her. 'See, those are the antennae for feeling about and those are its eyes in the middle. It's got five pairs of legs – the claws are really front legs too. And the flat part with the shell's called a cephalothorax. That just means the head and body are joined together, all in one. Spiders are made like that, too, only they don't have hard shells. The abdomen's hidden underneath.'

He knew about things like that because he learned them at school and, of course, it was all to do with wanting to be a surgeon one day. You had to know how animals worked before you started on people. She watched the crab making hopeless attempts to climb up the bucket and felt sorry for it.

'He wants to get out. He doesn't like it in there.'

'I'll take him back now,' Humphrey said. 'Do you want to come and set him free? We'll just tip him in gently. You won't have to touch him or anything.'

She smiled gratefully at her brother. He was jolly decent to her, mostly, and understood how she felt about things. They set off back to the rock pool together. Luckily, her mother had forgotten all about the hat.

'Atalanta! *Atalanta!*'

She pretended not to have heard the hated voice and turned over another page of her book. She was in the middle of reading *Little Women* for the fourth time and Jo was just telling Laurie that she couldn't marry him. Every time she got to that part she couldn't understand how Jo could possibly refuse Laurie, who was good-looking and rich and fun, and then go and marry the awful, dull Professor Bhaer, who wore spectacles, was poor as a church mouse and old as the hills. It spoiled the whole story. The voice called again and she turned over another page. A moment later her stepmother's maid put her ugly face round the door.

'Her ladyship's calling you, didn't you hear? She wants you in her bedroom at once.'

She stuck her tongue out as soon as Paget's head withdrew. The face reappeared, glaring.

'She said, *at once!*'

She plonked down the book and walked as slowly as

possible along the corridor to the bedroom that her father now shared with The Cow. She didn't bother to knock, but sauntered straight in.

Her stepmother was sitting up in the huge satin bed, wearing a peach-pink jacket with feathery bits round the edges. The headboard and bed cover were the same sort of pink, too, and so were the curtains at the windows and the couch thing at the foot of the bed. The whole room was vomit-pink, with white and gold cupboards, and it stank of the pukey French scent, *Ma Griffe*, that she always wore.

It had been lovely before *she'd* changed it all. She'd changed all sorts of other things in the house as well. Moved furniture about and sold old family stuff and put her horrible furniture there instead – chairs with gold on and silly little tables that only got in the way. She'd changed some of the servants, too, and got rid of Larkin, who'd been Papa's butler for years and years, and sacked Mrs Spicer, who made lovely puddings and cakes and let her lick out the bowl. The new butler minced around with his nose in the air and the French chef put sauces over everything and chased her out of the kitchens. She had started to change things at Melton, which was even worse, but luckily she hated the country and spent most of her time in London, shopping and getting her hair done.

'I've been calling you for a long time, Atalanta. Surely you must have heard me?'

She never called her Tally, like Papa, thank goodness – that was *his* name for her.

'Well, I didn't.'

She stared at her stepmother. The girl from Rene's had been to set her hair in its false curls. It wasn't real blonde; she knew that from snooping around in her bathroom cabinet. She was *all* false: her hair, her smile, her laugh, the way she gushed and smarmed over people and then said rude things about them behind their backs, and the way she wheedled and pouted with Papa and twisted him round her little finger. How could he not see how false she was?

When they had got married last year it had been the

worst thing that had ever happened in her life – worse than Mama going away to America and never coming back. She couldn't remember Mama at all, anyway, and wouldn't even have known what she looked like if Nanny hadn't saved a photograph of her when Papa started throwing them all away. She had left ages ago, before the war had started. She used to ask Papa questions about her, but he always put on his 'closed' face and she could tell he hated to talk about it. All he would say was that she'd gone to act in a film in Hollywood and decided to stay there and marry somebody else. In the end, she'd stopped asking questions and had hidden the photograph in the handkerchief sachet in her top drawer.

Then Papa had gone and met The Cow. The Cow had been married to someone else, too, before she married Papa, and Nicholas, her revolting son, was in the sixth form at Harrow, so she must be pretty old, however hard she tried to hide it. The first time she had seen Nicholas he had been standing in the hall, looking round with his nose in the air, as though he didn't want to be there at all, and he had given her a scornful look as she came down the stairs. Well, she didn't want him there either. Mostly he lived with his father but whenever he came to stay in the holidays she ignored him.

Her stepmother was holding up a long piece of paper. 'Did you make these marks all over your Beechlawn clothes list, Atalanta?'

She lifted her chin. 'I crossed out all the silly things. I'm not going to wear those horrible knickers, or a stupid suspender belt. Or those stockings, either.'

'You'll *have* to wear them, whether you like it or not. It's the school rules. For once, you'll have to do as you're told.'

The Cow was looking triumphant. Boarding school had been all her idea. She knew that because she'd heard them talking about it one evening when the drawing-room door had been left open. She'd sat halfway down the stairs and listened from behind the bannisters. Papa had been against it, at first, but The Cow had talked him round, the way she always did.

10

It would be the best thing for her, Hugh, don't you see?
She's outgrown a governess. Miss Miller simply can't cope
with her, and she's becoming quite uncontrollable and rude.
I do my best, of course, but I'm afraid she's been terribly
spoiled. And Nanny will be far too busy to run after her all
the time once the baby arrives.

The baby! That squalling, red-faced repulsive thing called
Thomas in *her* nursery. Papa's precious son and heir to the
title. She'd been born long before him but because she was
only a girl she could never be the heir – it wasn't fair. She'd
watched Papa bending over the cradle and seen the look on
his face; she was sure he'd never looked at her like that. And
now he seemed relieved that she was being sent away.

You'll enjoy it, Tally. Meet other girls. Good teaching.
Games and gym. All that sort of thing. Best thing for you.

He didn't realize that she was being sent miles away on
purpose because The Cow wanted to get rid of her. She'd
looked on a map and Beechlawn was on the other side of
England, almost as far as Wales. She could have gone to a
much nearer school, or even a day one in London, but The
Cow had made sure she was going as far away as possible.

Her stepmother had let the list fall on to the pink satin
bedspread and she was leaning back against the pile of
pillows, pretending to be exhausted. The baby had been born
ages ago but she still lay about in bed most of the day.

'Nanny says she doesn't know *where* she is now with
your uniform because you've made such a mess of the list.
Really, Atalanta, you're not a baby any longer, though you
still behave like one. You're eleven years old. She simply
hasn't the time to spare now for all your nonsense.'

She thought longingly and resentfully of the days when
Nanny had had all the time in the world for her, when it had
been just the two of them up in the nursery, alone together in
a lovely, cosy world of Vyella nighties and Chilprufe vests
left warming for her in front of the gas fire; of Robinsons's
groats and apple boats and bread soldiers with her boiled
egg; of bathimes splashing around in the big tub and Nanny
wrapping her up in a towel, playing 'This Little Piggy Went

11

to Market' as she dried her toes; of Nanny reading to her from all the Pooh books and *A Child's Garden of Verses*; of Nanny hearing her prayers and tucking her up tightly and singing 'Golden Slumbers' before she put out the light. She had a huge lump in her throat now, just from remembering it all, and had to swallow very hard.

There was a tap at the door and she saw Nanny coming into the bedroom, carrying the hated bundle that was Thomas, smiling and cooing at him.

'There's a little pet . . . our good little boy.'

Tally brushed her hand over her eyes. Nobody was paying *her* any attention. She slipped, unnoticed, out of the room.

PART ONE

One

As soon as Flora opened her eyes she knew what day it was. Her stomach knew, too, because it had a sinking feeling, like going down fast in a lift. Last night it hadn't been a bit fooled by her favourite supper – fish and chips and queen of puddings. People being hanged at dawn must feel just the same. She had gone to bed with everything churning around inside her and tried her hardest to stay awake, to make her last night at home last as long as possible, but in the end she'd fallen fast asleep. The next thing she knew, daylight was coming round the edges of the curtains and through the gap in the middle where they didn't quite meet. There were only hours, not days, left to count now – seven of them – before they would have to leave to catch the train that was going to take her far away from home.

She turned her head and looked at the oblong shape of the old trunk across the room. It was crouching there, ready and waiting, lid closed, big brass clasps snapped shut. Her mother had painted out her own initials and put FCM there instead. Flora Constance (after her grandmother) Middleton. It was scratched and scored from many journeys and one of the leather handles had had to be replaced. Inside lay everything on the school list, except what she was going to wear today. She had watched the trunk filling up relentlessly in the week since they had returned from Cornwall, and the higher the level, the lower her heart had sunk. She'd never had so many new clothes in her whole life, but she hated them all. There were only two things in the trunk that cheered her up a bit: the tin of sweets at the very bottom, and the beautiful new mottled-green Swan

15

fountain pen that was tucked away safely in a little loop in the writing case.

It was light enough to see the clothes that she was going to have to put on, laid out on the chair, and the stiff new lace-up walking shoes on the floor. The two pairs of knickers, the vest, the blouse, the grey pleated skirt and the red and white striped tie that she still couldn't manage to do properly. And, most frightening and horrible of all, the stockings that she'd never worn before and the pink suspender belt with hooks and eyes and dangling metal bits that somehow had to be put on right and attached to each other.

She averted her eyes from the sight of them and wriggled her toes around at the bottom of the bed until they came up against the comforting weight of Hercules. He was curled up on the eiderdown in a big ball and, as she prodded him from under the bedclothes, he lifted his head and looked at her reproachfully. If only he could come with her she wouldn't feel nearly so bad. He had climbed into the trunk several times while it was being packed, and once she'd found him fast asleep on her games sweater. The thought of leaving him for three long months made tears come into her eyes. He always slept at the end of her bed. It was she who fed him and brushed his glossy black fur, when he allowed it, and petted him and made the most fuss of him. He'd be bound to miss her as much as she'd miss him. Not that he was looking very worried at the moment. He was yawning, opening his jaws as wide as they would go so that she could see all his sharp white teeth and his rough pink tongue and the dark beginning of his throat. He uncurled himself slowly and got up and stretched out his front claws, making pinpricks in the eiderdown. Then, tail held high, he picked his way up the bed to let her stroke him, purring brokenly like a faulty motor as she rubbed his ear. A tear trickled down her cheek and she wiped it away. She wanted him to stay with her but he soon jumped down and made his way towards the bedroom door. It was time for his morning saucer of milk.

At breakfast her mother was all bright and jolly, as though it was a perfectly normal day. Flora toyed sulkily with her cornflakes. How could she be so cheerful? Didn't she *care* that she was going miles and miles away in just a few hours' time? Even Humphrey didn't seem to mind – he was eating his toast as though there was nothing wrong at all. He caught her indignant stare and grinned.

'Cheer up, Flo! You're looking as though the end of the world is nigh.'

'It *is* for me,' she said tragically. Tears were coming again. *Nobody* cared. Hercules had gone straight out into the garden as soon as he'd finished his milk and she might not see him again before she had to leave.

Humphrey scraped margarine across his toast. 'I felt like that in my first term, actually.'

She sniffed and wiped her nose with the back of her hand. 'You didn't have to wear my silly uniform.'

'Mine seemed pretty silly too, having to wear a skirt.'

She hadn't thought of that. The Christ's Hospital uniform was the same as the boys had worn in olden days – long-skirted coats with knee breeches and yellow stockings, and a white cravat instead of a tie. But Humphrey looked nice in it. It suited him. Nobody could look nice in hers.

After breakfast she went out into the garden. There was no sign of Hercules. All his favourite snoozing spots were empty – the hollow under the jasmine bush by the fence, the corner of the compost heap, the old trug in the tool shed. She went to feed Desdemona and to clean out her hutch. The rabbit heard her coming and hopped out of her sleeping compartment. She had a lovely big hutch in a sheltered corner and a moveable chicken coop run so that she could go out on the lawn and eat grass. Flora loved her long white fur and her pink eyes. Othello, Humphrey's black rabbit, had burrowed out of the chicken coop run one day and escaped, never to be seen again, but Desdemona never tried. You could leave the hutch door wide open and she didn't even bother to hop out.

She cleaned out the sleeping compartment and put new straw in there and fresh sawdust in the day run. Then she filled the bowl with clean water and gave Desdemona the carrots and cabbage leaves she'd brought.

17

'I'm going away,' Flora told her solemnly. 'But Mummy's going to look after you, and she's promised to give you all the things you like, so you mustn't worry.'

Desdemona didn't look any more worried than Hercules. Flora watched her for a while. Desdemona didn't communicate as well as Hercules. Actually, she didn't communicate much at all, but she'd miss her just the same.

The September sun, warm on her back, was climbing higher and higher in the sky and the morning was slipping away. Only four more hours left.

In the back of the Rolls, on the way to the station, her father kept telling her how much she was going to enjoy herself.

'You'll have lots of fun with all the other girls, instead of being on your own. Best years of my life, my school days. Only wish I was your age again.'

She didn't answer him – just stared out of the car window. It was stuffy in the car and her silly uniform was much too hot. The Cow was still at home – lying about in bed, of course – not that she'd wanted *her* to come and gloat. They were swinging round Belgrave Square and the swimmy motion was making her feel sick. Her father lit a cigarette, which made her feel worse. Once, coming home from the dentist, she'd been sick all over the beige carpet. Morecambe had been pretty decent about that, considering he'd had to clear it up. She looked at the back of his head through the glass partition – a bit of his hair, all grizzled like a badger, showed beneath the cap. He was terribly old and had very white false teeth that he could make fall down for her when she asked and he'd taught her how to do the same with her plate. She liked Morecambe a lot. He'd been Grandpapa's chauffeur before he'd been Papa's and during the war, when there'd been almost no petrol and the Rolls had been put away, he'd stayed at Melton with her and Nanny and done all sorts of odd jobs round the house and gardens. The Cow had tried to get rid of him because he was so old but Papa had stuck up for him and said he'd been with the family so long that he couldn't sack him. She'd overheard them arguing about it, but for once The Cow hadn't got her own way.

They went round Hyde Park Corner, up Park Lane and along the Bayswater Road, and just as she thought she really *was* going to be sick any minute, Morecambe turned the Rolls down a sloping entrance and they were at Paddington station. He touched his cap as he opened the door and winked at her quickly. And when she turned back to wave at him, he gave her another wink and a thumbs-up sign.

The station smelled of soot and smoke and steam and there was a huge glass roof overhead and pigeons flying about. When she walked down platform one with Papa she could see other girls standing about in the same horrible uniform. An old woman in a brown suit came up to them, brandishing a list.

'Are you one of the new girls?' she barked at Tally but didn't wait for an answer. 'Find yourself a seat quickly. The train will be leaving soon. And put your boater on straight.' She strode on.

The third-class carriages had RESERVED FOR BEECH-LAWN GIRLS' COLLEGE pasted on the windows. She'd only travelled first-class before and they looked dirty and uncomfortable, as well as full. They found some empty seats in a compartment near the very front. Three girls were sitting in there, huddled together, their boaters touching, giggling. As Tally climbed in they turned and stared at her rudely and then went back into their huddle. She put her overnight case down on one of the empty seats. Her father was hovering on the platform.

'All set then, Tally?' He had to raise his voice above the hissing from the engine. Doors were slamming all along the train and she pulled hers shut and tugged at the leather strap to lower the window. Papa looked at his watch and tapped it. 'Better be off. Meeting in the City . . .'

She nodded stiffly. She knew he was terrified that she might suddenly burst into tears or make a scene.

'Goodbye, Papa.'

He leaned forward and kissed her, his moustache tickling

her cheek. He smelled of the lovely lemony cologne he always wore and, just for a moment, he looked a bit sorry. Then his face cleared. 'Well, good luck, old thing. Write and let us know how you're getting on.'

She watched him as he walked away down the platform, straight-backed, tall and handsome – much more handsome than any of the other fathers. Some of the mothers turned round to look at him. Then he was out of her sight, lost in the crowds. She heaved her case up on to the luggage rack and sat down. One of the three girls looked round. She had a snub nose, just like a pig. 'You're a new girl, aren't you? What house are you in?'

'St Cecilia's.'

'Oh, the *Junior* School. One of the *babies*! You shouldn't be in here with us. We're all Middle School.'

'Well, I'm not moving.'

She out-stared the girl and the three of them put their boaters together again and started whispering. Tally ignored them. She sat looking out of the window, chin up, waiting for the train to move.

Humphrey stuck his head round the bedroom door as Flora was struggling with her uniform. 'Got something for you to take.'

It was a big bag of sweets – humbugs, treacle toffees, aniseed balls, fizzy yellow sherbets, liquorice bootlaces, all the things she liked best. It must have been most of his ration. Tears welled up; she stared into the bag, blinking.

'I say, thanks *tons*.'

'Want some help with the tie?' He showed her again how to tie it, turning her by the shoulders to face the looking glass on the wardrobe door. 'Look, the wide end goes on this side and you make it longer than the other. Then it's right over left, and over once more, and then under and up and then down again, through the loop . . . then you just pull on the ends till they're almost even. See? Easy!'

It still didn't seem a bit easy to her. She made a face at her reflection and sighed. Everything looked really soppy and was all too big for her so it would last. She peered closer, sure she'd sprouted even more freckles since Cornwall. They were all over her face.

Humphrey came to the station in the taxi as well. Her trunk wouldn't fit properly in the boot and had to be tied on with rope; she kept turning round to look through the back window, hoping it had fallen off so they'd miss the train. Her mother fussed all the way there.

'Have you got a clean handkerchief in your pocket, Flora?'

'Yes.'

'And your health certificate?'

'*Yes.*'

That was in her coat pocket, too. *This is to certify that Flora Middleton has not been in contact with any infectious diseases during the past two weeks. Signed Katherine Middleton.*

When Sally next door had gone down with chicken pox she'd had high hopes, but her mother had squashed them. 'You had chicken pox when you were two – you caught it from Humphrey. You can't get it again.'

So that was that. The last chance gone. And when they stood on the platform at Reading station, waiting for the London train to come in, her stomach knew that this was finally the end. No more weeks, or days, or even hours left to count – only minutes. She could already hear a chuffing sound in the distance.

And then everything happened so quickly that she didn't have time to think about it. The train came roaring in, wheels clanking, smoke puffing, and ground to a halt, hissing out great clouds of steam. She could see Beechlawn boaters bobbing about inside the carriages, faces peering out the windows, hands rubbing at the glass. Humphrey had grabbed her overnight suitcase and was running towards the front, searching for a spare seat.

'Here's one!' He pulled open the door and dumped her case inside.

One moment they were hugging her on the platform and the next she had been bundled into the compartment and the door was slammed behind her. They were mouthing things at her through the glass but she couldn't manage to get the window down to hear what they were saying. The train jerked forward while she was still struggling desperately with the leather strap, and the platform began sliding away. Humphrey was grinning and waving like mad and her mother was flapping her handkerchief and then dabbing her cheeks with it; Flora realized, with astonishment, that she was crying. She *had* minded, after all. The train went faster, sweeping her away from them, and then a group of people hid her mother from view. For a while she could still see Humphrey jumping up in the air to wave over the tops of heads; then she couldn't see either of them any more.

She sank down slowly in the empty seat, clutching her suitcase on her lap. There were four strange girls in the compartment, all wearing Beechlawn uniform, and three of them were staring at her. The fourth was looking out of the window. Nobody smiled or said anything. She straightened her boater nervously.

'I'm Flora Middleton.'

One of the three starers spoke. 'You're a new girl, aren't you?' She made it sound something awful to be.

'Yes.' She wriggled on the seat. It felt as though one of her suspenders had come undone in the rush to get on the train, but she didn't like to try and find out.

The girl pointed towards the one who was looking out of the window. 'So's *she*. Are you in St Cecilia's, too?'

'I think so.'

'Don't you *know*? How wet! You shouldn't be in this compartment if you are. It's for Middle School, not Juniors. *She* shouldn't be here either, only she won't move.'

The fourth girl took no notice at all and went on looking out of the window. Her boater was tilted low over her eyes. The speaker leaned over and dug her in the ribs.

'You haven't told us *your* name yet.'

The girl turned her head briefly. 'You didn't ask me.'

'Well, I'm asking you now.'

'It's Lady Atalanta Ashby.' Her voice was very clear.

22

The three of them gaped and then started giggling, clasping their hands over their mouths and falling about. One got up and spread out her grey skirt.

'Pray, pardon us, your ladyship. Permit us to share this humble third-class compartment with you.'

She went down in a deep curtsey and then collapsed sideways on to the seat in more giggles. The girl by the window seemed not to care. She looked at Flora.

'Did you say you were in St Cecilia's?'

'Yes.' The front suspender had definitely come undone; she could feel it dangling around under her skirt, loose against her bare bit of thigh. Would the other one hold the stocking up on its own?

'Thank goodness *they're* not.' The girl didn't trouble to lower her voice. 'Was that your mother seeing you off?'

Flora nodded. 'And my brother. Are you really called Atalanta?'

'Of course. Why shouldn't I be?'

Desdemona was the only thing Flora had known to be called anything so romantic-sounding. Humphrey had named her that because it went with his rabbit, Othello. Atalanta sounded like a goddess of the ocean.

'I've never met anyone with a Christian name like that before. Or a Lady anything.'

'Haven't you?' The girl seemed surprised. 'I've never really thought about it. I only said it just now because of *them*. I've never met a Flora, come to that.'

She smiled suddenly and unexpectedly, showing silver braces across her teeth. She had fair, shoulder-length hair, the colour of not-quite-ripe corn, and her eyes, looking out from under the boater's brim, were cornflower-blue. There wasn't a single freckle on her face.

'You can call me Tally, if you like.'

Two

'For what we are about to receive, may the Lord make us truly thankful.'

Miss Walters' bossy voice rang out over the dining room. One hundred and twenty girls chorused 'Amen', and one hundred and twenty chairs scraped across the floor as St Cecilia's sat down to lunch.

Tally could see nothing to be thankful for at all. Today was Tuesday and so it was gristly stew. Tomorrow it would be sloppy mince, the day after, toad-in-the-hole (burned sausages in old flannel), on Friday, slimy fish, on Saturday, rubber liver, and so on . . . The same thing on the same day, every week. The puddings were just as revolting – frogspawn tapioca, dead-baby suet roll, stodge, stodge and more stodge.

On the very first day she had decided that she wouldn't be staying long. It was just a question of whether she ran away or got herself expelled – whichever turned out to be the easiest to arrange. Not only was the food disgusting and the place dreary – a draughty old mansion stuck on the edge of town – but all the Junior girls were either babyish or silly or boring or catty, and often all four at once. Except for Flora. She was a bit babyish, too, sometimes, but she wasn't any of the other things.

Tally watched the stew being dolloped out by the prefect, Olive Fisher (known as Fish Face behind her back), at the head of the table – lumps of tough meat floating in gravy. It reminded her of a cat's mess. They were supposed to eat up every single thing on the plate and last Tuesday, when she had utterly refused to finish her gristle, she had been sent to stand in the corner with her face to the wall until lunch was over. She had kept her chin up and gone on staring straight ahead, while the other girls had sniggered away behind her back. And in the end she'd won, because when Miss Walters had ordered her to sit down and finish the cold remains on her plate, she'd been sick all over the table.

The heavy brass handbell on the hall table clanged at intervals all day long. First it woke you in the cold and dark when you had to get up, strip your bed down to the mattress, and rush off to fetch hot water in enamel cans. Each chest of drawers had china washbasins and cold-water jugs, just like the ones in the maids' attics at Melton. The dirty water had to be poured into slop pails and carted off, all grey and scummy, to be emptied before the bell clanged again to go down to breakfast. Matron, stationed like a dragon at the dining-room door, inspected everyone's fingernails. You had to hold them out under her nose as you passed. Tally had been sent back several times already – not because her nails were really dirty, but because Matron didn't seem to like her any more than Fish Face did.

After breakfast (lumpy porridge and bread doorsteps) it was back to the dormitory for bed-making. She'd never had to make a bed in her life before and hadn't a clue how to do it, so she got into trouble over that, too. Then there was more clanging from the bell for morning prayers and then again for the start of lessons.

The bell went on ringing throughout the morning to mark the beginning and end of lessons, and break time halfway through, when they had lukewarm cocoa and stale buns. It rang for lunch, and lunch was hardly over when it rang for games – stupid netball in winter – and then for tea (more bread doorsteps). Then it rang for prep and again for supper, which was only biscuits and an apple and watery milk, so that when it rang for bedtime they were still starving. It rang for the five-minute silence when they were supposed to say their prayers, and the final clanging was for lights out at eight – long before she was used to at home. At first she'd read under the bedclothes with a torch, but Fish Face, who

25

was head of the dormitory, had sneaked on her to Matron and the torch had been confiscated. Now she lay awake, thinking and plotting.

If she ran away, or got expelled, they'd have to send her to a day school in London, because if they didn't she'd go on running away. The only problem was how best to manage either. Breaking rules was easy, but how many would she have to break, and how bad would she have to be to get expelled? Running away would be much quicker, and wouldn't be too difficult, either – at least the first part. All she had to do was walk out of the house, down the drive and out of the gates, and keep on walking until she got to the railway station, if she could remember where it was. The snag was, she hadn't enough money to buy a ticket. They were only allowed one pound as pocket money for the whole term and it was kept locked away by Miss Walters and doled out each week for things like sweets and stamps. At the moment she had exactly fourpence in her purse. She had no idea how much a ticket to London would cost, but it would probably take the whole term to save up enough.

Tally had soon found out that she was badly behind in some subjects. None of her governesses had been much good at arithmetic and she'd never learned properly how to do long division or multiply double figures, or subtract a higher number from a lower by borrowing from the next. In geography class she didn't know where half the countries were in the world, or anything about them, and in history she had never heard of the Magna Carta, or the peasants' revolt. Her handwriting was so scrawly and untidy that the teachers constantly handed back her prep marked C-MINUS, UNREADABLE. On the other hand, she found English classes easy because her first governess had been a stickler for grammar and spelling, and because she'd read a lot on her own. And she was miles ahead of everyone else in French because her last governess had been French and had yakked away in French all the time. Art classes were quite fun, and so was drama, where they were reading *Children in Uniform* aloud in class, and she would have quite liked her piano lessons if the teacher hadn't been such an old grouch. Not that any of it mattered much, one way or the other, as she wouldn't be staying.

Humphrey had been quite right. It wasn't a bit like *First Term at Mallory Towers*. Nobody had midnight feasts or anything fun like that; there was nothing to eat at one, anyway. Flora cried every night when she had the most time to think about home. The daytime was so busy that there wasn't really a moment to think about anything but what she was supposed to be doing, or where she was supposed to be going next. She kept getting things wrong – finding herself in the wrong classroom at the wrong time, forgetting to hand in her prep, change her shoes, tidy her desk, clean her fingernails . . . Humphrey had been right when he'd told her she'd be ordered about. It wasn't so bad when the teachers did it, because they were grown-ups and you expected them to, but the prefects were even worse – really bossy and mean. If they wanted, they could report you for the littlest thing you'd done wrong, and some of them did – like Fish Face. She was always sneaking on everyone. Calling her that was an insult to fish, who weren't anything like as ugly as she was.

Everyone seemed to have nicknames or shortened names of some sort. They kept calling her Flo, like Humphrey did sometimes, which wasn't too bad, but Tally had been furious when she'd given hers away. It might have been much worse, though, if they'd gone and made something up, because nobody seemed to like Tally very much. Part of the trouble, Flora thought privately, was that Tally *seemed* stuck-up and snobby when she wasn't really like that at all. She didn't care a bit about being a Lady, or about her father being an Earl, and seemed surprised if anyone went on about it.

'I don't see what the fuss is about,' she'd told Flora. 'It's nothing special. I know lots of people with titles.'

'I don't. I don't know any.'

Tally had looked puzzled. 'Don't you? Oh, well . . . Anyway it doesn't make me any different.'

But she *was* different, Flora thought. There was something about her that made her so, and whatever it was showed in the way she walked and in the way she talked – not la-di-da exactly, but in a very clear, certain voice – and especially in the way she looked. In spite of the braces on her teeth, which Flora actually quite envied, and having to tie her hair in bunches because it was below her collar and against school rules, anyone could see that she was going to grow up beautiful. A lot of the other girls said catty things about her, probably because they were envious, but Flora didn't feel like that – except about her not having any freckles. She couldn't really feel envious of someone whose mother had gone off and left her when she was a baby. That was the very worst thing she'd ever heard of happening to anybody. Tally had told her about it quite casually one Saturday afternoon when they'd had their hair washed by one of the undermatrons and were drying it in front of the gas fire in the dormitory, kneeling by the hearth with their heads hanging upside down.

'You mean she just went away one day and *never* came back?' Flora had been stunned.

'Mmm. She was an actress, you see. She got a part in a film in Hollywood and then she decided to stay there. That's what Papa told me.'

'An actress!'

'Yes, but I don't think she's ever had any big parts. I've never seen her in anything.'

'What did she say to you when she went off?'

'Don't know. I was only one or something.'

'But who looked after you?'

'Nanny, of course. She's always looked after me.'

'Oh.' Flora was even more bewildered. 'I never had a nanny.'

'I thought everybody did.'

'I don't think we could have afforded one. Mummy looked after Humphrey and me. Daddy died in the war. He was an RAF bomber pilot.'

'Bad luck.'

Not as bad luck as your mother deserting you, Flora thought. Daddy hadn't left them on purpose. Tally was brushing her silky hair with her pink Mason Pearson brush. All her things were brand new and must have cost an awful lot. Her writing case was made of beautiful brown pig skin, with all her initials stamped in gold across one corner: A.V.E.R.A. – standing for Atalanta Victoria Elizabeth Rose Ashby – far more names than anybody else had. Her fountain pen was a Parker with a gold nib and her watch was gold with a real lizard strap. Her paisley eiderdown was from Harrods and so was her lovely fluffy tartan rug. Even her bath mat was. But Flora had noticed that Tally didn't seem to care much about any of these things, or to take any special care of them. She left her pen lying about without the top on and she'd spilled ink over the lining of the lovely writing case, and once she'd forgotten to take her watch off in the bath so that it didn't work any more. Flora didn't have anything made of gold and, apart from her Beechlawn uniform and her fountain pen, everything else was either old or a hand-me-down. So at first she had envied Tally all her lovely, expensive things – until she heard about her mother.

'Haven't you seen her at all since?'

'No.' Tally's voice was muffled by the curtain of hair hanging round her face.

'Doesn't she even write to you?'

'She sends me presents at Christmas and on birthdays, with a card.'

'What sort of things?'

'Oh, clothes, usually. The kind they wear in California, so they're not much use here, and she always gets the size wrong, anyway. Once she sent me a gold bracelet, but I don't wear it much.'

Flora was silent for a moment. It must be nice to get lovely clothes from America and gold bracelets, but it wasn't much of an exchange for having your mother live with you.

'Doesn't your father miss her?'

'Shouldn't think so. He's married someone else now. I've got a stepmother.'

A stepmother! Poor Tally! A vision of the pantomime one in *Cinderella* that she'd seen last Christmas floated into Flora's mind – red-cheeked, bewigged, and capering around in blue-striped stockings. Or, worse, one like the Wicked Queen in the film of *Snow White*. 'Magic mirror, on the wall, Who is the fairest one of all?' Black cloak swirling, green eyes, long fingernails, the basket of poisoned apples . . .

'What's she like?'

'*Horrible!*' Tally spat the word out so fiercely that she blew some strands of hair too close to the gas flames; they started to frizzle up at the ends and there was a smell of burning. 'I *hate* her. I call her The Cow, to myself.'

Flora felt sorrier than ever for Tally. And worried about her hair. 'Be careful, you're getting all singed in front.' She gave her own hair a brush, upside down; being longer than Tally's it wasn't as dry yet. She wished it was as nice a colour, not just ordinary old brown. Maybe she could have it cut shorter and wear it in bunches, too, not plaits. They took such a long time in the mornings when there was so much else to get done as well – like tying her tie and struggling with her stockings.

'Don't you have any brothers or sisters?'

'I've got a half-brother. He's not a proper one, and he's only a baby, so he doesn't count. He's The Cow's and Papa's baby.'

'Oh.' Flora was working it out. 'I see.'

'I've got a stepbrother, too,' Tally went on. 'That's when you've got no parents the same – they're just married to each other. The Cow was married to someone else, and had a son with him, before she got divorced and married Papa.'

'What's *he* like?' Flora was back to *Cinderella* again, transforming the Ugly Sisters into an Ugly Brother.

'Gruesome. I hate him too. Luckily, I hardly ever see him. He lives with his father. Sometimes he comes to stay for a few days in the school holidays but I always pretend he's not there . . . I sort of look straight through him. We hardly ever speak.'

'How old is he?'

'About seventeen, I suppose. The Cow makes a huge great fuss of him all the time. It's Nicky this and Nicky that and Nicky *darling*, all the time. Ugh!' Tally sat back on her heels and tossed her hair away from her face. She was pink from the fire and her hair gleamed about her like a halo. 'My mother went and married someone else, too – an American – so I've got a stepfather as well. I don't think *they* have any children, though. She's never mentioned it.'

It was a glimpse into another world: runaway actress mothers, Hollywood, divorce, nannies, wicked stepmothers, half-brothers, stepbrothers, American stepfathers . . . Her own world in Reading seemed awfully dull by comparison, but, on the whole, Flora thought she was glad of it.

Everyone had a best friend and Tally was hers. They went round arm-in-arm together, sat next to each other in class, slept in the same dormitory, walked as a pair in the school crocodile, played hopscotch and pick-up-sticks and jacks together.

They shared their weekly butter and sugar ration, too, and when Tally had finished her pound pot of school jam before the end of the month, Flora gave her some of hers every tea time until the new pots were given out. And because Tally never got any parcels from home, she shared the peanut butter and Marmite and Fry's chocolate spread that her mother had sent as well.

Tally was always being blown up about something, but she didn't seem to care.

'I want to get into as much trouble as I can,' she told Flora. 'Then they'll expel me.'

'*Expel* you!' Flora was horrified. It was the most terrible disgrace that she could imagine. 'But wouldn't your father be angry?'

'Not really. And it'd be worth it, anyway. They'd send me to a day school then.'

'They might just send you to another boarding school.'

31

'Then I'd go and do the same thing again.'

They were playing pick-up-sticks after supper on the common-room floor and Tally calmly lifted one of the sticks out of the pile. Even at her most homesick Flora had never considered such a drastic plan. It was unthinkable.

'Do you really hate it here that much, Tally?'

'Don't you? I thought you said you did.'

'Well, that was at the beginning . . . It's not quite so bad now. Some of it's alright, anyhow. Netball, for instance.'

'I *loathe* netball.'

'French, then. You're brilliant at that. And Mademoiselle Duvall's jolly good fun, isn't she?'

Tally frowned and pulled out another stick, sliding it forward very slowly so as not to disturb the other ones.

'She's always playing those babyish games. *Monsieur le Curé n'aime pas les "o" . . .*' She imitated Mademoiselle's voice perfectly. 'It's boring.'

Flora, who enjoyed the games, was silent for a moment. Tally was trying to pick up a stick that lay across another one. Her fingers never seemed to get inky like hers always did. She watched Tally press down carefully on one end of the stick, making it lift up at the other so she could take it without disturbing the one underneath. It was a tricky move and she waited until Tally had finished before speaking again.

'But why do you want to go to a day school and live at home all the time if your stepmother's so awful?'

Tally's frown deepened. 'They only sent me here to get rid of me – and it was all *her* idea. I'm not going to let her win.' She started to pull at another stick in the pile. 'Bother! They moved. Your go.' She clicked her plate with a sucking noise. It was an awful habit she'd got into.

Flora tried taking the same stick but her right plait swung forward and knocked the one next to it.

'That doesn't count,' Tally said at once. 'Have another go.'

She was always very decent like that, and never cheated.

Flora concentrated hard for a while but, in between turns, she kept thinking of what Tally had said.

'I'll miss you a lot if you go and leave,' she said at last.

Tally looked astonished and went red. 'Gosh, would you, honestly? I never thought of that.'

Flora made other friends too. The girls who had seemed so stand-offish and beastly at first got better as time went by. But they were still horrible to Tally.

'I don't know why you go round with her,' one of them said. 'She's such a stuck-up snob. She thinks she's better than any of us, just because she's a Lady.'

'No, she doesn't. Really she doesn't.' Flora tried hard to explain about Tally but they didn't believe her. She realized that she wasn't just Tally's *best* friend, but her only one.

Half-term was a week away and her mother was coming to visit her. Parents were allowed to visit once a term and to take them out over the weekend, and she could take a friend, too, on one of those days. She asked Tally.

'Unless your parents are coming?'

'I only have one and my father's not coming till later on in the term. He's gone to our villa in the south of France with The Cow.'

This was something new to add to the glamorous list: a French villa. 'What's it like?'

Tally shrugged. 'I've never been there. We couldn't go during the war, because of the Germans. There's a sort of caretaker couple who look after it. It really belongs to my grandmother, but she won't go there any more, not since Grandpapa died. They used to spend every winter there and she says it makes her too sad to go back.'

'Where does your grandmother live?'

'She's got a flat in London. In Eaton Square. She stays there all the time. She won't even go to Melton.'

'What's Melton?'

'You're always asking questions, Flora. It's the name of our house in Norfolk. Melton Hall.'

'You mean you've got *two* houses? *And* a villa in France?'

'Well, we've had them quite a long time. Years and years, I think. Specially Melton. That's my favourite place on earth. Nanny and I spent most of the war there, after the Germans started dropping bombs on London. Till it was requisitioned.'

'I can't remember any bombs in Reading,' Flora said regretfully. 'But I saw a bomb crater in a field once. It was just a huge hole full of water. And we did have an Andersen shelter in the back garden . . . Well, we've still got it, actually, but it gets full of water, too. Humphrey and I used to play at hospitals in it. It's got bunks and we put toys in them and pretended they were patients. He was the doctor and I was the nurse. They had broken legs and appendicitis and things like that. I can remember crying when Humphrey cut a hole in my doll to operate on her. He wants to be a surgeon when he grows up.'

'Ugh!'

'I know. But he doesn't seem to mind about blood and insides. Your go.'

'You're lucky to have a brother, Flora. Even if he does want to be a surgeon.'

'You've got one too – well, half of one.'

'I told you, he doesn't count. What school is your brother at?'

'It's called Christ's Hospital.'

'Oh. I thought he might be at the same one as my ghastly stepbrother. He's at Harrow. Your turn. I moved one.' She clicked her plate again.

Flora opened her mouth to say that Humphrey's school was for clever boys from poor homes but then stopped herself. She'd never said anything about her mother not paying the proper fees for her, either. It wasn't that she was afraid of Tally looking down on her, but she didn't think she would understand very well. She didn't seem to have a clue about things like that and had been very surprised when Flora had told her that her mother didn't have a car or any servants,

34

except a daily who only came on Friday mornings to do the rough. She wondered what Tally would make of the fact that her mother was going to stay at a bed and breakfast place instead of at the Abbey Hotel, where most parents went. She decided that she'd better tell her in case she didn't want to come out after all.

'I don't care where she's staying,' Tally said at once. 'I can't wait to get out of this prison, and I'd like to meet your mother. She looked nice when I saw her at the station.'

'She's not bad,' Flora admitted. 'Of course, she makes a fuss about silly things sometimes, but I don't suppose she can help it.'

'I'm so glad to meet Flora's best friend.' Mrs Middleton shook Tally's hand, smiling at her.

She's nice, Tally thought. *She's* not false or fake at all. The Cow wouldn't be seen dead in that old tweed coat, or in that felt hat, but I think they suit her. She hasn't dyed her hair, because I can see bits of grey at the sides, and she hasn't plastered her face with a lot of make-up either. She's not even wearing lipstick.

They walked into town and had lunch at a cafe. The table had a glass top with doilies underneath. There were bottles of Heinz tomato ketchup and HP sauce and Sarsons malt vinegar standing in the middle of the table, and a small menu card stuck in a silver holder. Tally had never been anywhere like that. The restaurants where her father used to take her – before The Cow came – had starched white tablecloths and napkins and double-sided menus all in French. The waiters always bowed and called her signorina or mademoiselle. In the cafe the waitress wore a flowered pinafore, had a pencil behind one ear and called her miss.

She chose fish and chips, and sprinkled vinegar all over them and plonked a big gob of ketchup on the side. While she ate, she watched Flora and her mother closely and listened to them talking. Mrs Middleton was asking all about the lessons and netball and Flora's marks. Papa probably wouldn't bother to ask her about anything like that.

35

After lunch they went for a long walk on the hills above the town. It was boring going for school walks in a long crocodile, but quite different with just the three of them. Even though it was a cold day, they soon got hot with the steep climb. Mrs Middleton took off her felt hat and looked much younger without it, and suddenly a bit like Flora. Tally wondered if she looked anything like her own mother. It was hard to tell from an old black and white photo. You couldn't see what colouring people had, and you couldn't know how they moved and spoke. Flora, for instance, had just the same way as her mother of putting her head on one side when she asked questions – which meant she had it on one side a lot.

They climbed to the very highest point of the hills – right up to the beacon where people used to light a fire to warn of possible invasion. She'd learned about it in history class. The people on the next hilltop would see it and light theirs too, and so on, in a chain all across the country, so that everyone knew there was danger. They'd have lit one up here when William the Conqueror was about to land, and when the Spanish Armada was sailing towards England. They'd probably have lit one for the Germans, too, only it had never happened in the end.

She took off her boater and let the wind blow full blast into her face and lift her bunches clean off her shoulders. You were supposed to be able to see four counties from the beacon – Worcestershire, Herefordshire, Gloucestershire and Warwickshire, but she couldn't tell where one finished and another started. It was just one huge sprawl of fields and woods, with hillocky ups and downs like on an eiderdown. It was nice standing there with the wind and the sky and the land far below. She felt free – like a bird let out of a cage after a long time. She was sorry when they started down again.

When they got back into town, Mrs Middleton took them to another cafe called the Copper Kettle. The waitress wore a frilly apron this time, like the parlour maid at home, and brought plates of crumpets and scones and cream cakes. She and Flora ate up every single thing. She remembered to thank Mrs Middleton politely for the day out when she said goodbye, and instead of shaking her hand, Flora's mother gave her a hug.

'I hope you'll come out with us again next term, Tally.'

She looked as though she really meant it, but she was probably just being polite, too.

Papa didn't come to visit Tally until two weeks after half-term, and he came with The Cow, which spoiled everything. Tally asked Flora to come out on one of the days that weekend.

'It won't be as nice as it was with your mother, but they're staying at the Abbey, so I suppose the food'll be alright.'

They came to collect her in the Rolls, with Morecambe at the wheel, sweeping up the driveway in full view of the common-room windows. She could hear the other girls making snide remarks, but pretended not to. When she went into the hall, Miss Walters was being smarmy with Papa.

'And here is little Atalanta, Lord Gresham. She's settling down with us much better now.'

She started to say indignantly that she wasn't at all, but Papa stepped forward to kiss her and she smelled his lovely lemony cologne again and felt the tickle of his moustache against her cheek. When The Cow tried to do the same, she turned away quickly.

'This is Flora Middleton, my best friend.'

Flora looked nervous but Papa bowed and shook her hand and was as charming as anything. And The Cow had put on her false smile and voice. She was wearing a long fur coat and a hat with a veil over her face and oceans of *Ma Griffe*. Tally could see that Flora was deeply impressed.

She was impressed by the Rolls, too, and by Morecambe, who held the door open and saluted as they climbed in.

'Who's he?'

'The chauffeur, silly.'

'Gosh!'

At the Abbey Hotel, Flora kept staring around her, as though she thought that was wonderful as well. Tally thought it was actually rather a dreary sort of place – all dark-red carpets and gloomy old oak.

The Cow must have been complaining already, because the manager came hurrying forward to ask if everything was satisfactory, clasping his hands together as though praying hard that it would be. The Cow complained all the time anyway, no matter how things were. When they went into the dining room for lunch she grumbled about the table they had been given, and the heard waiter had to go scurrying about to find another one, so there was a huge fuss and commotion while they moved to a table by the window, with everyone else staring and whispering.

The menu was pretty dull – not nearly so nice as in the fish and chips cafe. There were only boring things like lamb cutlets and poached sole. Flora was sitting next to her and she could see her puzzling over the French words and the different courses, so she leaned across to explain it. Then Papa helped Flora some more by suggesting things to have, so she stopped looking so worried. He was being very nice to her, putting at her ease.

'You must come and stay with us in the Christmas holidays, my dear. You'd like that, wouldn't you, Tally? Bit of company for you. Good idea, don't you think, darling?'

The Cow pretended to agree, smiling her big fake smile again at Flora. She always showed her gums when she did that, all pink and shiny.

'Yes, do come and stay when we're in London. Nicky may be there too. He could take you both out.'

'We can look after ourselves.'

The smile faded as The Cow turned in her direction. 'Not at your age, in London, Atalanta. I couldn't possibly allow you to wander about unescorted. Isn't that right, Hugh?'

'I should jolly well think not!'

There was another flurry as the first course was brought, the head waiter dancing attendance. Tally slouched lower in her chair and fiddled with a spoon; she clicked her plate up and down against the roof of her mouth.

'Don't make that noise, please, Atalanta.' The Cow looked daggers at her.

'I can't help it.'

'Please try.'

Flora was squirming around in her chair as though one of her suspenders had come undone – which they often did. Tally clicked her plate again, loudly.

'How's Nanny, Papa?'

'Fine . . . fine, far as I know. Isn't she, darling? Frightfully busy with Thomas, of course. He's grown like anything. Smiles now . . . Clever little chap.' Papa was beaming away.

'I think I've grown too, Papa.'

'Have you? Hard to tell. What do you think, darling?'

'I really couldn't say as she's sitting down. This soup is stone cold, Hugh.'

'We'll send it back then, darling. *Waiter!*'

Tally kicked Flora under the table and made a face at her.

After lunch The Cow complained of feeling exhausted and went upstairs to lie down. They moved into the hotel lounge with Papa and sank into deep armchairs. The other people in the room were mostly ancient – sitting around reading newspapers or knitting, or fast asleep – except for a spotty boy from the boys' college in the town, out with his parents, and looking bored to death. He kept glancing across and grinning; Tally ignored him.

Papa ordered coffee and brandy and when he'd drunk them he promptly fell asleep. Flora, whose feet didn't quite reach the floor, wriggled sideways in her armchair.

'I don't know what to call your father, Tally. The waiter kept calling him "my lord". Ought I to call him that?' she whispered.

'That's just for servants and people like that. You can call him Lord Gresham, if you want.'

'What about your stepmother?'

'You don't have to call *her* anything. I never do. What do you think of her? Isn't she *gruesome*!'

'Well, she's not as bad as I thought. I mean she was being quite nice, really . . .'

'She does that to people to fool them. She'll pick you to little pieces later on, when you're not there.'

Flora looked crushed. 'Will she? I expect I did everything wrong at lunch – used the wrong knife and fork and things – I got in an awful muddle, there were so many of them. I've never eaten in a proper restaurant before.'

'If you come and stay in the Christmas hols, I'll ask Papa to take us to much better places in London.' Tally wiggled one foot round and stared hard at it. 'That's if you *want* to come and stay, of course.'

'I wouldn't know how to behave, Tally. It'd be so different from home . . .'

'I'd tell you what to do. And nobody'd bother us much. They don't really care about me so long as I don't interfere with what *they're* doing.'

'I'd have to ask Mummy.' Flora chewed at the end of her plait, like she always did when she was worried. 'She might not want me to spend any of the holidays away from home.'

'I shouldn't think she'd mind if it was just for a few days, would she? We could go and look round shops, too, and have tea at places. And I could ask Papa to take us to the theatre. It's my birthday after Christmas, so he's bound to say yes. Have you ever been to the theatre?' Flora had just finished reading *The Swish of the Curtain* and she kept going on about the Blue Door Theatre, so that was bound to tempt her.

'Once. Mummy took Humphrey and me to see *Cinderella* in Oxford.'

'You haven't been in London, though.'

Papa stirred suddenly and they watched him resettling himself and waited until they were sure he was asleep. Flora whispered again. 'What about your stepbrother?'

'What about him?'

'Well, she said he'd probably be there.'

'Then we'll just pretend he's not. We needn't take any

notice of him, and we won't let him spoil anything.' Tally wiggled her foot some more. The toecap was shining very brightly in the light from a standard lamp beside her. Matron had sent her back twice to clean her shoes again after inspecting her.

'So, you'll come?'

There was a pause while Flora continued to chew her plait. Tally waited anxiously, staring at her shoe. She couldn't think of anything else to say that might persuade her. After a long moment, Flora stopped chewing and flicked the plait back over her shoulder.

'Alright, then. If you really want me to.'

Tally shut her eyes in relief and opened them again. The toecap winked at her. 'Thanks,' she said gruffly. 'Thanks.'

Three

Humphrey had already broken up for the Christmas holidays and was at Reading station to meet her. As the school train drew in Flora caught sight of him standing on the platform with her mother, and the two of them started waving and running towards her as she hung out of the window. She almost fell out of the compartment in her excitement and completely forgot her suitcase until Tally yelled at her from the carriage. Humphrey hurried to collect it.

'Who's that girl?' he asked.

'Tally Ashby. She's my best friend.'

'She was in the same compartment as you before, wasn't she? I remember her.'

She waved to Tally as they went to see about her trunk in the guard's van, and when they left the station she waved again because she was still standing at the compartment window, watching them.

It seemed like years and years since she'd gone away, though nothing at home had changed. Hercules pretended not to be pleased to see her, stalking away huffily at first before coming back to wind himself round her ankles. Desdemona didn't seem to care much, except about the cabbage stalks she took out with her and poked through the hutch netting. The trouble about rabbits, Flora thought, watching the stalks disappearing fast, was that their expression never really changed so you couldn't tell *what* they were thinking. For all she knew Desdemona might be thrilled to bits at seeing her again after so long – she just couldn't show it.

It felt funny to be home. She wandered about the house, not knowing what to do next. If she were at school they'd be in the middle of lessons, then there'd be lunch and then games, then tea, then prep . . . She'd got so used to every minute of the day being full up that it was strange not having much to do. She went in search of Humphrey and found him in his room, eyes glued to his microscope.

'What are you looking at?'

'One of Hercules's hairs. You can have a squint, if you like.'

She leaned over. It didn't look very interesting so she pulled a hair out of her own head. 'Have a go with this.'

Humphrey slid it carefully under the lens and twiddled knobs. 'There you are.'

It didn't look like human hair at all – more like an old bent twig split open at one end. She sighed. 'I wish I had nice silky hair like Tally.'

'Your hair's OK.' Humphrey peered into the microscope again. 'Is that her real name – Tally?'

'It's short for Atalanta.'

'Bit of a mouthful.'

'She's *Lady* Atalanta, actually. Her father's an earl.'

'Crikey!' Humphrey looked up.

'But she never talks about it,' Flora said quickly, in case he got the wrong idea about Tally, like all the others. 'You'd never know. She's asked me to go and stay with her in London these hols. I've said I will, if Mummy lets me.'

'Sounds pretty grand.' Humphrey went back to the microscope again. 'Can she run fast?'

Flora stared. 'Why?'

He adjusted one of the knobs carefully. 'Atalanta's the name of a maiden in a Greek myth. She could run very fast and she said she'd only marry a man who could beat her in a race.'

'What happened?'

'Someone called Hippomenes ran against her, but he cheated a bit.'

'What did he do?'

'He dropped three golden apples during the race and Atalanta stopped to pick them up, and she lost.'

43

'So she had to marry him?'

'That's right.'

'Did she mind?'

'Shouldn't think so. I expect she admired him for getting the better of her.'

Flora thought it sounded rather romantic. 'That's funny because Tally *can* run jolly fast. I don't think she'd bother to stop and pick up golden apples, though. She's got enough gold things already and she doesn't seem to care much about them.' She chewed at her thumb. 'Here, I've got a big juicy bit of nail for you to look at, if you like . . .'

Flora was now even less sure that she wanted to go and stay with Tally in London. Every day of the holidays was precious and she wanted to spend them all at home, doing the things she liked best – reading her Enid Blyton adventure stories and her Pullein-Thompson pony books; going over the garden fence to see Sally next door; playing card games with Humphrey; listening to a new *Norman and Henry Bones* adventure on Children's Hour on the wireless at five o'clock and to *Dick Barton, Special Agent*, every evening . . . If she went to stay in some grand house in London with the Earl and Countess, she probably wouldn't be able to do any of those things, and she would have to be very polite all the time and on her absolute best behaviour. And she would be bound to make mistakes, as she'd done at the Abbey Hotel with the knives and forks. Her mother, though, seemed to want her to go.

'You might enjoy it, Flora, seeing London, and a different side of life.'

'I'd sooner stay here.'

'Won't Tally be disappointed? She's probably looking forward to you coming. She seemed a very lonely child to me. I felt rather sorry for her.'

Flora stuck her finger in the bowl on the kitchen table and tasted the raw cake mix that her mother had been beating.

'I know. I do too sometimes. I don't know why, though, because she's got everything.'

'Everything?'

'Well, most things. She's got a gold watch and a Parker pen and a Mason Pearson hairbrush . . .'

Her mother was greasing a cake tin. 'Those things aren't very important, Flora. They don't make you happy.'

'They're jolly nice, though.' Flora dipped her finger in the bowl again and sucked at it. 'Actually, I don't really envy Tally having them because her mother went off and left her when she was a baby.'

'Poor Tally.'

'And she simply *hates* her stepmother.'

'Oh, dear. Well, you don't have to go, if you don't want to. Don't eat any more of that, Flora, or we won't have a cake for tea.'

In the end Flora went to London a few days after Christmas. Tally's father had telephoned her mother and it was all arranged between them. She was to stay for five days and then come home for a week before the spring term started.

She went by train to London from Reading and sat in a corner seat, so she could see out of the window properly. She had only been to London once before and couldn't remember much about it. As the train started to come into the city, she thought how dirty it all looked.

At Paddington, Tally was standing just beyond the barrier. She was wearing a camel coat and a dark-brown velvet beret, with her hair loose on her shoulders. There was no sign of either the Earl or the Countess but the chauffeur, Morecambe, came forward and touched his cap to her as he took her suitcase. The Rolls Royce was parked close by and he opened the rear door for them. When they had climbed in he spread a soft brown rug over their knees.

'Papa's gone to a meeting in the City, or something,' Tally said. 'And The Cow's gone to have her hair done, as usual, thank goodness. They're going to a dance this evening, so we'll be on our own.'

Flora felt like royalty, enthroned beside Tally on the back seat. When they had ridden with the Earl and Countess before, she and Tally had sat on the fold-down ones, facing backwards. People were looking their way, she noticed; one man in a cloth cap actually pressed his nose to the window and Tally stuck her tongue out at him. The Rolls glided smoothly up the slope and out of the station. London looked better now. The houses they passed weren't like the ugly little ones she'd seen from the train; they were tall with long windows and whitened steps leading to painted front doors. Tally lived somewhere called Eaton Terrace.

The house was joined on to a long row of other big houses, all painted white. She could see black iron railings along the pavement in front and a gate to the tradesmen's entrance in the basement. Three white marble steps with a tall pillar on each side led up to a very grand-looking black front door. Above the door, there was a stone balcony and long windows behind it, and more windows above that, getting smaller on each floor. The house went up too high for Flora to see all of it from inside the car. She scrambled out of the Rolls after Tally, who was already banging the brass knocker loud and hard. She went on doing it and after a few moments the door was opened by a grey-haired man with a smooth white face, like soap. He was dressed in a black coat with tails, striped trousers and a wing collar and Flora supposed that he must be going to the dance too. Beyond him she could see a vast expanse of black-and-white marble floor, and a sparkling crystal chandelier hanging from the ceiling.

'I was on my way, Lady Atalanta.' He didn't look at all pleased – presumably about all the knocking.

'We were getting cold,' Tally said. 'This is Miss Middleton.'

She stalked inside and Flora smiled nervously at the man. He was looking down his nose at her, seeming to take in her jumble-sale coat, the darns in her woollen gloves and her scuffed shoes, all in one go. She edged past him. Tally was heading fast across the black and white floor towards a curving staircase that looked like the one in the ballroom scene in *Cinderella*. Close to its foot stood a very tall Christmas tree, decorated in gold and silver.

'Come *on*, Flora! They'll see to your suitcase.'

She hurried after her. 'Who was that gentleman?'

'He's not a gentleman. He's Carver. The butler.'

46

'Oh. He didn't seem very pleased.'

'Oh, you don't want to take any notice of him. He's new. The Cow got rid of our nice old one and got him instead. He's horrible.'

A sharp-faced woman in black appeared at the top of the first flight. She gave Tally a nasty look.

'Her ladyship's lying down with a headache. She's not to be disturbed.'

'We weren't going to.' Tally went past her, chin in the air.

The staircase went up and up and after the third flight, Tally marched off down a corridor and stopped at a door at the far end.

'That was Paget. The Cow's maid. Don't take any notice of her either. She's horrible too.' She turned the doorknob. 'This is my room now. I used to be up in the night nursery till Thomas was born and they made me move.'

Flora stepped after her and stood in silence. It was the most beautiful bedroom that she had ever seen. The wallpaper had a pattern of tiny blue flowers, and the curtains at the tall window were pale blue and tied back so that they hung in lovely loops, reaching right down to the white carpet. The bed was a four-poster with a white lace canopy, all frilled round the top, and lace curtains gathered in at each post. It looked like the bed out of *The Princess and the Pea*. The counterpane was white lace, too, and beside the bed there was a fluffy white sheepskin rug and a little blue velvet armchair. In one corner stood a kidney-shaped, glass-topped dressing table with blue skirts that matched the curtains and stuck out stiffly like a ballgown. Flora swallowed. There were times when it was very hard not to envy Tally.

'You *are* lucky! It's absolutely super.'

Tally took off her beret and coat. She chucked them on to the little blue chair and Flora saw that the coat had a beautiful satin lining. Underneath, she was wearing a plaid kilt and a yellow jumper.

'Gosh, do you really think so? I hate it. The Cow got some awful interior decorator to come and do it all. He

47

chose everything. It was much nicer before. She's ruined almost everything in the house. I'll show you the bathroom. It's worse.'

She opened another door. The bathroom beyond it was all in pink – pink-flowered paper all over the walls and ceiling, pink bath, basin and lavatory, pink curtains at the window, pink towels, pink carpet, pink bathmat . . . Flora blinked.

'Really *yuk*, isn't it? She's dotty about pink. She was going to make me have it in mine but I said it made me feel sick and I wouldn't sleep in there if she did. She got her own way in here because this isn't just mine. It's a guest bathroom as well.' Tally opened another door. 'Your room's through here. It's revolting.'

The swagged and tasselled curtains in the next-door bedroom were pink, too, and the twin beds had shiny pink eiderdowns. Nothing was worn or faded, like at home; everything seemed brand new, except for Flora's battered old suitcase, which had already been put there and looked very out of place.

Tally was opening another door that led back into the corridor. 'I'll show you the nurseries upstairs. That's the nicest place in the house. The Cow hasn't spoiled them yet because Nanny refused to have anything changed.'

They went up another flight of stairs. It looked quite different from the rest of the house. The walls were plain white and there was brown linoleum on the floor. The day nursery that Tally showed her first had ordinary old furniture – a wooden table and chairs, a big toy cupboard, a bookcase with glass doors, a gas fireplace with a high mesh guard and a rag rug. It seemed a cosy sort of room to Flora. Safe. Comforting. She could understand why Tally liked it up here, but not quite how she could prefer it to the beautiful blue bedroom.

'This is my friend, Flora, Nanny,' Tally announced as they went into the night nursery next door.

The woman sitting knitting in a chair by the window put her finger to her lips. 'I've just got him off to sleep. Don't make a noise. He's teething, poor little mite.'

48

She looked as old as the hills to Flora. Her grey hair was done in a bun, and she wore wire-framed spectacles halfway down her nose and long skirts under a starchy apron. She peered at Flora and gave her a nod. 'You can have a quick peep at him, if you like. So long as you're quiet.'

Tally stayed where she was but Flora tiptoed over to the cradle and leaned across. Tally's brother lay asleep on his back, both fat little arms above his head, tiny fingers curled into fists. The long lashes on his cheeks still glistened with beads of tears. Flora stared at him for a moment and then tiptoed back. Nanny made signs at them to go.

Flora followed Tally downstairs again. 'He's awfully sweet.'

'No, he isn't. He cries all the time.'

'I think babies usually do. If you're a Lady, does that mean he's a Lord?'

'He's a Viscount, actually. He's the heir. I can't be because I'm a girl. It's jolly unfair, considering I was born *years* before him.'

'I suppose it is. Still, it's nice to have a brother.'

'A *half*-brother.'

They went back to the guest room and Flora started to unpack her suitcase.

'We used to have maids to do all that,' Tally said, watching her. 'But there's only Paget now, and she never touches anything but The Cow's things. Not that I'd want her anywhere near mine.'

There wasn't much to unpack – underclothes, socks, pyjamas, her best skirt and sweater and the second best ones, and her best frock. In fact, her *only* frock. She'd brought her school indoor shoes, with the straps and buttons.

Tally looked astonished as she took them out. 'Ugh! How can you bear to wear those in the holidays?'

'I haven't got any other indoor ones. I'd grown out of my home ones.'

'You can borrow some of mine,' Tally told her.

They went through the flowery pink bathroom to the blue bedroom and she flung open the doors of the white-painted cupboards that lined one wall. Flora gasped. There must have been twenty frocks hanging there, at least, and three or four more coats – one with a real fur collar – and shelves and shelves of blouses and jumpers. Tally was rummaging around at the bottom where rows of shoes hung by their heels from long racks. She pulled out a pair of dark-green leather ones with little fringes on the front.

'Try these. I've never worn them.'

But they were too big. Flora slopped around the room, crestfallen; they were so pretty and so grown-up. She took them off and handed them back.

'Thanks, anyway. I don't mind wearing my school ones, honestly.'

Tally stuffed the green shoes away. 'I'm taller than you, I expect that's why I've got bigger feet.'

She was quite a lot taller, actually, with long, straight legs. Flora wished she would hurry up and grow too; she seemed to have been stuck at the same height for ages. She finished unpacking quickly.

'What was your school report like, Tally?'

'Well . . . not as bad as I hoped it'd be. I'll have to try much harder next term.'

'Try harder?'

'To get expelled.' She looked at Flora. 'Sorry. I did warn you.'

'Yes, I know. But I thought you'd sort of forgotten about that.'

'Well, I haven't.'

'Oh . . . Anyway, my report wasn't very good. Miss Mead said I don't pay attention in arithmetic and could do much better if I tried. I jolly well *do* but I just don't understand it when she explains it. She gets me in a muddle.'

'She said that about me, too. *Atalanta could do a great deal better if she tried.* I don't care. I don't want to think about gruesome school. Let's go out.'

'Out?'

'We can walk down to Sloane Square and go and look in

50

Peter Jones. That's fun. Then we could get a taxi to Harrods, if we like. I've got plenty of money.'

'But I thought your stepmother said we weren't to go out on our own.'

'I never do what *she* says. Besides, she's lying down with one of her silly headaches. She won't get up for hours, so she'll never know.'

There was nobody around to notice them going out. They tiptoed across the marble hallway and slipped out of the front door. Flora was torn between admiration for Tally's daring and fear that they would both get into terrible trouble and that she would be sent home in disgrace. Tally didn't seem a bit worried, though. She skipped along the pavement, flipping her fingers across the railings, and Flora had a job keeping up with her, as well as trying not to tread on the lines.

It wasn't very far to Sloane Square, which was only a small place with trees in the middle and shops and an Underground station round the edge. Peter Jones was on the far corner and Tally waltzed in through the swing doors as though she often went there, and marched through different departments, picking things up and putting them down.

'I took something from here once,' she said airily, as they went through the Accessories department.

'You mean *stole*?'

'Mmm. A Jacqmar scarf. I wanted to see if I could do it without anyone noticing. It was easy-peasy. I just put it in my pocket and walked away.'

'But Tally, supposing you'd been caught?'

'I wasn't. Don't look so shocked, Flora. Actually, I put it back later. I didn't want it anyway. Come on, let's go upstairs.'

They went round all the departments – Leather Goods, Dress Fabrics, Men's Wear, Ladies' Shoes, Hosiery, Haberdashery – and up and down in the lifts several times.

'This is getting boring,' Tally decided finally. 'Let's go to Harrods. That's more fun.'

In Sloane Square she waved at a taxi and, when it stopped said, 'Take us to Harrods, please,' to the driver, as though

51

she was always doing that too. When they arrived, a tall man in a green coat and hat opened the taxi door for them and Tally swept out. She paid the driver from her purse and grandly gave him an extra sixpence for a tip. Flora watched admiringly. She seemed so grown-up.

Harrods was even bigger and better than Peter Jones. Lots of the women wore fur coats, or fox furs draped round their shoulders, and one fat old woman in a very long fur set them off into giggles.

'Sable,' Tally pronounced knowledgeably. 'It costs hundreds of pounds.'

'How do you know it's that?'

'The Cow's got one just like it. Papa gave it to her as a wedding present. She wheedled it out of him. I heard her going on and on about it. It doesn't make her look any better, either. Fur only makes beautiful people look more beautiful, haven't you noticed? If they're ugly it makes them look even worse.'

They went up by lift to the fourth floor and came out by the hairdressing and beauty salon where there was a wonderful smell and a woman who looked like a film star sitting at a reception desk. Tally seemed to know her way perfectly. She walked straight through the Picture department and up some stairs into the Silver Buffet. There were several empty tables, but she headed for the high counter in the centre and climbed on to one of the stools. Flora hauled herself up on to the empty one beside her.

'I usually have the toasted teacake,' Tally said, passing her a menu. 'It's jolly good. But there's all sorts of other things. You can have ice cream, if you want.'

Flora looked at the prices and gulped. 'I haven't actually got very much money . . .'

'Oh, don't worry about that. I've got stacks. I'll pay for you.'

'Are you sure?'

'Of course I'm sure. You're staying with me, aren't you? That's the rule with guests. So don't look so worried.'

They both had toasted teacakes with butter melting all over

the top and dripping down on to their fingers, and then some lovely cakes. And then chocolate ice cream, and a strawberry milkshake each. Flora began to feel rather sick and was glad when Tally said they'd better be getting back.

Outside Harrods it was already dark and the store was lit up by hundreds of electric light bulbs all over the building. Flora had never seen so many lights, or such crowds of people, or so much traffic. The green man at the door put his fingers in his mouth and whistled for a taxi, and magically one appeared in front of them.

When they got back to the house, the front door was opened this time by a young man with shiny, smarmed-down hair, not so grandly dressed as the butler. He was much more friendly, too, and grinned and winked at them.

'That's Norman,' Tally said as they climbed the stairs. 'He's a sort of footman. He helps horrible Carver, but he's quite nice.'

To Flora's alarm the Countess suddenly appeared at the head of the stairs. Her face was a white mask.

'Where have you been, Atalanta? I thought I told you that you were not to go out by yourself.'

'I wasn't by myself. I was with Flora. She had to post a letter, didn't you, Flora?'

'Is that so, Flora?' The Countess's voice was sharp.

Flora edged out from behind Tally. 'Yes, that's right. To my mother.' Well, it was partly true. She was supposed to send a postcard home to say she had arrived safely, only she hadn't even written it yet.

'I see. Well, if that's really the case . . .' The Countess was smiling at her now – a forced sort of smile. Her voice was more friendly, but sounded forced, too. 'I'm sorry I wasn't able to welcome you, Flora. I'm afraid I had a dreadful headache. I hope Atalanta has been looking after you properly.'

'Oh, yes . . . Thank you.'

Her smile stretched even wider, showing all her top gums. Flora stared, fascinated.

'Well . . . I hope you'll enjoy your stay with us. It

53

will be nice for Atalanta to have a little friend here for company.'

'A *little friend*!' Tally said in disgust when they'd gone up to her bedroom. 'You'd think we were six or something. I'm *twelve* the day after tomorrow.' She threw her coat on the blue chair again. 'Anyway, Papa's got us tickets for the theatre. We're going to see an American musical at Drury Lane. The Cow tried to make us go to *Where the Rainbow Ends*, or *Peter Pan*, or something babyish like that, but Papa promised I could choose what I liked for my birthday, and I chose that. It's called *Oklahoma!* It's about cowboys and things.'

Humphrey had a book about the Wild West, with pictures of cowboys lassoing cattle and riding unbroken horses, leaping high into the air. Flora thought it was an odd idea for something on stage in a theatre, but she didn't like to say so. She was still feeling rather sick from the tea and the taxi ride, and beginning to feel homesick, too, and to wish that she had never come. The Countess had frightened her, and there was nothing homely about this huge London house. She remembered, too, that it would soon be time for *Dick Barton*. Somewhere there must be a wireless, and Tally might like *Dick Barton*. It turned out, though, that she had never even heard of the programme.

'I don't listen to the wireless much. There's one in the drawing room but I don't go there when The Cow's in it. She won't be this evening, though, as they're going out, so we can listen to it, if you like.'

The drawing room, on the first floor, was all blue and gold and the paintings on the walls had little lights fixed over them. Above the marble mantlepiece there was a very large portrait of the Countess wearing a tiara and a ballgown that slipped off her shoulders. She looked much better in the painting than she did in real life.

Flora perched gingerly on the edge of a satin chair, feeling ill at ease. At home she would have been curled up in the old armchair beside the fire, probably with Hercules on her lap. This room wasn't a bit comfortable, or even very warm.

Tally had turned the volume up high on the big radiogram standing in a corner, and the 'Devil's Gallop' music that always introduced the programme began thundering out from the speaker. They settled down to listen to the latest adventure of Dick Barton, and Snowy and Jock, his faithful men. As usual, the fifteen minutes went much too quickly for Flora.

Tally had been silent on the sofa throughout, listening intently. 'Will Dick escape?'

'Oh yes, he always does.'

'I don't see how he can. He's tied up in a locked cellar, with the water pouring in . . . What's he going to *do*?'

'He'll think of something. Don't worry.'

The Greenwich Time Signal pips had sounded and someone was reading the seven o'clock news now, still at top volume.

The drawing-room door was thrown open.

'Please turn that down *at once*, Atalanta. It's far too loud. You're giving me another headache and you'll disturb Thomas.'

The Countess looked simply furious and did not bother to try and hide it. She had changed into a long evening dress and a lot of jewels; Flora could smell her perfume from across the room.

'And take your feet off the sofa.' She went out, shutting the door with a bang.

Flora quaked in her chair, but Tally didn't move. She stayed exactly where she was, and so did her feet. 'Let's listen to that programme again tomorrow,' she said, as though nothing had happened. 'I liked it.'

The shiny pink eiderdown kept slipping off during the night and, every time it did, Flora woke up feeling cold. She had to grope about in the dark to haul it back on again. She was also feeling rather hungry. Supper last night had been served to them at one end of the long table in the dining room by a winking Norman and a sad-looking maid in a white cap and apron. The food was awfully rich – something covered in a sort of thick gravy, and she had started to feel sick after a few mouthfuls.

'It's the French chef, Monsieur Leone,' Tally had explained. 'He always cooks muck like this. I can't eat it either.' She nodded towards the sad girl who was taking away dishes, her head bowed. 'He's simply foul to Milly. That's why she always looks so miserable.'

The pudding was apple tart, which would have been alright except that it was all covered with spicy brown stuff that spoiled the taste of the apples. They had left most of that too. So, when she woke early in the morning, she was feeling really quite peckish.

She washed, dressed, did her plaits quickly and tied her second-best ribbons on the end of them, then she tiptoed downstairs. There was no sign of Tally yet. The dining-room table had a stiff, white cloth over it and was laid for four. On the sideboard there was a row of silver dishes with lids on, keeping warm on a hot plate, and china plates stacked ready beside them. She lifted one of the lids cautiously and saw mouth-watering grilled sausages and bacon and tomatoes, and then another lid which revealed lots of scrambled eggs. She had just started to lift the third lid when the dining-room door opened suddenly and she let it drop with a guilty crash.

'Good morning.'

A young man was standing in the doorway, one hand on the knob, looking at her. 'Sorry, I startled you. You must be Atalanta's school friend who's staying.' He shut the door behind him and came towards her. 'I'm Nicholas Dyer. Her stepbrother.'

She took his offered hand shyly. 'I'm Flora Middleton.'

'How do you do, Flora?'

'Oh . . . How do you do?'

He smiled. 'Well, now we've got that over with, shall we get on with breakfast? I'm starving, aren't you?' He moved to the sideboard and handed her a plate. 'What would you like? Sausages?' He lifted the first silver lid and spooned two on to her plate. 'Bacon?' Several rashers followed and then tomatoes, then a mound of scrambled eggs from the next dish. He picked up the third lid, the one she had dropped. 'Kedgeree?'

She had no idea what that was, but he was already putting a big dollop of it on her plate. Then he took a bit of everything himself, poured a cup of coffee and sat down opposite her at the table.

'You *are* hungry?'

'Oh, yes. Frightfully.'

He smiled again. He had a wonderful smile; the nicest smile she'd ever seen.

'Good. Then eat up, before it gets cold.'

While they were eating, she sneaked quick glances at him and tried to remember what Tally had said about her stepbrother. He was at boarding school and about seventeen, that's all she could remember really. But he looked grown-up – tall as a man, and awfully handsome. Even though it was winter, his face was brown, which made his eyes blue as anything. Tally hadn't mentioned any of that, so somehow she'd always imagined him horrible-looking and rather fat, with spots and glasses. Mean and sneaky, too.

'Why isn't Atalanta looking after you?'

'She is.'

He lifted the cloth and peered underneath the table. 'I don't see her.'

'I came down before her, that's all.'

'Because she's still snoring her head off and you were famished, I expect. How long are you staying?'

'Five days. I arrived yesterday.' The kedgeree had turned out to be fishy rice and she wasn't sure if she liked it.

'I got in late last night, after you'd gone to bed. The snow wasn't much good so I left a few days early. I've been skiing,' he added, seeing her blank look. 'Zermatt. Switzerland.'

'Oh.'

'Have you ever been skiing?'

'Gosh, no. I've never even been abroad.'

'Well, you must try it some day. It's terrific. When there's some decent snow, that is.' He smiled at her again. 'You

57

know, you're not really the sort of friend I'd have expected Atalanta to have.'

'Oh?' What on earth did he mean by that?

'No, you look much too nice.'

She went red, embarrassed, and didn't know what to say.

'Atalanta doesn't exactly put out the welcome mat for me when I come to stay here, you see,' he continued calmly. 'So I'd expected her friend to be as unpleasant as she is.'

'But she's not—'

'Oh, I'm sure she can be nice, too, if she wants to be. I've just never seen it.'

Flora said earnestly, 'Perhaps you don't know her well enough . . .'

'You're a very loyal friend, aren't you? Well, the truth is that her nose is severely out of joint because of my mother. She's jealous as hell, so she behaves appallingly. Don't you like that kedgeree?'

'Not much.'

'Leave it, then. There's no need to struggle with it. Have you known Atalanta long?'

'Only one term. We were both new girls together.'

'How does she behave when she's not at home? Any better? Don't bother to answer, I can see by your face that she doesn't.'

'I didn't mean that. But I don't think she's very happy at Beechlawn.'

'Perhaps she doesn't try to be.'

'Some of the girls are awful to her . . . They think she's stuck-up. It's not easy for her, being a Lady, you see. She gets left out things all the time . . . Being picked for teams, that sort of thing, you know?'

'She probably deserves it.'

'Actually,' she went on quickly, 'it's a bit better now. She can run awfully fast.'

He drank some coffee. 'Like her namesake in the myth.'

'You know about that?'

'Oh, yes. As a matter of fact, I always felt rather sorry

58

for Hippomenes, stuck with someone so keen on gold. He'd have done far better to lose.'

'But Tally's not a bit like that.'

He smiled at her over his coffee cup. 'Loyal little Flora.'

'Are you awake, Tally?'

'Mmmm . . .'

'I've just met Nicholas. He came into the dining room for breakfast.'

The mound of bedclothes heaved and Tally poked her head out. 'Ugh! He's not supposed to be here till next week, or something.'

'He came back earlier because there wasn't enough snow. He's been skiing.'

'Poor you, having him for company.'

'Actually, I didn't think he was so bad.'

'Yes, he is. He's putrid.' Putrid was one of Tally's favourite words.

'He said he'd take us out today, if we wanted to go somewhere.'

'Well, we don't – not with him, anyway.'

'He says he's got a car and he could drive us around London this afternoon, if we like.'

Tally sat up suddenly, looking cross. 'You didn't say we'd go?'

'Well, I didn't exactly say we *wouldn't*. I didn't want to be rude and I didn't think you'd mind too much. Sorry.'

'I *do* mind, but it's not your fault.' She flopped back on the pillow again. 'Oh well, I suppose it'll be alright if you're there. Then *I* won't have to talk to him.'

Flora sat beside Nicholas in the front seat. She thought he handled the car brilliantly, steering it easily through all the traffic and changing gears so smoothly. Tally was slumped in the back, not bothering to look when he pointed out the sights for Flora, like Westminster Abbey and the Houses of Parliament, Nelson's Column in Trafalgar Square, and the Tower of London. Tally kept yawning and patting her hand obviously over her mouth. Sometimes she clicked her plate loudly. Nicholas didn't seem to notice. In fact, he paid no attention to her at all.

He took them to tea at Fortnum and Mason, a store in Piccadilly that had the nicest cakes that Flora had ever eaten, loaded with icing and oozing with real cream. She ate several, but Tally only picked at one and hardly spoke a word, and when Nicholas paid the bill and drove them back she didn't say thank you.

They stood up for 'God Save the King'. Flora had never been in a box at the theatre before; when she had gone to the pantomime in Oxford with her mother and Humphrey they had sat in the cheap seats up in the gallery. In the box there were proper chairs to sit on and people kept staring up at them from the stalls as though they were royalty. In fact, Tally had told her it really was the royal box, where the King and Queen sat when they came to the theatre.

They sat down, the lights were dimmed, and the orchestra struck up the overture. She listened as they played a whole lot of lovely tunes, one after the other, finishing with a great clash of cymbals. The audience clapped, the conductor bowed, and an expectant hush fell over the theatre. Flora felt her stomach tickling with excitement. She watched the curtain go up with a soft swish and there before her was a beautiful sunlit scene of golden cornfields, and a wooden farmhouse with a porch and a little white picket fence.

Flora watched and listened, spellbound, and forgot how mortified she had felt before about her smocked wool frock with the let-down hem while the others were all dressed up in proper evening clothes. She forgot about Tally and Nicholas sitting on either side of her. She forgot everything except what was happening on stage – the singing, the dancing, the colour and the romance.

When the curtain came down for the last time, she clapped and clapped until her hands stung, dismayed that it was all over. Nicholas leaned towards her, smiling, and said something in her ear that she couldn't hear above the applause, so

60

she just smiled back at him. And then the orchestra started to play some of the wonderful music again as they stood up to leave.

I'll remember this evening for ever, she thought, looking back wistfully at the stage. For the rest of my life.

Four

'You can feed her, if you like.' Flora offered a stick of carrot. 'Just push it through.'

Tally poked the carrot through a hole in the wire netting of the rabbit's cage. Desdemona hopped over and started nibbling it. Tally liked her pink eyes and white fur but she wasn't nearly as much fun as Hercules, who came and sat on the end of her bed and played with her dressing-gown cord when she dangled it for him.

'I've got to clean out her sleeping compartment,' Flora said. She opened the other door of the hutch and began pulling out dirty straw and soggy yellow newspaper. Tally wrinkled her nose.

'Pooh! It stinks.'

'I know. I should have done it yesterday, but I forgot. Do you want to put the clean stuff in?'

'No, thanks. You do it.'

She watched Flora sweeping out all the rabbit currants. She could remember having a rabbit as a pet at Melton a long time ago, but she'd never had to clean it out. Someone else had always done that – the gardener's boy, probably. There weren't any proper servants at Flora's home – only a woman who came on Friday mornings – but Tally liked staying there. The house was rather small but it was nice because everything was old and you didn't have to be careful.

They ate their meals round a table in the kitchen where it was warmest because of the Aga, and Mrs Middleton cooked everything herself. They were all the kind of things Tally liked best – macaroni cheese, all brown and bubbly on the top; melty cheese dreams; rice pudding with lots of skin;

queen of puddings, which was Flora's absolute favourite; hotpots; shepherd's pie and crisp, puffy toad-in-the-hole – nothing like the school flannel. In the evenings she and Flora listened to *Dick Barton*, curled up in comfy armchairs. Sometimes Hercules curled up on her lap instead of Flora's, and purred loudly as he stuck his claws into her knees.

The first two weeks of the Easter holidays had been really dull in London. Papa and The Cow had gone away to stay with some people and she'd been left with Nanny and Thomas. She'd wandered about the shops on her own, and pinched something from Harrods this time – a crocodile purse. But nobody had noticed and so, after a bit, she'd put it back again. She'd been so bored she'd gone up to the nursery once to play with Thomas, who could sit up now and was starting to crawl. She had built little piles of bricks for him to knock down and wound up clockwork toys.

Gruesome Nicholas had turned up suddenly to collect something. She'd looked round to find him spying on her from the nursery doorway and had stopped playing at once.

When he'd gone away she went back to building the brick piles, but she soon got tired of it, and so did Thomas, who had started to grizzle and throw the bricks around. If she hadn't been invited to stay with Flora she would have died of boredom by the end of the holidays.

Last term had been absolutely putrid. She didn't know why it was called the *spring* term when the entire eleven weeks had been nothing but winter. When they had gone back in January, the tops of the hills had been covered with snow and had stayed that way for weeks. The classrooms had been so cold she could hardly hold her pen, and in between lessons everyone fought to get near the lukewarm radiators. The dormitories were worse, with no radiators at all, and on some mornings there had been ice on top of the water jugs. Matron had confiscated her hot-water bottle because they weren't allowed, not that there was ever enough hot water to fill it with. They had been made to play games and go for walks in all weathers and Tally had had three bad colds – one so bad that Matron had actually let her stay in bed for a day. For most of the term she had felt too awful to bother about getting expelled.

Flora had finished putting clean newspaper and fresh straw into the rabbit hutch, and shut the door. Desdemona, on her fourth carrot stick and nibbling away fast, was watching them with her pink eyes.

'Humphrey'll be back tomorrow,' Flora said, poking yet another piece of carrot through the netting.

Her brother had been staying with his godfather. Flora talked about him quite a lot and about how clever he was. She talked about her father, too, even though he'd been dead for years, and had showed her a big photograph of him in the drawing room. He was wearing Royal Air Force uniform with wings on his chest and a striped ribbon under them that Flora had said proudly was a medal: the Distinguished Flying Cross. He looked rather nice and kind, Tally thought. Papa had been a major in the army, and there was a big silver-framed photo of him in uniform at home, too, but he'd never left England in the war, or won any medals.

Humphrey, when he arrived back, turned out to be a terrible swot. The godfather had given him a whole lot of glass slides to look at under his microscope, as well as some rather boring textbooks, and he seemed thrilled to bits with them. He offered to let them look at some of the slides, as though it was a great treat, but Tally couldn't see anything to get excited about. It was more fun when he found a dead spider and put that under the microscope. It looked horrible that big – all fuzzy black legs with a fat, round body.

'It has four pairs of segmented legs and two feelers,' Humphrey told her solemnly. 'And its body's divided into two regions – the cephalothorax and the abdomen. Can you see them?'

'Not really. It's gone blurry.'

'Hang on.' He bent his head close to hers and moved a knob. 'Is that better?'

The spider was very clear now, and even more horrible. She stared at it for a moment and then took her eyes away from the lens. 'Ugh! It's disgusting.'

'It isn't, really,' he said, looking all earnest like Flora did sometimes. 'Of course some of them are nicer, with lovely colours and patterns – there are hundreds of different kinds and sizes, you know. And it's wonderful the way they build their webs. They have things called spinnerets in the abdomen that produce silk . . .'

'I still think he looks disgusting.'

'Actually, it's a she.'

'How do you know?'

'I can tell. I've learned.'

Flora had a turn next, and she thought it was pretty revolting too. Tally couldn't understand how Humphrey could think spiders were so marvellous. He was so funny with his slides and his books and his long words and his wire specs. Still, he seemed kind, and he was very polite and passed her things at table and even opened doors for her.

Tally felt quite miserable when it was time to go back home, though she was careful not to show it. They took her to the station in a taxi and Humphrey carried her suitcase and put it up on the luggage rack for her when the train came in. Mrs Middleton kissed her, Flora hugged her and Humphrey shook her hand, and they all stood and waved to her as she hung out of the window, waving back. When they were out of sight she sat down in the corner seat and stared out of the window all the way back to London.

In late May, when the weather grew warm, they were allowed to play in the hay field at the back of St Cecilia's. The hay had been cut and left lying in long rows to dry, and Tally and Flora made a house by draping swathes of it over a framework of broken branches. There was just room to crawl inside and pretend it was a tent and that they were Scott trekking to the South Pole; it was so hot in there, though, that they soon changed to being explorers in Africa.

Rounders was much better than netball, Tally decided, and as she was quite good at hitting the ball and could run very fast, she was put in the first team. Swimming was gruesome because the water was freezing, and as she was the only one in the top form who couldn't actually swim, she had to stay on her own in the shallow end.

Towards the end of one lesson, Tally had suddenly managed three strokes without going under, and then a few more until, finally, she'd done a whole width without once touching the bottom. After that it was quite easy, really, and she was allowed up the deep end with the others. But she was still always the last to jump in.

The hay house was much bigger now. They'd found more branches and worked the ends deeper into the earth so that they didn't keep falling over, and they made a criss-cross of sticks for a proper roof and gathered more hay to cover it all. It was better than any of the others and nice and cosy. They lay in it, side by side, pretending all sorts of things.

Sometimes the Germans had invaded England and Flora and Tally were hiding from them, evading capture. The German soldiers walked right by the hay house and they had to keep absolutely still and not make a sound, but it was so cleverly camouflaged that the soldiers always missed it. Quite often, to please Flora, they were away at Pony Club Camp, and had taken their own ponies who were grazing quietly outside. Tally took her chestnut, Flame, and they invented a lovely skewbald for Flora called Patches. Once, they were both heiresses who had been kidnapped and held to ransom and were waiting to be rescued by Dick Barton.

When they got tired of pretending things, they told each other secrets about awful things they'd done.

'I smoked one of Mummy's cigarettes once,' Flora confessed. 'I took one and hid behind the toolshed and lit it. It made me feel sick.'

'Oh, I've smoked lots of cigarettes,' Tally said. 'I pinched one of Papa's cigars, too, but I couldn't get it to light properly. And I drank a whole lot of gin. I've tried all sorts of drinks – whisky, vodka, sherry, brandy, liqueurs . . . And when The Cow's out I sometimes go through her drawers and read her letters. Paget caught me once and sneaked on me. She's as bad as Fish Face.'

'Didn't you get into awful trouble?' Flora sounded quite shocked.

'Not really. They made me stay in my room for ages, but I'm mostly in there anyway.' Tally looked up at the hay ceiling, frowning. 'I've got another secret, if you promise not to tell.'

'Cross my heart.' Flora slashed at her chest with her finger.

'I think I'm going to die.'

'Don't be silly! Of course you're not.'

'I might. I've got something *terrible* wrong with me.'

'What's wrong?' Flora propped herself up on one elbow. '*I* can't see anything.'

'Well, when I went to the lav this morning there was blood everywhere, and it won't stop. I've had to put wads of lav paper in my pants . . . and I've got an awful pain in my stomach.'

'Oh, I know what that is, Tally. You're not dying at all. It's Eve's Curse.'

'What?'

'Don't you know about it? Mummy told me before I came here, in case I start it.' It wasn't often that Flora knew something Tally didn't and she was looking rather pleased and important.

'There's no one to tell me.'

'Oh, poor Tally . . .'

'*Tell* me, then.'

'Well, Mummy said that all women have it. It's called The Curse because Eve was cursed after beguiling Adam in the Garden of Eden and taking the apple, and all that business, you know . . . Anyway, you get it once a month.'

'Get *what*?'

'Well, what you've got. The Curse. You bleed from . . . well, down there somewhere, and it's a nuisance because you have to wear towel things all the time, and sometimes it hurts. And then it stops again until the next month. It's something to do with having babies, too, but I've forgotten exactly what. You get it when you're growing up and it goes on for years and years.'

67

Tally let out her breath in a long sigh of relief. She had been imagining the most frightening things. 'I thought it was something horrible.'

'You'll have to go and see Matron. She'll tell you what to do, I expect, and give you those things. I've seen some packets of them in her cupboard.'

'Ugh! What a bore.'

'You are lucky!' Flora looked envious now, instead of important. 'I wish I'd get it.'

Tally squinted up at the hay ceiling; she could see little bits of bright blue sky through the gaps. 'Actually,' she said, 'it's *you* that's the lucky one, Flora.'

Papa and The Cow came for Speech Day, near the end of the summer term, and The Cow wore a really stupid hat with masses of fake flowers round the brim and a spotted veil. It was miles bigger and fussier than any of the other mothers', and Tally could see the other girls nudging each other about it.

Tally sat next to Flora, twiddling her thumbs in her lap. Some old woman who'd been at the school a hundred years ago made a speech and then presented the silver cups and prizes. Miss Walters read out names and everybody clapped as each girl went up to get her prize. Tally flapped her hands together very slowly. It went on and on. Form cups, the music cup, the swimming cup, prizes for history and English and arithmetic and scripture . . .

It was stifling in the marquee and some of the mothers were fanning themselves with their programmes. Miss Walters was getting pinker and pinker in the face.

'Geography prize: Olive Fisher.'

Who cared about geography anyway? Tally made sure her own palms didn't meet at all this time. Fish Face came back carrying a book and looking smug.

'French prize: Atalanta Ashby.'

At first she thought she must have heard wrong, but Flora was nudging her excitedly. 'Go on, Tally. It's you. It's *you*!'

Miss Walters repeated her name rather sharply and Tally stood up. It seemed a long way up to the platform, past all the rows of parents clapping and turning round. The old woman smiled down at her and shook her hand, and said something about foreign languages being so useful as she handed her a book. She was still so stunned that she forgot to curtsey as they were supposed to do. When she walked back to her place, Flora was still clapping hard, and beaming. She didn't care that some of the others, including Fish Face, weren't.

The prize was a leather-bound French dictionary with a label inside on the marbled flyleaf, and beautiful slanting writing in black ink. She read it through the tears that had suddenly come into her eyes.

ATALANTA ASHBY
FRENCH PRIZE
ST CECILIA'S, BEECHLAWN GIRLS' COLLEGE,
JULY, 1948.

PART TWO

Five

'*Caesari cum id nuntiatum esset, in Galliam contendit.* Flora, translate, if you please.'

Miss Grainger's cold grey eyes had fallen upon her, picking her out of the class. Flora stared in panic at the Latin textbook open on her desk. The words were a jumble before her eyes. It was a horrible language to work out – cases and genders and the verb at the end so you didn't know where to begin to get the sense of it. She could manage it alright for prep, with a dictionary and lots of time, but whenever she was asked to translate unseen in class her mind seemed to go completely blank.

'I'm waiting. So are we all.'

'Caesar . . . when . . . when . . .'

'When what?' Miss Grainger's voice was bitingly sarcastic. She had a chalk-white face, wiry grey hair, and thin, bloodless lips. Just like a witch.

'When . . .' What on earth was *nuntiatum*? Out of the corner of her eye she could see Tally, at the next desk, mouthing something at her. 'Um . . . um.'

'Really, Flora, this is an extremely simple sentence. *Nuntio, nuntiare* . . . surely you know that verb?'

'I've forgotten what it means, Miss Grainger.'

A sigh of irritation. 'Well, who *can* tell me? Olive?'

'Report or announce, Miss Grainger.' Fish Face's ever-ready hand had shot up first.

'Exactly. You should know that by now, Flora. You're bone idle and I won't tolerate laziness in my class. You will translate the whole of this exercise and the next two for preparation and bring them to me before classes start in the morning. Now, perhaps you can translate the rest of this sentence.'

She was close to tears, which she knew would please Miss Grainger, who liked nothing better than to make people cry. Tally never cried if the teachers were foul to her, which they often were. Her chin would go up and her face would take on a shuttered look. Flora wished very much that she could be the same.

Unfortunately, Miss Grainger was not the only mistress who could make her cry. Miss Plunket, her piano teacher, did so almost every lesson. Flora would stumble through her pieces with the same desperation as when she was trying to translate Latin in class, and Miss Plunket, sitting impatiently beside her, ruler in hand, muffled in scarves and sweaters against the room's icebox chill, would lean across and rap her over the knuckles if she made too many mistakes.

Even so, she was enjoying being in Middle School more than St Cecilia's and the first year had passed quickly. It had six separate houses, close to the main school, and luckily she and Tally were in the same one. So, unfortunately, was Olive Fisher.

As Tally had grown more beautiful, Fish Face had grown more ugly. Her spots had got a great deal worse and were now all over her face, especially on her bulging forehead. She had blackheads on her nose now, too, and her frizzy hair had gone greasy. Even though she was no longer a prefect since they had left the Junior School, she still tried to boss everyone about. Tally, of course, ignored her.

Flora had been to stay with Tally in London twice more during the Christmas holidays and the Earl and Countess had taken them to another American musical on Tally's fourteenth birthday. *Carousel* was all about a bragging fairground man and a shy mill girl who had fallen in love with him. Flora had wept buckets, and when the house lights went up Nicholas had passed her his silk handkerchief. He had left Harrow and was on leave from Caterham, where he was doing his National Service before going to Cambridge. Tally, as usual, had scarcely said a word to him, even when he gave her a beautiful leather writing case from Asprey's for her birthday.

'You might have looked more pleased,' Flora said to her when they were alone in Tally's bedroom after the theatre. 'It was a super present.'

Tally shrugged. 'I've already got one. Anyway, I didn't ask him to give me anything.'

'It must have been awfully expensive.'

'He can easily afford it. His father's a millionaire.'

'Gosh, is he?'

'Well, you didn't think The Cow would have been married to anyone *poor*, did you?'

'How did he get to be so rich?'

'Oh, something to do with making bricks and things, that's what Morecambe told me – he read all about it in a newspaper. At least, that's how it started. Then he bought a whole lot more companies. Morecambe says he buys and sells them all the time and gets richer and richer.'

Tally had insisted on giving Flora the writing case. It had the wrong initials on it, of course, but Flora didn't mind about that. The wonky zip on her old one had finally broken and she badly needed a new one, and even though it had really been meant for Tally, Nicholas had chosen it, which made it special. When she saw him again at Christmas, she thought he was more handsome than ever, in spite of the army haircut, and when he smiled at her, which he did several times, it made her heart beat faster. She longed to grow up quickly so that he would stop thinking of her as just a little girl.

In the summer she would be fourteen, too. She had started The Curse and wore a bust bodice now – a white cotton Kestos one with cross-over elastic straps that buttoned in front. Her mother had bought her three of them though there wasn't all that much to put in them yet. She had been five foot three when they were last measured at school and, with luck, she'd probably grow an inch or two more, though she didn't think she'd ever catch up with Tally, who was five foot six, with terrifically long legs. She still wore plaits, mostly because her mother made such a fuss about cutting her hair. Tally had hacked hers off with her nail scissors so that she wouldn't have to wear bunches any more, and she didn't have to wear a plate now either because her teeth had straightened. Fish Face was enormous now and her bosoms bounced around under her gym tunic when she ran up and down the games pitches.

'Do you think any man will *ever* fall in love with her, Tally?'

They were heading reluctantly in the direction of the hockey pitch, which were always freezing cold in the winter terms. The wind was already making Flora's bare ears ache; by the end of the game they would be agony.

Tally swiped at the grass with her hockey stick. 'Don't see how they could.'

'I don't either.'

Flora had just finished reading *Devil's Cub* by Georgette Heyer – one of the few romantic novels allowed on the house library shelves. She had been sighing for days over Lord Vidal, the tall, dark and handsome young hero, who would surely never have looked the way of anyone like Fish Face.

Tally had been rather scornful, and said he was too good to be true.

'"He caught her in his arms so fiercely that the breath was almost crushed out of her . . ."' Flora quoted.

'Honestly, Flora, that's really soppy.'

'No, it isn't. I think it's terribly romantic.'

Although she dreamed about him often, she wasn't sure that Lord Vidal would have looked *her* way either now that she'd started getting spots; there was a huge, hard one coming up on her chin, as well as the one on the side of her nose and the four on her forehead. What with them and the freckles he wouldn't have been impressed at all.

'If Fish Face weren't so beastly, I'd almost feel sorry for her. Just think, Tally, she might never get married.'

'Who'd have her?'

'Well, I suppose there *must* be someone somewhere who'll want her. Isn't there meant to be somebody special for everybody in the world? You just have to find them.'

Tally gave another savage swipe with her stick. She was

in a bad mood because she hated hockey as much as she had hated netball in Junior School.

'I don't believe in that sort of romantic tosh. And I don't care if *I* never do. I don't think getting married's so wonderful.'

'But what else would you do?

'Don't know. Get a job or something, I suppose.'

Flora couldn't imagine Tally working all day in an office or a shop. Nor did she much fancy the idea herself. She'd often thought she might like to be an actress – especially after reading *The Swish of the Curtain* and going to the theatre with Tally – but as she was only given small walk-on parts in school plays, she didn't think she was good enough, or pretty enough either. Tally was much better at acting and easily beautiful enough, but she didn't seem interested in going on the stage. Maybe it wouldn't count as a proper career anyway, or be the kind that Miss Benham would approve of.

All girls at Beechlawn were supposed to have a career. Miss Benham, who had been headmistress for years and years, was rumoured to have been a suffragette and to have chained herself to railings. She made it quite clear that she expected them to know what their career was by the time they reached the upper fifth when she would interview each girl, in turn, in her study. It was a frightening prospect.

So far, Flora hadn't the least idea what she wanted to do. I ought to want to do *something*, she thought – be a librarian, or a nurse, or an occupational therapist, or a physiotherapist. Those all sounded useful and respectable – the sort of career that Miss Benham would allow girls to follow.

Sometimes, when she wasn't dreaming about Lord Vidal, Flora thought of Nicholas. And sometimes the two of them got muddled up in her mind because they were both tall, dark and handsome. She would imagine Nicholas, dressed in buff breeches and a blue coat with silver buttons, wielding a rapier with dashing brilliance in her defence against a dastardly villain. He always won, but sometimes he was wounded in the process, and she would bandage the wound and bathe his feverish forehead tenderly. Or, at other times, Lord Vidal would be lounging nonchalantly in a box at the Theatre Royal in Drury Lane, opera glasses raised, watching her sing 'People Will Say We're in Love' on stage, and falling madly in love with her . . .

Tally had received a letter from Nicholas earlier in the term. It had been confiscated at first because the girls were only allowed letters from males who were relatives. After cross-examination by their housemistress she had been allowed to keep it, but as soon as she'd read it she had torn it in half and thrown it in the wastepaper basket. Flora had been dying of curiosity.

'What did he say?'

'Oh, nothing.'

Flora had secretly retrieved the letter and fitted the two parts together. It was written from the army barracks at Caterham in very grown-up writing. It said he hoped Atalanta was well and enjoying the term and that the writing case was useful. Flora had felt doubly guilty afterwards – for reading Tally's letter and for having the writing case.

The spring holidays were cold and wet and, to make matters worse, Desdemona died. Flora found her lying stiffly in her hutch one morning and cried over her furry body. Humphrey helped her to bury her at the bottom of the garden, where an apple tree hung over the fence. When the blossom came out it would shade the spot. They wrapped the rabbit in an old cardigan and Flora picked some daffodils to put in a jam jar on the grave.

'She had a good life,' Humphrey said. 'And a pretty long one, for a rabbit.'

Humphrey was always so calm and sensible, she thought. He never fussed about things or got upset the way she did. He was going to be a wonderful surgeon; he'd sit on the end of people's beds, soothing them and telling them it would be alright. And it would be.

They left the grave and walked back towards the house. Humphrey had turned sixteen a month ago and he was a lot taller than her so he took longer strides. She quickened her pace to keep up, her damp handkerchief balled up in her hand.

'It's awful these hols. Nothing to do and simply foul weather.'

'Haven't you got some school work?'

'In the holidays? It's supposed to be a rest. I don't know how you can study so much, Humphrey.'

Apart from having his nose in his books, he'd been spending hours dissecting a pickled dogfish. He wore his specs all the time now.

'Because I've got School Cert in less than three months, that's why. And then Higher two years from now, or whatever they're going to call the new exam. I want to get the best marks I can so I can get into one of the big London teaching hospitals – Bart's, or Guy's, or Thomas's, I hope. I want to train somewhere really good.'

'Won't you go to university first?'

He shook his head. 'I want to get on with it as soon as possible. And you know how it is with the money . . .'

'You're so lucky you know what you're going to be. I haven't a clue.'

'You'll think of something. How about being a nurse?'

'Ugh! I'd be hopeless – you know I would.'

'Teaching?'

Flora retched.

'Law?'

'I *hate* Latin and I'd have to go on doing that, wouldn't I?'

'I should think so. What about Tally, what's she going to do?'

'She doesn't know either. But I don't suppose she'll *need* to do anything, as they're so stinking rich. She'll just go and marry a lord and not bother.'

'That'd be a pity. She seems pretty bright.'

'Well, she's good at some things – like Latin and French and English – but she doesn't bother much if she doesn't like the subject. Actually, she doesn't bother about *anything* she doesn't like. You should see the way she just dawdles around on the hockey pitch, but with 'crosse she's brilliant, because she likes it.'

'Sounds to me as though she's been a bit spoiled. Just doing what she feels like all the time.'

'Oh, no! I mean, she's got all sorts of *things*, like gold watches and pearl necklaces, but she has a miserable time at home. Nobody cares much about her.'

'Poor Tally.' Humphrey stopped walking. 'She's an odd sort of friend for you to have, though, Flo, isn't she? You're so different in character, and poles apart in background.'

'I suppose so . . . . But it doesn't seem to matter. She wanted me to go to the south of France with them these holidays, you know, but her stepmother had invited other people so there wasn't room. I'm glad I didn't go now, because of Desdemona. I'd've felt even worse about her.'

They walked on to the back door of the house and went into the kitchen. The warmth of the Aga greeted them, and Hercules stretched out a lazy paw from his strategic spot on the counter beside it. There was a smell of something savoury cooking in the oven for lunch, and the table was laid ready. Flora stuffed her handkerchief away in her pocket. She suddenly felt quite hungry.

Dear Flora,

This place would be really nice if it weren't for The Cow being here too. I spend all day by the pool, doing nothing, and I'm absolutely black!! One day you must come here – you'd love it. They've said I can go to Melton in the summer hols as Nanny's going there with Thomas, so please come and stay too. The Cow won't be there as they're to spend the summer down here and in Italy.

See you next term – ugh!!!

Love, Tally

Morecambe drove them to Norfolk in the Rolls. Thomas sat on the back seat between Nanny and Tally, with his fat little legs sticking straight out. Flora was on the fold-down seat because Tally always felt sick if she travelled backwards for too long. She watched Thomas wriggling about with excitement. At three, he was a beautiful little boy. He had the same sort of colouring as Tally, but Flora thought his blue eyes had a look of Nicholas, though she'd never say so to Tally. He had a sweet smile and a lovely, gurgling laugh, and she could tell that Tally actually liked him quite a lot, though she always pretended not to.

'He's a bit better now he's bigger,' she'd once admitted grudgingly. 'And it's not *his* fault that he's got a cow for a mother.'

When Morecambe drove the Rolls between the big gates at the entrance to Melton Hall, Flora had to twist round to see the house through the glass partition behind her. As soon as she caught a glimpse of it at the end of the long driveway, bathed in sunshine, she understood why Tally had always said that it was her favourite place on earth.

It was built of bricks that had faded to a lovely warm orange-brown. She saw stone-mullioned windows, turreted towers and tall chimneys standing in pairs on the roof. It looked very old and very beautiful. And friendly, as though it was waiting for them. The Rolls made a crunching sound over the gravel and Thomas, who had fallen sound asleep with his head on Nanny's lap, woke up and started wriggling around again, trying to see out. One day it will all belong to him, Flora thought, though he doesn't know it yet. It must be awfully hard for Tally, when she loves it so.

The stables were at the side of the house and built of the same old lovely brick. There was a cobbled yard with loose boxes and stalls and a tack room with a hayloft above. The clock in the clock tower above said ten past nine.

'It hasn't worked for years,' Tally told her. 'But it used to. And it had nice chimes. These are Papa's hunters, Warlord and Chieftain.' She patted the noses of two large and very handsome horses as they walked along the loose boxes. 'And this is my pony, Flame.'

This was one of those times, Flora thought as she leaned

over the loose-box door, when it was impossible not to envy Tally, in spite of the sad things she knew about her. The chestnut pony was the prettiest she had ever seen. It had four white socks, a gleaming coat and a lovely thick mane. It came towards her, ears pricked, and she stroked its soft, whiskery muzzle.

'I'm too big for him now really,' Tally said. 'So I suppose he'll have to be sold, unless he's kept for Thomas. But you can still have a go on him if you like. It won't hurt him.'

'Will you get another?'

'I shouldn't think so. I don't know how often I'll be able to come here now.'

'Oh, Tally . . . what a shame. It's so lovely.'

'Yes, I do mind an awful lot. And it isn't fair that it's going to be Thomas's. It ought to be whoever's born first, girl or boy. But it's entailed with the title, so it's got to be a male. Actually, if Thomas hadn't been born, I still wouldn't have inherited Melton. It would have gone to Papa's brother and then *his* son, who's utterly wet. So I'm glad *they're* not getting it. That would be even worse. It's much fairer with the royal family.'

'How do you mean?'

'Well, Princess Elizabeth will be queen one day; it's not like one of her uncles will be king.'

'Mmm. I see what you mean.' Flora sighed. 'Poor her! I wouldn't want to be, would you? But then she's got Prince Philip to stand by her side. And he's simply gorgeous.'

'I thought you always liked dark people – like Lord Vidal and Rhett Butler and Heathcliff and Mr Rochester. And Nicholas.'

'I haven't said I like Nicholas.'

'You've never said you don't, have you? And you always stand up for him. I think you've got a crush on him, Flora.'

'No, I haven't. Honestly, I haven't.'

'Well, last time you came to stay you went red whenever he spoke to you. I noticed it. And you're all red now.' Tally sounded accusing. 'I can't think what you see in him.'

'I don't see anything . . .' Flora hid her face in Flame's

neck and stroked his mane. She changed the subject quickly.

'Who looks after the horses, when you're not here?'

'Liversidge. He's been our groom forever. And there's a boy who helps him, and helps Trunch too in the gardens. There used to be a whole lot of servants here, of course – before the war – but I don't really remember it then. Nanny and I were here during the war, though – until the American Air Force came and took the house over.'

'Did you have to have them here?'

'Oh yes. We had to get out in a few days. Everything was packed away until after the war was over.'

'How awful!'

'Actually, it was rather fun. They were jolly nice and kept giving me chewing gum and chocolate. Nanny got furious about that. She and I went to live in one of our cottages on the estate and the Americans turned the house into an officers' mess. I came to a Christmas party they gave for all the children in the village and ate so much I was sick. They painted pin-up girls all over the walls in the old dairy while they were here . . . Come on, I'll show you.'

The dairy was a long, low building across the yard from the kitchens. Tally opened the door.

'There.'

The light fell on to whitewashed walls inside revealing paintings on them. None of the girls had a single stitch of clothing on, except for very high-heeled shoes. One girl had her right foot poised to put on a pair of blue French knickers; another was lying down, casually waving a straw hat; another was kneeling with her hands behind her head, lifting her long blonde hair off her shoulders. One girl was leaning back on a chair, one leg crossed over the other, her high-heeled shoe pointing up in the air, and the next had turned her back and was peeping coyly over one shoulder.

Flora swallowed and giggled. She could feel herself going hot in the face. 'Goodness!'

'Nanny doesn't know they're here, so don't say a word whatever you do or she'll have them whitewashed over.

They're awfully well done, aren't they?' Tally was considering the naked girls, her head on one side.

'I suppose so.'

'You've gone red again, Flora. You're shocked.'

'No, I'm not.' She flicked back her plaits defiantly. 'I've just never seen anything like them before. Who on earth did them?'

'Someone called Chuck. You can see he put his name in the corner there. Chuck Morgan, Jacksonville, Texas.'

'How would he know to paint things like that?'

'I suppose it's his girlfriend or something. If you look, you can see it's all the same girl.'

'You mean, she'd have taken off all her clothes for him to paint her?'

'Well, not in here. He must have done it from memory. You're like a beetroot, Flora. Men know what girls look like without clothes, anyway. From pictures and paintings and photos, and things.'

'Perhaps Chuck was an artist . . .'

Tally laughed. 'He was probably just a cook. They used the dairy as a sort of extra kitchen. There's more in one of the buildings over at the old airfield. That's where they used to fly their bombers from to go over to Germany. Nanny and I used to watch them go off and come back again. I can remember that quite clearly. Nanny used to count them and sometimes there were an awful lot missing.'

'How sad!'

'I know. But I don't think I realized what would have happened to them at the time. All I really cared about was the chewing gum and the chocolate.'

The weather stayed hot and sunny for almost the whole month that they spent in Norfolk. Flora had riding lessons on Flame with Liversidge, who was old and bandy-legged and whistled all the time through his few teeth, like a simmering kettle. He showed her how to mount and sit properly in the saddle, how to hold the reins correctly, and how to give commands with her legs and feet and hands.

'You're the boss, miss. He's waiting for you to tell him what to do next, see. Just a nudge and he'll know.'

She soon graduated from walking round the field to trotting. But when Flame broke into a canter, Flora promptly fell off and lay winded in the grass until Liversidge and Tally hurried over to help her up.

'You were pretty good, though,' Tally told her later. 'You'll soon get it.'

They went out on bike rides round the countryside, and once they rode as far as the sea, which was five miles away. Privately, Flora didn't think that the beach there was nearly as nice as the one in Cornwall. There were no cliffs or rocks or pools and hardly any sand – mostly shingle – and the sea looked grey, even on a sunny day.

'Of course, it's the North Sea,' said Tally, who seemed to sense what Flora was thinking.

They left their bikes and took their socks and shoes off to paddle. The water was cold and rather murky. If you could only move Melton to Cornwall, Flora decided, then it would be simply perfect.

In the Christmas holidays, Humphrey went to stay with his godfather for a week and Tally went skiing in Switzerland with the Earl and Countess. Flora got a postcard from Zermatt with a picture of the Matterhorn covered in snow. *Having a gruesome time. Wish you were here.*

Nicholas wouldn't be with them. Tally had told her he'd been sent out to Africa on his National Service. 'Good riddance,' she'd added.

I still like him, though, Flora thought as she stuck the postcard on the mantlepiece. I like him an awful lot. She still daydreamed about him, too. He was no longer dressed like Lord Vidal, but in army uniform, leading his men into battle. Once he had been quite badly wounded and she visited him in hospital where he smiled at her from his bed and told her that she had made the pain go away. In her favourite dream he came home on leave when she was staying with Tally in London, and when he saw Flora coming down the staircase he stood rooted to the spot in the hall, gazing up at her, amazed at how she had grown up and how beautiful she had become.

When she looked in the mirror afterwards, though, she knew it could only ever be a dream.

Six

'My heart aches, and a drowsy numbness pains
My sense, as though of hemlock I had drunk,
Or emptied some dull opiate to the drains
One minute past, and Lethe-wards had sunk . . .'

Tally, lying flat on her back, stared up at the sky above her.
'Um . . . Um . . . Oh, hell's bells, I've completely forgotten.
What's next, then?'

Flora, cross-legged on the grass beside her, was holding
the poetry book up high so that she couldn't cheat.

''Tis not.'

''Tis not through envy of thy happy lot,
But being too happy in thine happiness,
That thou, light-winged Dryad of the trees,
In some melodious plot
Of beechen green, and shadows numberless,
Singest of summer in full-throated ease.'

'Go on,' Flora mumbled through the Horlicks tablet she
was chewing. She waved the book. 'There're another seven
verses.'

'I know there are. But I can't be bothered. It's too hot.'
Tally fanned herself with her hand. The sky was cloudless
and deep blue, the sun very bright. She shut her eyes. Some
lower-sixth formers were playing tennis on the nearby courts.
Lucky so-and-sos, not having bloody exams. 'He took drugs,
you know.'

'What? Who?'

'Keats. Opium, or something. That's what all that *dull opiate* stuff's about. I read it somewhere. Not that old Bees Knees would ever tell us that. Far too shocking. Remember how red she went when somebody asked her what phallic meant? "See me after class is over."'

'What *does* it mean? I've forgotten.'

'It's to do with a man's whatsit. That sort of shape, you know.'

'Oh.'

'I wonder what it'll be like having one stuck into us.'

'*Honestly*, Tally!'

'Honestly, what? We know that's what happens, don't we? Then they squirt their sperm stuff into you. Haven't you ever thought about it?'

'Not exactly . . .'

'I bet you only ever get as far as the kissing bit. Being crushed in someone's arms – like Lord Vidal's – lips bruised by his passion and all the rest of it.' Tally fanned herself lazily again. 'I want to know about the other part . . .'

'We're *supposed* to be revising.'

'Oh, lord . . .'

'Do you want me to test you on *Pride and Prejudice*?' Flora was looking hopefully at her. It was her favourite book at the moment and, of course, she was bonkers about Mr Darcy.

'Can't be bothered with that, either. I think Elizabeth should have gone off with Wickham. Darcy's such a stiff-neck.'

'No, he isn't. He just keeps his feelings hidden, like a true gentleman. Come on, Tally, we've got English Lit. in three days' time . . .'

'I'll just fail. I don't care.'

'No you won't. But I wish we were doing the old School Cert, not this GCE thing. I mean, nobody knows what O levels really are, do they? Supposing we fail everything?'

'You won't, Flora. *I* probably will, because I haven't revised like you. But then I'm leaving at the end of term anyway, whatever happens.'

88

'Lucky you! But I wish you weren't. It's going to be awful without you. Fish Face is bound to be made a prefect – she's such a goody-goody. It makes me sick. Do you remember how she cried when Miss Benham announced the King had died, and how she kept praying for him every night for weeks? You'd think he was closely related to her, the way she carried on.' Flora tugged fretfully at her socks. 'Do you really want to go to finishing school, Tally? Won't you hate it?'

'Probably, but I'll get away from here. And I'll be able to do quite a bit of skiing.'

'What else will you do?'

'Oh, cooking. Flower arranging. Table setting. All that sort of stupid stuff. *Really* boring – except for the cooking. And French, too, of course. But that'll be easy. German, maybe. And it's only for six months.'

'Then what'll you do?'

'The Season, I suppose.'

'What happens with that?'

'Well, I get presented at Court with all the other debs – not by The Cow, thank God. She can't because she's divorced, so it'll be an aunt of mine. I have to go to Buckingham Palace and curtsey to the Queen and Prince Philip. And then I go to a whole lot of dances and cocktail parties, and Ascot and Henley and Wimbledon, things like that . . . And then it stops.'

'Then what?'

'I marry someone, I suppose. That's the point of the Season.'

'I thought you said you didn't want to get married ever.'

'I might as well – as long as I don't have much to do with whoever it is. I'll spend my days shopping in Harrods and Fortnums, and having lunch with people and going to theatre matinees.'

'I shouldn't think Miss Benham would approve.'

'She certainly wouldn't.'

Flora looked defeated. 'I've got *two* more years here. That's forever. I wish Mummy would let me leave before A levels. She goes on about me being qualified to train at something, but there's nothing I want to train at. I'm not like Humphrey, who's always known what he wanted to do. And he's terrifically clever, too. He'll pass his As easily.'

'What's he taking?'

'Chemistry, physics and biology.'

'Ugh!'

'I know. Then he's going to a teaching hospital in London.'

'Doesn't he have to do National Service?'

'He's allowed to wait till after he's qualified as a doctor. He's more use to them then, I suppose. Has Nicholas finished his?'

'Who cares?'

'Did you see him at all in the hols?'

She's trying to sound very casual, but she's still got a crush on him, Tally thought. Even though she hasn't seen him for years.

'No, thank goodness. But The Cow kept saying that darling Nicky would be back from Nigeria soon. Now, if you married *him*, Flora, you wouldn't have to worry about getting a job and having a career. He'll have stacks and stacks of lolly. As much as Mr Darcy.'

'Don't be silly.'

'I'm not. Perhaps he'll fall for you one day.'

Tally rolled over on to her side and watched the tennis players for a while. Tennis was one of the few things she hadn't minded at Beechlawn. And lacrosse. She'd miss playing 'crosse. And she'd miss acting in plays, too, but she couldn't think of anything else that she'd miss, except for Flora. Funny, in the end she'd never run away or got herself expelled. Too much effort.

Civilisation. At last she'd be free of school uniform and petty rules and bitchy mistresses and priggish sneaks like Fish Face. Free of them all – for ever and ever, amen.

'Have a Horlicks?' Flora was holding out the tube.

'Thanks.' She sucked on the tablet for a while. 'I wish you could come to France and stay in the villa. You'd love Les Rosiers.'

'So do I. But I can't. I told you, Mummy's booked for

us to go to Devon. Humphrey'll be away staying with his godfather, so I've got to go with her.'

'What'll you do there?'

'Go for walks on Dartmoor and things like that.'

'Well, you'll come another time. When I get back from Switzerland. And we'll go to Melton again, too.'

Flora was staring off into the distance. 'I'd like that, Tally, but quite honestly I think we're going to be leading awfully different lives from now on. I'm not sure if it'll work out . . . if you see what I mean.'

'No, I don't see what you mean.'

'Well, it hasn't mattered much while we've both been at Beechlawn, but now you're going off to Switzerland and being presented to the Queen, and all that kind of thing.'

'You do talk the most awful bilge sometimes. It won't make any difference.'

But Flora's head was still turned away and she didn't answer.

The bell sounded in the distance and, from the way that Flora grabbed up her books, Tally could tell she was quite upset – almost in tears.

A silly rhyme was going through her head as they walked back to the house for tea.

This time four weeks, where shall I be?
Out of the gates of misery . . .

Seven

Dear Flora,

You'd loathe it here. The girls are snobby bitches and thick as two planks. All they think and talk about is clothes and men and doing the Season. They've all got a crush on our skiing instructor, Henri, who's madly good-looking, with a terrific tan. He wouldn't look as good back in England, though, and he's actually dull as ditch water off skis.

French is a doddle – the others can hardly speak a sentence and I'm the only one who knows any German. Flower arranging stinks, but I quite like cooking. I've put on pounds because I eat everything I cook and we're always going to a cafe in the town and stuffing ourselves with cream cakes . . .

Flora turned over the page. There were four more sides covered with Tally's big writing, and from the sound of everything she didn't think she'd loathe it at all. As far as she could tell, Tally was having a marvellous time not having to do any work, skiing every day and eating lovely cakes.

Papa is renting a chalet near here for a month at Christmas for the holidays so I won't be back until the end of March. See you then.

Love, Tally

Fish Face was peering nosily over her shoulder.

'Is that from Tally Ashby? I thought I recognized her

peculiar writing. She went off to some snobby finishing school, didn't she? Typical! I bet she's going to be one of those awful debutantes. Completely useless.'

Flora rounded on her. 'This is a private letter, if you don't mind.'

Fish Face gave her a silly sort of smile. 'You always stuck up for her, didn't you, Flora? I suppose it was the title that dazzled you. It never impressed *me*, I can tell you.'

She was just jealous, of course, and always had been. Jealous of everything about Tally – including the title, however much she denied it.

Fish Face sometimes sat next to her in class, which was unpleasant in more ways than one, as she often smelled. She was still Miss Grainger's pet in Latin.

If only Flora could have given up Latin and Miss Grainger, but Miss Benham had said she must go on with it so that she could go to university if she did well enough in her A levels. She hadn't dared to argue with her. For history prep that evening she had to write a long essay on industrial unrest in England in the early twentieth century.

Oh, lucky, lucky Tally.

'May I suggest, Lady Gresham, that this gown might be particularly suitable for your stepdaughter. I call it "English Rose". I think it would be quite delightful on Lady Atalanta.'

Mr Randolph flapped his wrist in the direction of the house model who was slinking towards them, showing off a sugar-pink evening dress, with pink beads on the bodice and bouffant tulle skirts sprinkled all over with sequins. Tally shifted on her chair and hugged her stomach. She had a ghastly Curse pain and the showroom was hot and airless and reeked of sickly scent. She watched the model swivelling this way and that, fanning out the skirts so that the sequins sparkled under the chandelier lights, and then twirling all the way round. She was very tall and thin as a beanpole, with blank eyes that stared straight ahead, and a lot of thick make-up. As she turned, Tally noticed that her shoulder blades stuck out like knives and she could see the little knobs of her spine disappearing down into the bodice. The pink gown retreated and, after more twirlings at the salon doorway, disappeared altogether.

The Cow nodded. 'Possible, Paul. Possible. Though it's a little low-cut . . .'

Mr Randolph's fingers fluttered. 'We could make an adjustment at the fitting, Lady Gresham.' He gave Tally the sort of stupid smile grown-ups give to small children. 'Well, what do *you* think, Lady Atalanta? You would certainly be the belle of the ball.'

'I don't like pink, actually. Or sequins.'

The smile vanished. 'In that case,' he clapped his hands, 'you will prefer *"Fleur Blanc"*.'

'*Blanche*. It's feminine.'

'Exactly . . . As I said, *"Fleur Blanche"*. *Perfect* for Queen Charlotte's.'

Tally did prefer it – infinitely. The white ballgown was sequinless and beadless and, best of all, strapless.

'A lily,' Mr Randolph explained, in raptures. 'That is what I had in mind when I created this model. Very pure and exquisitely beautiful.'

The Cow, naturally, made a big fuss over it being strapless, but Mr Randolph had got the message and was on Tally's side now. He snapped his fingers and an assistant hurried forward with a length of white tulle that he draped around the model's shoulders. 'See, Lady Gresham, we can overcome that very easily . . .'

After some more wrangling, a blue watered-silk dress was chosen for her presentation, and then The Cow wanted to order things for herself. The afternoon dragged on and on, as afternoon dresses, cocktail dresses, and evening gowns from Mr Randoph's grisly summer collection were paraded up and down before them. It was five o'clock before they left the showroom.

Morecambe was waiting patiently outside with the Rolls, and all the way home The Cow talked about styles and materials and colours and about how wonderful Mr Randoph was, and how lucky *she* was to be having two of his gowns.

Tally picked at her gloved fingers and watched Green Park going by. The daffodils were all out – and the leaves on the trees. London looked especially nice. It always did in spring.

'We ought to consider the pink for your own dance, Atalanta,' The Cow said. 'I thought it was extremely attractive.'

'Pink doesn't suit me.'

'I think perhaps *I* should be the judge of that . . . I have rather more experience than you.'

Tally's fingertip was poking through a hole she'd made in the glove seam. She gnawed at it, staring out of the window. The rush-hour traffic round Hyde Park Corner was a solid mass of vehicles, like a great log-jam. Some stands were already being put up for spectators at the coronation procession, and men were working on the scaffolding at the side of the road. Papa and The Cow would be in the Abbey, of course, and Tally was supposed to be going to sit in Parliament Square with one of her aunts and some cousins. She wondered if the Queen was beginning to feel nervous.

Dear Tally,

Did you enjoy the coronation? I thought it was fantastic! They let us go home from school for five days, which was almost the best thing about it. Mummy and I went to watch it next door as they have a television set. Their sitting room was jam-packed and I was squashed on the sofa in between two old women who kept crying and saying 'God bless her' all the time. The television screen was so small that I couldn't see very well from where I was sitting, but I thought it was amazing to think we were watching it actually happen, and the Queen looked absolutely beautiful.

Did you see her from where you were sitting? It must have been wonderful to see it in real life and in colour. You are lucky!

Humphrey saw it too, as he's in London now. He's a medical student at Guy's Hospital – did I tell you?

He had to camp out all night and stand for hours in the crowds. He got drenched but he said it was worth it. Wasn't it fantastic about them climbing Everest?

Thanks awfully for the invitation to your dance in July. I'd love to come, and to stay at Melton for it. I'm not sure if Humphrey will be able to come, too, but I know he'd like to if he can get the time off. The only thing is, neither of us has anything proper to wear, but I expect we'll manage something. How are you getting on with the Season? Do write and tell me all about it.

Love, Flora

'Actually, it only took me thirty-five minutes to get here from Sandhurst. The thing is to avoid the A30 and Staines, you see. I always take the 319, then pick up a B road I happen to know that goes round the back of Weybridge to Walton-on-Thames. Jolly good short cut, that. Worth knowing. Then I pick up the 244, past Sandown, and whip round to Kingston. Plain sailing from there on – past Robin Hood Gate, over Putney Bridge and up the King's Road . . . Bob's your uncle.'

'Really?' Tally swallowed a yawn. She couldn't remember his name, but whoever he was, he was boring her to death with his short cuts. 'How interesting.' Her shoes were killing her and she was definitely getting a corn. She took one foot out and rubbed her toes against her calf.

He was sipping his gin and tonic, gazing at her earnestly with his popping-out blue eyes. His moustache reminded her of a worn-down toothbrush.

'I expect you live in London?'

'Mostly.'

'Country at weekends, though, I suppose?'

'Usually.'

'Going to the Buxton's dance this Saturday, by any chance?'

'Yes.'

'I say, you wouldn't care for a lift? I know a frightfully good way. Cuts out Sevenoaks completely. You see, I always

96

take the A22 instead of the 21 and pop across on the B2028, pick up the 2026 and then the 2110—'

'Excuse me a moment,' she said. 'There's someone I've just seen that I simply have to talk to.'

Charles Lisle was a friend of Nicholas's who had stayed with them in France that summer. She didn't want to talk to him in the least, but he provided the only handy escape route from another cross-country tour. She made her way to where she had caught sight of him across the room, weaving through the crowd of debs and their delights, catching snatches of conversation as she went.

'The most *ghastly* bunfight, my dear! The eats were too frightful, and the champers was simply undrinkable . . .'

'What on *earth* is she wearing? I mean, *honestly* . . .'

Charles was delighted to see her. 'I say, I didn't know you were here, Tally. Saw you at the Dalrymple thrash last week but couldn't get near you for admirers.'

'Bores, you mean. I've just been stuck in a corner with another one. He's been telling me how to avoid going through Staines and Sevenoaks.'

'I'd have rescued you, but I've only just got here. This is my third drinks party this evening. The other two were incredibly dull, so I didn't stay long.' He gave her a "here-I-am-lucky-you" smile. 'I can't remember who's actually giving this one.'

'I'm off soon,' she said.

'What a coincidence, so am I. And I suggest I take you to dinner somewhere nice. My car's parked right outside.'

It was a cream-coloured sports two-seater, and the usual contortions were required to get in and out in her sheath dress and high-heels. And, like all drivers of similar cars, he drove off from the kerb like Stirling Moss. Apparently this one was an Austin Healey, or so he informed her as they raced up Sloane Street. She gathered that she was supposed to be impressed. It was a warm summer's evening and still light – the sort of golden evening when she thought London looked really lovely. They whipped past Harvey Nichols, across the traffic lights and round by Scotch House.

'Thought we'd pop into the Wellington,' he said. 'Know it?'

She'd been there twice last week with different escorts – both of them a real yawn – but the grub was OK. And Charles wasn't exactly a yawn, just too pleased with himself.

In the restaurant downstairs, a band was playing 'So in Love' and a few couples were smooching around on the pocket-handkerchief dance floor. Two of the girls were fellow debs, clinging to the necks of cavalry officers. One of them waved vaguely at her; the other was far too absorbed to notice her at all. Half the girls were madly in love with some man or other – mostly weeds, in her opinion.

She glanced at the menu and asked for the same thing she'd had the last two times, because she couldn't be fagged to think of anything else. She'd been out almost every night for weeks: cocktail parties and dinners and dances and nightclubs in London during the week, and then a big dance somewhere in the country every weekend that had lasted until dawn, and a house party that carried on through most of Sunday.

'Thanks for the invitation,' Charles said. 'I wasn't expecting one.'

'My stepmother put you on the list. She says you're an extremely charming young man. You made a big impression with her in France.'

'I'd far sooner make one with you.'

She rolled her eyes. 'If you're going to say that sort of thing, I'm leaving.'

'Alright. Change of subject. How was Switzerland?'

'The skiing was fun. That's about all.'

'Nicholas said you were getting pretty good when he saw you at Christmas.'

'I don't actually care what Nicholas thinks.'

'Not much love lost between you two, is there?'

'He thinks I'm a spoiled, attention-seeking little bitch who's rude to his mother.' She tweaked the flowers on the table. 'Well, the second part's true, I have to admit. I *am* rude sometimes. I know I am. The thing is, I simply can't stand her. I never have been able to, since I was ten. And she can't stand me.'

'Tricky.'

'We've got a sort of pax going for the Season, though.'

'What about afterwards?'

She shrugged. 'Don't know. I think she's hoping I'll get married to somebody and leave home.'

'Isn't that rather the point of it anyway?'

'There's nobody I want to marry, thanks very much.'

'You haven't met anyone at all of these parties and dances?'

'They're all complete weeds.'

'I hope that doesn't include me?'

'You're not a weed, Charles. You're a wolf. And that's just as boring. I've heard the other debs talking about you. They talk about all the men – you should hear them. You're classified as NSA.'

'NSA?'

'Not safe anywhere.'

He looked pretty pleased about that. They danced cheek to cheek on the pocket handkerchief to some dreamy music and when he drove her back to Eaton Terrace she let him kiss her in the car. It was a lot better than some of the slobbery efforts she'd had to put up with. He knew how to kiss rather well, *and* did all the tongue bit, but it meant nothing to her at all. Absolutely nothing.

Flora lifted her head, dripping wet, from the hand basin and looked into the mirror. Her hair hung in corkscrew curls round her face.

'Are you sure this is right?'

'I think so.' Sally from next door was reading the instructions carefully again. 'I've done just what it said. Now we have to set it on the curlers and dry it. Then it'll look like the picture on the front. Soft, natural waves – like it says here.'

She sat rigidly, towel round her shoulders, and watched in the mirror as Sally wound the corkscrews back on to the curlers. It took ages and she didn't always get the hair quite straight and smooth, so that bits were left poking out. There was a sinking, panicky feeling in Flora's stomach – the kind she always got when something awful was going to happen. Sally tied a bright-pink hairnet over the curlers, stuffing cotton wool wodges under it at each side to protect her ears, and wheeled over her mother's home hairdryer. Her parents always had the latest things, like the new television set in the sitting room with a big twelve-inch screen, and the automatic washing machine in the kitchen. Flora sat with her head under the dryer. It looked as though she was wearing a huge helmet and she felt trapped inside it. In spite of the cotton wool, the heat seared the tips of her ears. Her face was getting redder and redder and she now wished that she had never agreed to let Sally give her a home perm. She had hoped she might look better for Tally's dance.

It was forty minutes before Sally would let her out from under the dryer, and by that time Flora's face was a shiny scarlet. Off came the hairnet and the cotton wool wodges and she saw that the hair round the curlers looked baked dry and anything but shining. Wisps like hay stuck out all over her head, and the hairnet had left a mark, like a long wound. Sally began to unwind the curlers. When she had finished there was silence. Flora stared at her reflection with horror. She put her hands over her face.

Humphrey was waiting by the bookstall at Liverpool Street station. Flora had tied a scarf over her hair to hide it from him – and from everyone, including herself. They found an empty third-class compartment and he slung her suitcase up on the luggage rack. When they sat down in corner seats opposite each other he smiled at her.

'You're looking very grown-up, Flo.'

She fingered her cotton skirt. 'I don't feel it. Everyone else is going to be fearfully smart.'

'Does it really matter?'

He'd never cared about clothes, never minded about the jumble sales and the making-do. He was wearing the same grey trousers he'd had for years – a bit short for him now, so that too much ankle and sock showed – and a tweed jacket that Mummy had unearthed in a second-hand clothes shop. We're both going to look like the poor relations, Flora thought. Or the poor friends. I wish we weren't going at all, even if Nicholas is going to be there. In fact, *especially* if Nicholas is going to be there. Her dream of coming down the stairs and him seeing her had turned into a nightmare. If he was rooted to the floor at the sight of her it would be because she looked such a fright. She slumped miserably into the corner. A big spot had come up on her chin that morning and she'd tried to squeeze it and only made it much worse. What with that and the hair and the dress . . .

'Don't worry, I've hired a dinner jacket,' Humphrey said, guessing her thoughts. 'And a black tie. Trouble is, I don't know how to tie it.'

'Perhaps someone will show you. There're going to be other people staying.'

Three other debs and assorted delights, Tally had scrawled in her letter, making them sound like a box of chocolates. *And Nicholas, worse luck*. So Nicholas would see her looking like this. It was too dreadful to think about.

The train pulled out of the station, belching smelly smoke and steam that drifted back into the compartment. Humphrey got up to close the window and sat down again. He gave her another quick smile.

'What are you going to wear, then? Have you got a new dress?'

'Mummy couldn't afford it. She found an old dress of Granny's in a trunk up in the attic. It's one she wore to dances apparently.' She tried hard to speak quite normally, but her voice trembled. The yellow chiffon dress was a joke. The waist was somewhere down by her hips and it had silly beads all over it, some of which were missing.

Humphrey leaned over and put his hand on her knee. 'You'll look fine, Flo. Really you will.'

He was being so sympathetic that it made her feel worse; her throat went tight and tears came into her eyes. 'No, I won't. I'll look ridiculous.' She snatched at the headscarf and tore it off. 'And just *look* at my hair!'

'Oh, Flora!' Tally put her hand over her mouth. 'What *have* you done to it?'

'It's a home perm. But it went all wrong. Sally did it for me – you know, the girl who lives next door – and she must have left the stuff on too long or something. It's a disaster, isn't it?'

'Yes, it is. It looks ghastly.'

In a way she was grateful to Tally for not pretending, like Humphrey had. More sympathy would have made her start crying again and then she would have had red eyes on top of everything else. She could see her reflection in the looking glass in Tally's bedroom and it was no comfort at all. Her hair was a frizzy mess at the ends – like lumps of wire wool – with the bits that had missed the curlers sticking out. Tally hadn't pretended about the dress either. She'd put her hand over her mouth at the sight of it.

'Well, it's a nice old dress, but it's a bit . . .'

'Old-fashioned. I know. It's from the Dark Ages!' Her voice had started to break again. She couldn't help it. She had already seen what Tally was going to be wearing – a cloud of creamy tulle with layers and layers of full skirts, and a tight, boned bodice with narrow shoulder straps and peach-coloured silk roses at her waist. And all the other girls would be wearing dresses like that too.

Tally was still staring at her. 'Wait a mo, Flora. I've got an idea. Your dress is from the Twenties, isn't it? Well, let's do your hair the same and you'll look absolutely terrific. Different from everybody else, see?' She started rummaging in her dressing-table drawer. 'Come and sit down and I'll cut all that ghastly frizz off and make you look like a flapper.'

Flora sat down reluctantly in front of the dressing table. Snip, snip went Tally's scissors. She shut her eyes. Well, nothing could be worse than it was now. Snip, snip, snip. Snip, snip, snip . . .

'There you are.'

She opened her eyes slowly. The hated wire wool lay on the floor around the stool. What was left on her head was short and sleek and – miracle of miracles – rather pretty. It made her look quite grown-up. And quite different. She touched the ends and smiled.

'Anatomy and physiology,' Humphrey said earnestly. 'That's for the first two years.'

Tally was trying to follow what he was doing for a quickstep and to keep him from treading on her shoes. She wished she was dancing with someone who knew how to. Still, Humphrey was a lamb, really, and so serious about his doctoring. She smiled at him kindly. He looked rather nice in the hired dinner jacket. The bow tie was all wonky, but never mind.

'I know what anatomy is – skeletons.'

'That's right. Well . . . there's a bit more to it than that, of course. We have to learn all about the whole body, the way everything fits and works, and so on . . . We have to dissect it all, see.'

'Really? How amusing.' Tally skipped backwards nimbly to avoid his right foot. At least this made a change from the long lecture on the quickest route to Norfolk from Sandhurst by her last dance partner. How on earth had that ghastly bore got invited? 'How do you mean, exactly?'

'Well, we have to dissect each part in turn. My first term it was an arm, then the next term a leg, and so on.'

'Of what? A rat or something?'

He looked embarrassed. 'A human, actually.'

'You mean you cut up a *real* body? A dead *person*?'

'Well, yes. I mean, people donate them, in their wills.'

'But that must be simply disgusting.'

He said uncomfortably, 'It's the only way to learn properly. Look, I'm sorry, I shouldn't have mentioned it. It's hardly the time or place . . .'

'My fault. I shouldn't have asked.'

God, how revolting! How could he bear to do it? She remembered how he was always peering down his microscope

103

whenever she went to stay with Flora in the holidays, looking at the most revolting things. That spider, for instance. He'd thought it was beautiful!

'I've been wanting to thank you,' he said.

'Thank me? Whatever for?'

'For being so kind to Flora. You saved her bacon over the hair and the dress. She was absolutely wretched about both of them. I didn't know what to do, but *you* did. And I think she looks marvellous.'

'She does, doesn't she? The hair really suits her. I'd have lent her one of my evening dresses, you know, but they're all in London. Anyway, I don't think they'd have fitted her. I think it was best this way, in any case. It's a lovely old dress, and it's nice it was her grandmother's. Something special and different. The rest of us all look the same.'

'You don't,' he said seriously.

She smiled at him again. He was awfully sweet. Nothing like all the weeds and wolves. She could see Flora dancing with Dominic Esterhazy. She must remember to warn her about him.

The Cow was dancing with Charles – *flirting* with him by the look of it – at her age! She was wearing one of Mr Randolph's direst creations in puke-pink and, of course, the whole marquee colour scheme had had to be pink to match her – lining, flowers, tablecloths, the lot. And she would go and have a fountain in the middle of it all. Someone would certainly be thrown in before dawn broke.

After Humphrey she danced with Julian, and then Mark and then Alex and then Bertie . . . It was all good fun and the music was divine. Just so long as she didn't have to dance with Nicholas . . .

'I hardly recognized you, Flora. Last time I saw you you had pigtails.'

'Oh, I had them cut off ages ago. Actually, Tally cut my hair like this.'

'Did she really? An unexpected talent. Well, it suits you. So does the dress. You look enchanting.'

'Thank you, Nicholas.' He was smiling at her – not exactly in amazement, more like amusement. And she hadn't been coming down any stairs, either, but sitting in a corner. Please God, don't let the spot on her chin be showing. She'd plastered it with calamine lotion and with Tally's face powder but maybe that had worn off.

'Will you come and dance with me?'

'Oh . . . Yes, of course.'

He led her on to the floor, towing her behind him with one hand. The band were playing one of her very favourite tunes from *Oklahoma!* She knew the words by heart.

'You dance very nicely, little Flora. Who taught you so well?'

'We have ballroom dancing classes at school.'

'All girls?'

'Heavens, yes. No males are allowed within the walls, except the boiler man. We take turns at leading and following. Actually, I'm better at leading. I find it easier if I know what's coming next.'

'Would you sooner we changed round?'

She blushed and laughed, knowing he was teasing her. 'Gosh, no . . . You're easy to follow. Some men just charge around expecting you to guess.'

'Thank you for the compliment.'

She blushed deeper, thinking how silly she'd sounded. 'Of course, Tally's awfully good, isn't she?'

'I wouldn't know. I've never danced with her.'

'Oh. Well, I expect you will this evening.'

'I doubt it. Tally's avoiding me like the plague, and she's extremely good at that. In any case, I'd far sooner be dancing with you. This tune's from *Oklahoma!* isn't it? Do you remember when we saw it?'

'I'll always remember.'

'You were just a little girl then. What . . . eleven?'

'And a half. It was Tally's twelfth birthday.'

'We're not talking about her. We're talking about you. You must be seventeen now. Almost grown-up.'

She pulled a face. 'I've still got another year at school.'

105

'It'll go very quickly. Then what?'

'Depends on my A level results. I've got to get Latin if I want to try for Oxford or Cambridge, and I just know I'm not going to do it. Anyway, I'd have to get a scholarship or we couldn't afford it, and that's impossible. I'm not even sure I want to go to university, anyway.'

'You should. You'd enjoy it. Come up to Cambridge.'

'But you'll be leaving there soon.'

He laughed. 'Does that matter? I'll come back and take you punting. We'll go up the river to Grantchester.'

'Is that nice?'

'Very. We'll take a picnic with us. What would you like? Smoked salmon sandwiches? Champagne?'

'I've never drunk champagne before tonight. I'm not sure I like it.'

'Then we'll have Pimms instead. You'll like that, I promise. It's sort of like grown-up lemonade.'

He spun her round, smiling down at her with his wonderful smile. Don't let the music stop yet, she thought. Please, not yet.

'Trust Bertie to be the one to get thrown in the fountain. He's such a silly arse.' Tally, sitting on the end of her bed, was twirling her pearl necklace round and round on the end of her forefinger. She was still wearing her beautiful dress, the layers of cream tulle all puffed up about her like a big meringue.

Outside the window it was broad daylight and the birds were singing loudly. Flora didn't see how she was going to sleep, except that she was very tired. Her head was aching from the champagne and she wished that Tally would go to bed, too, so that she could shut her eyes. But Tally seemed wide awake, not even a bit sleepy, so Flora made an effort.

'Why did they do that?'

'Oh, goodness knows. It's supposed to be amusing. They always do something like that by the end of the evening.'

'His suit will be ruined.'

'He'll just buy another one. His family are loaded.'

The pearls slowed to a stop, descending gradually like the chairoplane at a fairground. 'Did you enjoy yourself, Flora?'

'Oh yes, it was lovely. I had a wonderful time.'

'That's good. Actually, they're mostly complete drips or crashing bores – the men, I mean – when they're not behaving like prep-school boys. Did you dance with anyone decent?'

'Well, I danced with Nicholas.'

'He's not decent! I managed to get out of that, thank God.'

Tally started twirling the pearls again. Flora's head spun with them. 'I saw you dancing with Dominic Esterhazy, by the way. Watch out for him. He'll try to get you to go to bed with him if you're not careful. He does that with everyone.'

'Oh! Golly . . .'

'He didn't try it on with you, I hope.'

'Well, he didn't actually say anything . . . At least, I don't think he did. I wasn't sure what he was talking about some of the time . . . Anyway, I wouldn't.'

'Lots of them do. I know of four debs who have.'

'I didn't think girls did – not before they got married.'

'Lord, yes.'

'You wouldn't, though, Tally?'

'Not with Dominic – he'd tell everyone.'

'Or with anyone else?'

'Can't promise that. I'm curious, you see. I want to know what it's like.'

'But Tally . . .'

She was prattling on again, though, swinging the pearls once more. Flora's eyes began to close, however hard she tried to stay awake and listen. When she opened them again some time later, Tally had gone. Her head was thudding away and a shaft of sunlight piercing between the curtains hurt her eyes. She shut them again quickly.

You look enchanting, Flora . . . We'll go up the river to Grantchester . . . take a picnic . . . What would you like? Smoked salmon sandwiches? Champagne?

PART THREE

Eight

'Today we are going to make *Carbonnade de Boeuf*. For this dish we shall need one and half pounds of braising beef, six ounces of onions, a clove of garlic, half a pint of beer, half an ounce of flour, a bouquet garni, French mustard, bread, and dripping. First we cut the meat into large squares . . .'

Tally scrawled the recipe down as the woman called it out. She started cutting up the meat and then the onions, chopping away any old how. It was an easy dish and she wouldn't have to pay much attention; just as well as she'd only had three hours' sleep. She and Charles hadn't left the Milroy until around four. They'd danced the night away to Paul Adams and she'd had far too much to drink and smoked too many cigarettes.

'The onions should be in *thin* slices . . .' That was directed at her. 'And they should brown well.'

Chop, chop, chop. Too late for thin slices. She wasn't sure what she was going to do about Charles. He was becoming a bit of a pain in the neck. She didn't mind going out with him occasionally – he was quite good company, in fact, and a super dancer – but it was draggy having to fight him off all the time. She'd had a real scuffle with him in the car last night and there was a huge bite mark on her neck that she'd had to cover up with a scarf.

'Cover closely and cook gently for two hours at mark three . . . Fifteen minutes before serving, we skim off any fat and pour it over the squares of bread. Then we spread these thickly with French mustard and replace on the top of the pot to brown in the oven for ten minutes. And while our carbonnade is cooking we will prepare our *Supreme au Chocolat*, and also make some *Tuiles à l'Orange . . .'*

The chocolate pudding actually made her feel quite sick to look at, and some of the *tuiles* were a bit of a disaster because she wasn't quick enough rolling them up. Normally she found it all pretty easy and even quite enjoyed the cookery lessons, but today was a bad day. To make it even worse, Charles was waiting outside the school at the end of the day in his Austin Healey.

'What are you doing here?'

'Giving you a lift home.' He got out, raising his curly-brimmed bowler.

'I'm getting a taxi.'

'Why bother?' He opened the passenger door. 'I cost nothing, and I'm here.'

She got in wearily, balancing the cardboard plate of *tuiles* on her lap. She really felt too tired to argue with him. They bombed down Marylebone Lane and across Oxford Street into Bond Street.

'Shouldn't you be at work, insuring people?'

'I took the day off. Those look good. Did you make them?'

'Actually, I made a hash of them, but they taste OK. Have one.'

He ate it, balancing one hand casually on the steering wheel. 'Awfully good. Sort of orangey . . .'

'*Tuiles à l'Orange.*'

'I'm impressed. So, at the end of this course you're going to be a fully fledged Cordon Bleu cook.'

'That's the general idea. I'm going to cook lunch and dinner parties for snobby people like you.'

'You'll hate it. You don't need to work anyway.'

'It'll be better than being cooped up with my stepmother.'

In the autumn, after the Season had finally ground to an end, she had hung about the house for a while, meeting girl friends for lunch, shopping for hours, and being taken out by various men in the evenings. She had learned to drive, which had passed a bit of time, too, and Papa had given her a car so that she could drive up to Melton for weekends, either on her own or with others. In London, though, there had been rows all the time with The Cow – rows over the times she came in, the bills she ran up, the clothes she wore, the men she saw, the cigarettes she smoked, the drinks she drank . . . In the new year, to get out of the house, she had got a job working in a small dress shop in Knightsbridge, which had turned out to be incredibly boring. She had sat around all day, waiting for customers to come in, painting her nails different colours and reading fashion magazines. And then some of her ex-deb friends would drop by and stand there gossiping, without buying a thing. In the end, what with the gossiping and the fact that she often overslept and was late, she'd been sacked.

After that she had to been Les Rosiers for most of the summer, which had neatly solved the problem of what to do next, and that's where she'd got the idea of the Cordon Bleu course, when she'd been watching Yvette, the maid, concoct one of her fabulous *cassoulets*. It would be something to do and might be quite fun.

Charles stopped outside Moyses Stevens, and she ate two *tuiles* while he was inside, trying to see in through the window. Not the dark red roses, please . . . Men *would* keep on giving her those, and she hated them. But he came out bearing a dozen of them, long-stemmed and the colour of dried blood.

'These are to say I'm frightfully sorry about last night.'

She took the roses reluctantly and held them up to her nose; they had no smell at all and were too perfect to seem real. She knew that the tightly furled buds would never turn into proper roses. The ones at Melton never looked false like these, and when they opened up they became gorgeous big rosettes, like the ones she used to win at gymkhanas on Flame years ago. *Gather ye rosebuds while ye may, old time is still a-flying.* In other words, have a good time while you can – which she fully intended to do. She couldn't remember how the poem went on – something about dying. She plonked the bouquet down on her lap, beside the *tuiles*.

'It's OK. There's no need to make a big thing about it. But quite honestly, Charles, I don't think there's much point in us seeing each other any more . . . In fact, I'd much sooner we didn't.'

'I've said I'm sorry and I promise to behave.'

'I don't believe you. You won't. You never do.'

'It's bloody hard with you, Tally. You're the most incredibly attractive girl, and I'm falling terribly in love with you . . .'

'Spare me, Charles. You say that to everybody.'

'I know, but it's the truth with you.'

'No, it isn't. And anyway, I don't *want* anyone falling in love with me. I just want to go out and have a good time and not worry about that sort of serious stuff.'

He restarted the engine. 'Alright. We'll just go out and have a good time and I *swear* I won't try anything. We'll just be madly platonic. What do you say?'

She sighed. 'I'll think about it.'

He dropped her at Eaton Terrace and called after her. 'I'll give you a ring soon. OK?'

She shrugged and went inside. Carver appeared from nowhere as she was dumping the roses on the hall table. She detested the way he crept about the house.

'His lordship wished to see you on your return, Lady Atalanta. He's in his study.' He looked at her with his usual pursed-lip expression. He probably knew exactly what time she'd come in last night.

Papa was writing a letter at his desk and she held out the cardboard plate. 'I made these today.'

He took the nearest of the last two *tuiles* and nibbled at a corner. 'Delicious. How's the course going, then?'

She flopped down in a chair, munching the remaining one. 'OK. I can do better than these, though; they went wrong.'

'Still going ahead with this cooking idea? Dinner parties, and all that sort of thing?'

'May as well. It might be amusing.' She took another bite. 'Carver said you wanted to see me . . . What's it about?'

He was fiddling with the cap of his fountain pen. Whatever

it is, she thought with sudden misgiving, he doesn't know how to put it. So, it can't be anything good. The Cow's been up to something. She gulped down the rest of her mouthful, waiting.

'I've just been writing a letter to the headmaster of my old prep school . . . We're sending Thomas there next September.'

'Won't he be a bit young?'

'He'll be eight. Ready to make the break from Nanny and all that . . . get him living with other boys of his own age, instead of being on his own. Prepare him for Eton. He'll have a lot of fun . . . best years of my life, my school days.'

He'd used the same sort of words with Tally when they'd sent her away. She could distinctly remember him saying them in the car on the way to Paddington station.

The pen cap was still going on and off. So, that wasn't all. What was coming next?

'The thing is, old girl, with Thomas going off pretty soon, we're not going to be spending nearly so much time here in London. We're thinking of spending part of the winter in Antigua, and then a fair bit of the summer down at Les Rosiers, and then, of course, there's skiing . . . One way and another we'll be away a good deal.'

'It's alright. I don't mind.' Not at all, actually, if it means The Cow being away.

He cleared his throat. 'Well, we've decided that the best thing for you would be to have a place of your own now – not actually on your own, of course. You could share it with another girl – perhaps one of the ones you came out with last year. It so happens one of the mews houses round the corner has just come up for lease – I noticed it the other day. I'm going to take it on for you. It's small, of course, but I think you'll like it.'

So that was it. They were getting rid of her again. Turfing her out of the house. She felt sick inside, exactly the way she'd felt when she'd overheard them plotting to send her off to boarding school. She was suddenly frightened at the

115

thought of being on her own. It was The Cow's doing, again, of course. She knew that for certain.

Papa was still talking – very fast now. 'Grandmama will be nearby, of course. You'll be able to visit her just the same, and you know how pleased she always is to see you. I'll increase your allowance, and you can make use of the shopping accounts whenever you need anything . . . Can you think of anybody you could ask to share with you? We wouldn't charge rent, so I imagine it wouldn't be too difficult to find someone. How about that girl at Beechlawn who you were such friends with? Flora . . . wasn't that her name? She seemed a pretty good sort.'

Tally stood up slowly. There was no point in making a scene about it. They'd decided, just like they'd decided last time. It had all been arranged without consulting her.

'What do you say, old thing?' He was looking up at her, anxiously, wanting her to go quietly, not to make a scene and a fuss. Or start crying. He'd looked just like that on the platform at Paddington station.

'I'll ask Flora,' she said.

She walked out of the room with her chin up and nearly collided with Carver, who must have been listening outside the door. She saw the smirk on his face before he had time to wipe it off.

Flora read Tally's letter through three times before she showed it to her mother. Of course, it was out of the question to go and live in London. The secretarial course was all arranged in Reading. She was going to do shorthand and typing and then get a job and work her way up – that was her mother's practical solution to her dismal failure in the Latin A level and the mediocre pass marks in History and English. There was no chance now of a scholarship anywhere. She knew she had let her mother down and disappointed her badly, though she had never said so.

Her mother read the letter and looked up. 'Would you like to do this, Flora?'

'I don't see how I can. Not if I'm doing the Pitmans.'

'You don't have to do a course in Reading. You could do one in London. They have colleges everywhere. And Tally says her father wouldn't charge any rent, which is very generous of him, so it would just be a question of paying for your food and fares and pocket money – not so much more than if you were living at home, I'd say. We could manage it, if that's what you'd like.'

She shook her head. Her mother had already made enough sacrifices for herself and Humphrey, and probably lots more that they didn't even know about.

'I'll write back and say no.'

'Just a moment. I think you should write back and say yes.' Her mother flourished the letter. 'This is a chance for you, Flora. You'll have a far better choice of jobs in London when you've finished your training. And there'll be all sorts of advantages that I can't give you . . . I want you to do it, for my sake, as well as for yours. And you'll be near Humphrey, which is another good thing.'

'Do you really mean that?'

'Certainly. And apart from all that, I've always liked Tally. You'll both benefit from each other. It all makes sense. So sit down and write that letter.'

'Well, what do you think of it?'

'It's lovely, Tally. Really super.'

The mews had once been stables, Tally had explained, but they had all been converted into little houses, with rooms where there had once been hay and horses, and cars where there had been carriages. The front doors were painted in pretty colours and there were bright summer flowers in window boxes and wooden tubs.

Inside the house, a steep staircase led straight up from the front door to the first floor where there was a sitting room with a small kitchen off it on one side, and a bathroom on the other. On the second floor there were two bedrooms. Tally's overlooked the cobbled mews at the front and the room that was to be Flora's looked out on to somebody else's garden at the back. She liked it at once. There was space for a bed,

117

a wardrobe, a little velvet chair and, most wonderful of all, a kidney-shaped dressing table with a glass top and white organdie skirts.

'I know you always wanted one like that,' Tally said. 'So I got it for you. I chose everything myself.'

They went down to the sitting room again.

'I went and ordered a whole lot of stuff from Harrods and Peter Jones. Do you like the sofa?'

'It looks awfully comfortable.'

'It is.' Tally sat down on it and bounced up and down. It was huge and took up most of one wall. 'We've got a car, too. It's down in the garage. A Morris Minor that Papa gave me last year when I learned to drive. It's rather sweet.'

She was trying to light a cigarette while she was talking. She'd never smoked before, so far as Flora could remember. Or worn so much make-up. There was a lot of blue stuff on her eyelids and thick black on her lashes, and her lipstick was very red. And her hair was different . . . Shorter and combed back behind her ears which made her look much older. She was wearing her pearl necklace and more pearls in her ears, and a twinset that looked like cashmere. Her stockings were the sheerest nylon, and her shoes were black patent leather with very high heels. I'm not going to be able to keep up, Flora thought in panic. It's going to be like Town Mouse and Country Mouse. She's going to be sorry she asked me, and I'm going to be sorry I came.

Then she saw that, without any warning at all, Tally had started crying. One moment she'd been all jaunty and gay and the next the tears were trickling down her cheeks.

'They've chucked me out, you see. I didn't tell you in the letter, but it wasn't my idea . . .' She waved the cigarette around blindly. 'Papa's paying for all this so they don't have to have me living with them any more. He made all sorts of excuses but that's what it comes down to. Isn't it a joke?'

She was trying to laugh, but suddenly crumpled up and she put her hand over her eyes. Flora knelt down by the sofa and put her arms around her.

*　　*　　*

118

q w e r t . . . y u i o p . . . a s d f g . . . h j k l . . . z x c
v . . . b n m . . .

The noise of thirty typewriters all crashing away in time
to a slow march made Flora's ears sing, and her fingers were
aching after a solid hour of exercises, pounding painfully at
the keys. a g e . . . p n m i . . . w z d v . . . k h u j . . .

Two mistakes in that one but she couldn't cheat and look
at the keys because of the metal shield hiding them. s m i
f . . . d j c l . . .

Getting better, but only a bit. By the end of the course she
was supposed to be able to touch-type at least sixty words
a minute accurately; at the moment she could only manage
about fifteen.

Shorthand was just as bad: light and dark strokes, short
and long ones, curves, hooks, dots and dashes – all hard
to remember and get down quickly and even worse to
read back.

*Dear Sirs, We are in receipt of your letter of the 2nd instant
and we thank you for your esteemed order . . .*

Thirty words a minute was her fastest so far and employers
would expect not less than a hundred and twenty – and they'd
expect her to be able to read back all the frantic squiggles
correctly then type them out perfectly at sixty words a
minute.

As for bookkeeping, that was just plain boring. Balance
sheets, profit and loss columns, gross and net, carrying things
forward and making everything balance – it was as much of
a puzzle to her as maths had been at school.

She went to and fro on the bus, carrying her shorthand
notebooks and sharpened pencils, and her sandwich, which
she ate in the classroom at lunch break. Tally drove in the
Morris Minor to her cookery school and often brought home
the dishes she'd made so that they could eat them up for
supper. *Carré d' Agneau à la Princesse, Pigeons à l'Italienne,
Potage Parmentier, Galette Lyonnaise, Tournedos en Croute,
Poires Flambées* . . . And, as Tally was always being given
big boxes of Charbonnel and Walker chocolates and Bendicks
Bittermints, they ate those too. If somebody was taking Tally

out to dinner, which often happened, then Flora had double helpings on her own, listening to the wireless part of the big radiogram that Tally had bought from Harrods. She lay on the big sofa, glued to *Paul Temple*, *Take It From Here*, *Hancock's Half Hour* . . . If *Dick Barton* had still been on, she would have listened to that too.

On Saturday mornings Flora and Tally often went to Harrods, parking the Morris Minor round the back. Tally would waltz round the departments, buying more new clothes, make-up and different bottles of scent, and all kinds of things from the food halls – cakes and sweets and cellophane boxes of chocolates and sugared almonds and silver dragées. She put everything on her father's account, signing the bill with a flourish. They would always visit the zoo to say hello to the parrot and look at the birds and animals in their cages. Then they would have coffee and toasted teacakes in the Silver Buffet, perched up at the same old counter with the butter still running down their fingers.

The men who drove down the cobbled mews in their expensive cars to collect Tally usually worked at something in the City. Sometimes they were in the army. Occasionally they were in advertising. If Tally was still putting on her warpaint up in her bedroom, Flora would have the daunting task of making polite conversation with them.

'Would you like a drink?' she would ask.

'I say, that's frightfully decent of you.'

They would stand there, glass in hand, while she racked her brains for something intelligent to say, and the conversation would usually go in fits and starts.

'Don't think I've seen you around at the usual bashes, have I?' they'd say, trying vaguely to place her.

'No, I've only just come up to London. I used to live in Reading.'

'Reading?' It might as well have been Vladivostok, judging by their expressions. They would take another rallying sip.

'Seen *Salad Days* yet?'

'No, I'm afraid not.'

'*The Boyfriend*?'

'Sorry.'

'Jolly good shows . . .'

She knew she must be a puzzlement to them, as well as a conversational dead loss. She didn't know anybody they knew and hadn't been anywhere they had. She could see them wondering what on earth she was doing there. Their faces would light up with relief at the sound of Tally coming down the stairs and when she made her entrance, dressed to kill and in a cloud of French scent, the jaws on those faces would drop at the stunning sight of her.

Sometimes, when Tally crept in very late, she would put her head round the bedroom door to see if Flora was awake and then, if she showed any sign of life, sit on the end of her bed, talking about the Blue Angel, or the Jacaranda, or the Four Hundred, or Quaglinos, or The Milroy, or whichever nightclub she had been at. She hardly ever said nice things about the man who had taken her there.

'He's bearable,' she would say, yawning. Or, 'He can dance alright, that's the main thing.' Or, 'God, what a boring evening. If he ever rings again, Flora, tell him I'm out forever.'

Charles Lisle was the most frequent and persistent caller, but Tally seemed as indifferent to him as all the rest. She never mentioned Nicholas and Flora, who hadn't seen him since Tally's coming-out dance, asked about him as offhandedly as she could.

'Oh, he's in Hong Kong.'

'*Hong Kong*?'

'Yes, he came down from Cambridge and went straight into his father's company. Working his way up from the boardroom, I expect. He's been sent there for about two years, thank God. Nice and far away.'

So much for the picnic on the river, the smoked salmon sandwiches and the champagne.

C I P S . . . Q N X B . . . Capitals now, and the shift key was so stiff it hurt her little finger. X O A W . . . K Z J V . . .

The quxk brown fix jumpef over the kazy dog. Now
id the tike for all food men to come ro the aid of their
xountry . . .

She was going to make a rotten secretary.

Humphrey lived in digs in a grimy little street near the
hospital in Southwark, south of the river. Flora caught the
bus there one Saturday and was dismayed at the sight of
the dingy old houses, and at the bomb sites left over from the
war, full of sooty weeds and dumped rubbish and pools of
stagnant water. The brass knocker of number sixteen didn't
look as though it had been polished for years and the woman
who opened the door to her wore curlers under a headscarf
and carpet slippers on her feet.

'I've come to see my brother, Humphrey Middleton . . .'
She jerked her head. 'Better come in then.'
As Flora stepped into the narrow hallway, the woman
shouted upwards from the foot of the stairs.
'Mr Middleton! Yer sister's 'ere. You can use the front
room.'
She slopped away down the dark passageway towards the
back of the house and the strong smell of fish cooking.
Flora looked round at the porridge-and-fruit-frieze wallpaper, the ugly coat and hat stand, the frameless mirror
suspended from a rusty chain, and compared it with the
little mews house.
Someone was clattering fast and noisily down the stairs
and she looked up, expecting to see Humphrey. Instead it
was another young man. He was wearing a khaki duffel coat
with a striped scarf wound round his neck and he stopped
dead when he saw her.
'You must be Flora?'
'That's right.'
'Humphrey's just coming down.' He grinned at her. 'I'm
Algy Baxter. Another would-be sawbones. And fellow lodger.
Did Old Mother Riley let you in?'
'I think so.'

122

'She's our landlady. The former runner-up to Miss England 1901. She renounced it all for love and marriage.'

Flora smiled. 'Is it really Mrs Riley?'

'It's Mrs Polomski, actually. She married a Pole. We don't know what she did with him. He either died or went back to Poland – anything to escape.'

'I'm supposed to go into the front room, I think.'

'Ah, yes. No visitors in the bedrooms, especially not female ones, and most especially not pretty female ones. That's on the long list of house rules. Did you wipe your feet when you came in?'

'I'm not sure . . .'

'Then you've broken Rule Number One.'

'What are the others?'

He ticked them off on his fingers. 'No lights left on in the passageways after eleven at night; not more than five inches of hot water in the bath; no food or alcohol in the bedrooms; no telephone calls out; no wireless and no records to be played after ten . . . Ah, here's Humphrey. He'll tell you the rest. I'm off to play a spot of rugger.' He grinned at her again. 'Remember to wipe your feet next time.'

Humphrey showed her into the front room, which was a museum piece of Victorian gloom, complete with an aspidistra in a purple pot. It felt damp and chilly.

'I'm sorry, Flo. It's not very cheerful in here, but the landlady won't allow visitors upstairs.'

'So I gathered from the other lodger. He was telling me all the rules.'

'That was Algy. He's a really good sort. Third year like me.'

He looked pale and tired, she thought. And not very well fed. The stark contrast between her own living conditions and this place distressed her. She had no idea that he lived in such dreary and depressing surroundings.

'It seems a bit grim here.'

'Oh, it's not so bad. Convenient and pretty clean and she does a reasonable breakfast. And it's cheap – only three pounds ten a week. Algy and I can get a meal at the pub down the road in the evenings.'

She held out the paper bag she had brought with her. 'Tally sent these for you. She made them at her cookery course. They've got some fancy French name, but they're really just macaroons.'

'Thanks. They look wonderful. How is she?'

'Fine.'

'What about you? How's the shorthand and typing?'

She made a face. 'I'm not really enjoying it, but I'm ploughing on. How are you doing?'

'Pretty busy. It's pharmacology and pathology this year. There's a lot to learn.'

He'd passed his previous year's exams brilliantly and she had no doubt that he'd do the same with the next ones. She was more convinced than ever that he was going to be a famous surgeon one day.

'Tally asks if you will come over to supper one evening. She's going to use you as a guinea pig.'

'I'd like that very much.' He smiled wryly, glancing round the room. 'She'd think this place was a slum, wouldn't she?'

'She's just so used to her world.'

He said quite seriously: 'Don't get too used to it yourself, Flo. You don't really belong there.'

Going back on the bus, she thought about that. It was true. She didn't belong in Tally's world. She might live in the little mews house and meet Tally's society friends, but she wasn't really a part of it. She was only on the outside, looking in.

'Hallo.'

'Is that Flora?'

'Yes.'

'This is Algy Baxter. We met on the stairs. At Old Mother Riley's. Remember?'

'Oh, yes, of course.'

'Humphrey gave me your number. Hope you don't mind

my ringing you, but I wondered if you'd like to meet up this Saturday?'

'Well, I'm not sure . . .'

'I've got to play rugger in the afternoon, but there's a pub near you where some of the players go afterwards . . . Place called the Antelope. Do you know it?'

'I don't think so.'

'It's in Eaton Terrace, just round the corner. Meet you there at seven?'

'Well, I . . .'

'That's settled then. See you in the bar.'

He rang off before she could say he wouldn't. Tally raised her eyebrows.

'He's in the same lodgings as Humphrey,' Flora explained. 'Another medical student. I only saw him for a moment. He wants me to meet him on Saturday at a pub.'

'Pretty fast worker. What's he like?'

'He seemed quite nice, I suppose.'

'I'd go and find out, if I were you.'

'I've never been in a pub before.'

'Nothing difficult about it. You just open the door and walk in.'

The bar was so full she could hardly get the door open, let alone walk in. When she had managed to squeeze inside, she couldn't see beyond a solid wall of beefy male bodies, all downing beer, smoking cigarettes, and out-shouting each other. She struggled through the crush, ducking beneath drinking arms, and saw Algy. He was wearing the same old duffel coat and scarf as before and leaning against the bar, one elbow on the counter, a mug of beer in his fist. When he saw her, a big grin broke out on his face.

'Hallo there! What'll you have, Flora?'

'Do you mean to drink?' She took off her headscarf and shook her hair.

'That's usually what people do in here. That and talk absolute rubbish. Beer?'

'I've never tried it.'

125

'No time like the present. Half a bitter to start with?'

'Alright. Thanks.'

'I was afraid you'd stand me up. Bit of a cheek, my phoning you, I know. Not much of a prospect – either me or this place. Gets awfully crowded on a Saturday with all these dreadful rugger types.'

'Is that what they are?'

'Can't you tell by the broken noses and the cauliflower ears? And the missing teeth?' He fingered his own nose and, now that he had mentioned it, she noticed that it was rather crooked and that one of his front teeth was chipped. He handed her a small mug of dark-brown liquid and raised his own. 'Cheers. Down the hatch.'

'Oh . . . cheers.' She tried to hide her shudder.

'Have a crisp.'

There were about three left in the packet that he offered; she took one of them politely.

'Thanks.'

'I asked Humphrey if he wanted to come along too, but he had his nose buried in the textbooks. Never knew anyone to study as hard as your brother. Puts me to shame.'

'It's pathology this year, isn't it?' She couldn't remember the other subject that Humphrey had mentioned.

'And pharmacology. Know what that is?'

'I don't exactly know what either of them are.'

'Well, pathology is the study of diseases, and pharmacology is all about how drugs affect the body. That's it in a nutshell, really. We're always looking at bits of liver on slides, that sort of thing . . . and injecting atropine into mice and measuring their pupils . . . Sorry, I shouldn't talk about it. I can see it turns the old stomach a trifle. Let's talk about what you do instead. Shorthand and typing course, isn't it?'

'Not very interesting, I'm afraid.'

'Useful, though. Are you going to be a fearfully efficient secretary to some high-powered businessman?'

'I shouldn't think so. I'm not very fast yet.'

'I can type very slowly with two fingers.'

'We have to use all of ours,' she told him. 'And not look

at the keys. You can't type fast if you have to look. Your fingers have to learn where all the letters are.'

He was looking at her admiringly. 'Sounds incredibly difficult. I'm such a clumsy fellow myself – I'd never manage it. Two left hands and two left feet. I'll never make a surgeon, like Humphrey.'

'What will you do, then?'

'Be a good old GP. That's what I really want, anyway. I like the idea. Knowing the patients. Dealing with it all, from cradle to grave. The indispensable family doctor. Have another crisp?'

Someone knocked her arm, spilling her beer down the front of her coat.

'Sorry about that,' Algy said. 'These lot are animals. Think they're still in the scrum.'

She wiped herself down with a handkerchief. 'Do you play a lot of rugger?'

'Whenever I get the chance. Fly half, that's me. Get to move about a bit. You could come and watch a match some time, if you like.'

'Oh . . .'

'Never mind. I'll ask you when you know me better. Drink up and I'll get you another of those. And another packet of crisps.'

Afterwards they walked to Sloane Square and down the King's Road. Algy said he knew a bistro where he swore they did a marvellous goulash. It was down in a basement and so crowded and noisy that they had to shout at each other. The tables had red checked cloths and candles stuck in old wine bottles, encrusted with layer upon layer of melted wax that Algy kept picking off. He was quite right about the goulash.

Nine

Tally parked the Morris Minor in Cadogan Square, backing hurriedly into a tiny space. Number forty-two, she discovered, was on the other side of the square, of course. By the time she'd raced all the way round she was out of breath and, as it was a warm spring evening, she was sweating too. She rang the bell and waited. There was a sharp click-clacking of heels somewhere inside and then the door opened. Mrs Campbell-Morton looked rather like Joan Crawford and was obviously furious.

'You're very late. I've just been phoning the agency to find out what had happened to you.'

'My car wouldn't start,' Tally lied. Actually, she'd fallen asleep on the sofa in the afternoon, exhausted after a night out. Her head was still aching and her eyes felt as though they were full of sand. The last thing she wanted to do was cook a four-course dinner for eight people.

'Well, you'd better come in and get started immediately. I can only hope you'll be able to get everything ready in time.'

'Oh, there won't be any problem,' Tally lied again airily. What Mrs Campbell-Morton didn't know was that this was her first job – nor did the Good Cook agency, come to that. She had invented an impressive list of previous dinner parties and appreciative clients for their benefit.

Inside the house, beyond the tiled hall, there was a lot of dark-green carpeting and heavy furniture. The kitchen, down in the basement, didn't look as though it had been changed since its cook and butler days. There were three cardboard delivery boxes on the table.

Mrs Campbell-Morton pointed at them with a long finger-nail. 'I think you'll find everything you need in those, or in the cupboards.'

'What do you want me to cook?'

She picked up a piece of paper. 'I've written it all down here. We're starting with vichyssoise soup, then goujons of sole, followed by the crown roast of lamb and vegetables. Cold chocolate soufflé for dessert, followed by cheese, of course. My husband will see to the wine. It's all quite straightforward.' She stared coldly. 'You *are* Cordon Bleu trained, aren't you? The agency said you were.'

'Yes, of course.' That much, at least, was true.

'You look too young to have had enough experience. I should have preferred them to send someone older, but apparently you were the only one available. This is an important dinner party with some distinguished guests. I hope you realize that.'

She clacked away upstairs. Tally looked in panic at the table and wondered how she was going to turn everything into a perfect dinner in two and a half hours. She felt like the miller's daughter in *Rumpelstiltskin*, left with her roomful of straw to spin into gold, except that there was no chance of the little man turning up to help her. Or anyone else. She was on her own. For a moment she seriously considered the possibility of simply walking out and leaving everything. There would be a tradesmen's door with steps up to the street and she could be gone before Mrs Campbell-Morton even knew it. The agency wouldn't use her again, of course, but there were other agencies, so who cared? She got as far as going to the door and opening it. Then she shut it again slowly.

If she started off doing the potatoes and leeks for the vichyssoise, then while they were cooking she could make the chocolate soufflé. Then they could both be put in the fridge and left to chill while she got on with the rest . . . It might work, if she kept her head and planned it out a bit. She put on her apron, rolled up her sleeves and started peeling and chopping.

Nearly an hour later, with arms aching from beating yolks and whites with an old hand whisk, she was pressing the cooked leeks and potatoes through a sieve. It had taken far longer than she had thought, partly because she had had to hunt for the utensils through deep drawers and dark cupboards, and she had searched in vain for a rotary egg beater. In one of the cupboards she had come across a bottle of sweet South African sherry and had poured several tots for herself.

She was slicing the sole fillets into narrow strips when Mrs Campbell-Morton reappeared. She had changed into a wine-red dinner gown that made her look even more like Joan Crawford.

'I forgot to ask, do you have a suitable apron for the dining room?'

'For the dining room?'

'Yes, for serving the food. Naturally, you're expected to do that.'

'I don't see how I can, as well as cope with everything down here.'

'But it's part of the arrangement. That's what we pay the agency for – someone to cook the meal *and* serve it. Surely you always do that?'

'I've never done so before.'

'Well, I'm afraid you'll have to this time. You can't expect me to leave my guests and run up and down the stairs.' Mrs Campbell-Morton looked at her watch. 'They'll be arriving in about half an hour. We'll allow some time for cocktails, of course. I'll let you know when we're ready for you to serve dinner. You'll find a spare apron in one of the dresser drawers.'

Bitch! She should have left as she'd planned at the beginning, gone straight out of the door and up the steps. All this sweat for a measly ten shillings that she didn't need anyway. Well, she could still leave now. Mrs Campbell-Morton could serve her own bloody dinner, and she hoped it choked her.

Tally started to wrench off her kitchen apron, then stopped. The vichyssoise had actually tasted rather good and was chilling quite nicely in the fridge, and the chocolate soufflé wasn't bad either. The crown roast was cooking away in the oven, and she'd piped the duchesse potatoes, so there was only the sole and the carrots to do. There was something to be said for staying and showing Joan Crawford how wrong she'd been.

The goujons were ready and waiting to be fried at the last minute and she was cutting a lemon into wedges when Mr Campbell-Morton came into the kitchen, dressed in a dinner jacket and smelling strongly of whisky.

'I say . . . *Hallo*!'

'Hallo,' she said coldly.

'Haven't been here before, have you? Thought not. I wouldn't forget a face like yours.' He stood in the middle of the kitchen, leering at her while she went to and fro. 'You don't look the type for this sort of job, if you don't mind my saying so.'

'I do mind, actually. Excuse me. I'm rather busy.' She brushed past him with the baking tray of duchesse potatoes.

'I can see I'm in the way.'

'Yes, you are rather.'

The ten shillings didn't cover having to put up with lecherous husbands as well as bitchy wives. She turned her back on him firmly but he still lingered, watching her until, to her relief, the sound of Mrs Campbell-Morton calling impatiently from above galvanized him into fetching bottles from the cellar.

'We're ready.' Mrs Campbell-Barton stood in the door-way. 'Would you serve the soup now, please. And don't forget the apron.'

She unearthed one in a drawer – the white, frilled kind that maids at home always wore – and tied it round her waist before carrying the heavy soup tureen and bowls upstairs on a tray.

The dining room was at the back of the house, overlooking the garden, and the guests were already seated – two dreary middle-aged couples, she noted, and a girl she didn't know, thank Christ. And Nicholas.

*   *   *

131

'*Nicky*, Flora! Can you imagine? I nearly dropped the tray. Of all the bloody bad luck . . .'

'I thought he was in Hong Kong.' Flora suddenly sounded wide awake. She sat up in bed.

'So did I.'

'What did he say to you?'

'Nothing. Absolutely nothing. He pretended he didn't know me.'

'That was nice of him.'

'I don't actually see why.'

'Well, it could have put you off – if they'd all known he knew you and who you were, it would have made it even more embarrassing.'

'I wasn't embarrassed. Just furious that it had to be him, of all people. It was bad enough as it was. Everything had gone wrong – the soup wasn't chilled enough, then I dropped all the goujons on the floor in the kitchen and had to blow the dirt off them. The carrots burned and the soufflé didn't set and the husband was a complete lech. Mrs Campbell-Morton was simply livid about everything and she's bound to tell the agency. So that's that. My career as a Cordon Bleu cook is over before it's begun.'

'Surely they'll give you another chance.'

'Who cares, anyway?' Tally collapsed on to the end of Flora's bed. 'I'm too tired to think about it.'

'How was Nicholas?'

'I've no idea. He looked just the same, but a bit older, I suppose. Actually, he was waiting outside when I finally got out of that ghastly place.'

'Oh? What did he say then?'

'Nothing worth listening to.'

He'd been standing by a lamp post, smoking a cigarette, when she'd pulled herself wearily up the basement steps. She'd washed the piles of dirty pans and dishes and glasses, then dried them all too. In the process, she'd broken three Waterford crystal wine glasses, a Doulton dinner plate and the lid of a serving dish; she'd hidden the pieces at the bottom of the dustbin outside the back door.

He'd stepped forward as she reached the pavement but she was in no mood to see him.

'Congratulations.'

'What for?'

'The dinner.'

'Is that supposed to be a joke? It was a disaster, and you know it.'

'Not at all. And frankly, I was amazed.'

'At what?'

'That you had a job.'

'I wouldn't exactly call it that. It was my first dinner party, and probably my last, if Mrs Campbell-Morton has anything to do with it. What on earth were you doing there with all those old fogies?'

'Campbell-Morton's in my father's company.'

'Sucking up, I suppose. He's a real creep. He kept coming down for more wine and chasing me round the kitchen table.'

'Tiresome.'

'Very. Unfortunately, Mrs C-M. came down once just as he'd caught up with me. There was a bit of a scene and he had the cheek to blame it all on me. Men are simply the end sometimes – the absolute end. Anyway, I thought you were in Hong Kong.'

'I was. I'm back.'

'Oh.' She moved on past him. 'Well, actually I'm pretty fagged out, so I'm off.'

'Can I give you a lift?' He indicated a car nearby.

'No, thanks, I've got my own on the other side of the square.'

'I'll walk you over.'

'No need.'

But he had insisted, much to her irritation, and she'd been too tired to argue.

'I hear you've got your own place now.'

'Yes. I was booted out. Thanks to your mother.'

133

He hadn't said anything to that. 'Flora's sharing it, I gather. How is she?'

'Fine. She's doing shorthand and typing at Pitmans.'

'Enjoying it?'

'Not much. I don't think anybody does. All that bashing away at the keys and scribbling in notebooks. Then having to go and work in some office. I'd hate it.'

'Fortunately you don't have to. Or perhaps unfortunately.'

They'd reached the Morris and she'd stopped and turned to face him. 'What's that supposed to mean?'

'That it might be better for you if you *did* have to do things you don't want to . . . just occasionally.'

'You've got a bloody nerve! That scarcely applies to you, does it? The big white chief's son. Everything on a plate. All made easy for you.'

'If anything it's made it harder, as a matter of fact.'

'Oh you poor, poor thing.' She'd fumbled furiously for her car keys in the bottom of her handbag. 'Please go. There's absolutely no need for you to wait.'

'I will as soon as you've found your keys.'

She'd jabbed them into the keyhole and flung herself into the car, slamming the door. As she drove off, very fast, she'd glanced back in the driving mirror, and saw that he was still there.

Flora was watching her. 'He made you angry, didn't he? Upset you?'

'Oh, I don't give a damn about him. I've decided that most men are bastards. Bastards, or boring. Or both.' Tally stood up stiffly. 'God, I'm shattered and my head's splitting. I'm going to bed.' She reached the bedroom door. 'He asked after you, by the way. I told him what you were doing.'

'Did you?'

'You haven't still got that thing about him, have you?'

Flora lay down. She pulled the sheet up to her chin. 'Heavens, no.'

In the morning the Good Cook agency phoned. Mrs Campbell-Morton had complained about both the dinner

134

and her behaviour with her husband. She had also found the broken china and glass in the bottom of the dustbin, which would have to be paid for and would cost a great deal more than the ten shillings she had earned. They would not, in any case, be requiring her services again.

The quick brown fod jumped over the lazy dog . . . Only one mistake. *Now is the time for all good men to come to the aid of the party.* No mistakes at all, and no peeking, either.

On the last typing test she'd reached fifty words a minute, and in the shorthand one she'd managed a hundred and ten words a minute *and* she'd read it all back alright. By the end of the course, in two months' time, she should be able to do a hundred and twenty at least. Flora typed on doggedly. It was becoming almost automatic now; her fingers knew what they were supposed to be doing by themselves. Sometimes she could even think of other things.

She had started working part-time at the Oasis coffee bar in Fulham, wiping down tables, taking orders, running to and fro with cups of espresso and cappuccino from the machine that hissed and gurgled behind the counter, like a mad professor's experiment. She quite enjoyed it. The people who went there were mostly young – about her own age – and they spent hours over one cup of coffee, smoking and talking. She worked there three evenings a week and, with the occasional small tips and her wages, it all added up.

Tally was halfway through the modelling course she had started when her cooking career had foundered. She would glide up and down the sitting room, balancing a book on her head, hands on hips thrust forward at a peculiar angle. She spent hours at her dressing table, practising putting on make-up and doing her hair different ways. Sometimes she would simply stand about, posing, with unnaturally fixed limbs and a blank expression.

'How does this look, Flora?' she would ask.

'Rather odd.'

'It's how they all stand – haven't you noticed? I've got to get it right.'

'Tally, isn't there something else you could do? What about trying again with the cooking?'

'Oh, I can't be bothered. It'd all be people like Mrs Campbell-Morton and her bloody husband.'

On her nineteenth birthday, Flora had come back to find a Harrods box lying on her bed. She'd carried it through to Tally's room. 'This must be yours.'

Tally was painting her nails. 'No, it's for you. It's a present. Go on, open it.'

Inside, beneath folds of rustling tissue paper, lay a beautiful blue taffeta dress with a heart-shaped neckline and full skirts. 'Oh, Tally . . . It's much too much. I can't possibly take this.'

'Why not?' She had blown on her fingernails and waggled them. 'I paid for it myself, by the way. It wasn't on Papa's account for once.'

Flora realized that it would be wrong to refuse. Tally was always trying to give her things – clothes she pretended she no longer wore, a bottle of a scent she swore she didn't like any longer (though Flora noticed she went on buying it), a handbag she said didn't go with any of her shoes . . . The problem was going to be when to wear the beautiful new dress. It was the sort of thing that Tally often wore, but it really had no place in her own life. She hadn't the slightest wish to go out with any of the men who took Tally to expensive restaurants and nightclubs, even if they had asked her, which they never had. It wasn't the kind of dress she could wear when she was taken out, as occasionally happened, by one of the account executives at the agency. And it certainly wasn't the sort of thing she could wear with Algy Baxter. Outings with him invariably meant pubs and bistros and coffee bars, the cheapest seats in the cinema or the gods at the theatre, or standing on the touchline in the freezing cold, watching rugger matches.

Recently he had taken her to the Players, a theatre club built under the arches of Charing Cross station and so close to the underground trains that you could hear them rumbling past during performances. Algy had joined as a member because it was cheap and because, as he had assured her blithely, it was a jolly good evening out.

The show had been exactly like Victorian music hall, with different turns coming on, one after the other, and she'd enjoyed it all very much. But the blue dress would have been ludicrously out of place.

It was busy in the Oasis that evening and late before she finished work. She walked down the King's Road to the bus stop and waited for a number twenty-two to come along. When a car drew up just past her she took no notice at first until a man got out and she saw, with a shock, that it was Nicholas.

He came towards her hesitantly. 'It *is* you, isn't it, Flora? I wasn't sure.'

'Yes, it's me.' She must have gone white, then red. For two years she had only seen him in her dreams, and now, suddenly, he was there in real life.

'Can I give you a lift anywhere?'

'Oh! Yes, please, that would be awfully kind.'

He opened the passenger door for her and she slid inside.

'Where to?' He pressed the starter button.

'To Tally's place, please. Do you know where it is?'

'It's the mews, isn't it?'

They drove down the King's Road.

'You've changed your hair again,' he said. 'That's why I wasn't sure at first.'

She'd grown it longer and put it into pin curls religiously every night – except last night, of course, when she'd been too tired to bother. So today it was looking like rats' tails, and she hadn't washed it for nearly a week.

'Tally said she'd seen you.'

'Yes, she cooked for a dinner party I was at. I was amazed to see her working at something.' He turned his head towards her. 'It's late to be out on your own. Don't your escorts see you home?'

'I haven't been out with anyone. I've got a job waitressing

137

at a coffee bar in Fulham, three evenings a week. I've just finished there.'

'You must be tired. I'm glad I spotted you. When was the last time we met? A long time ago . . .'

'At Melton.'

'Oh, yes, of course.' He turned towards her again. 'I remember. We had a dance. You were doing A levels, weren't you? How did they go?'

'Not awfully well. And I failed Latin.'

'What a pity. I gather you're doing a shorthand and typing course at the moment.'

'Very dull, I'm afraid.'

'So now you're going to be a secretary?'

'Worse luck.'

'Come and work for me.' He smiled as he said it, and of course he was only joking. He had forgotten all about the promise of the punting up the river to Grantchester and about the picnic.

'Did you like Hong Kong?' she asked politely.

'Very much. I'd like to have stayed out longer. Have you ever been there?'

'Goodness, no. I've never even been out of England. I might go abroad this summer, actually. Tally's invited my brother and me to their villa in the south of France in August. I'm not quite sure yet if we can, though.'

'Why not?'

She couldn't explain about the money problems, about Humphrey's reluctance, about trying to save up some of her wages from the Oasis because she couldn't possibly let Tally pay for everything.

'We don't know if we can get away then.'

'Well, if you do, perhaps I'll see you there. I'm going to Italy sometime around then so maybe I'll be able to call by at Les Rosiers.'

Every single traffic light had been green and they were now nearly at Sloane Square. It was all going too fast, the same as when she had been dancing with him. As they turned into Eaton Square, he said suddenly, 'Have you eaten?'

'Well, not really.' Not since her sardine sandwich at lunch.

'Nor have I. Let's go and get something. There's a place near here that stays open pretty late.'

He turned down Elizabeth Street and stopped outside a small restaurant in Pimlico.

'I hope you like Italian food.'

'I've never tried it.'

'Now's the time, then.'

Eating spaghetti wasn't easy. When she tried to wind it round and round her fork, copying him, it kept slithering off between the plate and her mouth.

'How are you getting on, living with Tally?' he asked.

'Oh, fine.' She tried to concentrate on eating and not look at him too much in case she gave herself away. 'She's been awfully kind. I don't pay any rent, you see. I'm very lucky.'

'I think *she's* very lucky. God knows how she'd be without someone sensible like you.'

Yet another piece of spaghetti slid off her fork before she could get it as far as her mouth.

'Look,' he said, 'you can use your spoon, too, if it helps. Like this.'

He showed her how to twirl the fork against the spoon and after that she began to get the hang of it. And after a glass of wine she began to relax enough to make an attempt at conversation.

'Do you live in London now, then?' she asked.

'I've got a flat on the Embankment. It's convenient for the City.'

'That's where you work?'

He nodded. 'At the moment. My father's company has offices there – as well as overseas. I was setting up one in Hong Kong. The next will be New York, I hope.'

Hong Kong, New York . . . It was all so far away.

'It sounds awfully exciting. I'd love to see America.'

'I'm sure you will, one day. People are travelling more and more.'

'Did you go to Hong Kong by ship?'

'No, I flew both ways. With BOAC. It's a long journey, and they have to come down several times to refuel, but it's reasonably enjoyable.'

He was very casual about it, as though flying round the world was nothing special. He poured her another glass of wine.

'How's your brother? Humphrey, isn't it? The medical student.'

'Oh, fine. He's nearly finished his third year. Then he's taking a year out to do a BSc. He wants to be a consultant, you see. A surgeon.'

'What sort of one?'

'A chest surgeon. You know, lungs and things.'

'Do you see much of him?'

'He comes round to supper sometimes. Tally cooks. She's very good – well, you know that.'

'Is she still doing dinner parties?'

'No, actually. She's doing a modelling course now. You know, learning to be a model.'

'Ah.'

'I think she'll be awfully good at it.'

He smiled. 'Still the loyal little friend.'

'Well, she's incredibly beautiful, isn't she?'

'Don't you ever look in the mirror yourself, Flora?'

'Well, yes, but . . .'

'Next time you do, take a closer, longer look.'

He drove her back to the mews and dropped her outside the front door. She felt euphoric and, at the same time, crushed by misery. She had seen Nicholas again and he had taken her to dinner and said nice things to her and smiled at her with his wonderful smile. But as he said goodnight he hadn't mentioned taking her out again. 'Sleep well,' he'd said. And that was all.

'And now we come to ze suits in Monsieur Randolph's new wintair collection. Atalanta is wearing "Grousemoor" . . .'

As the head vendeuse, Madame Lise, announced her turn,

140

Tally glided forward, hips leading. She swayed down the spotlit walkway between the little gold chairs, and between the rows of faces turned towards her. The salon was packed, the air thick with the scent from lavish flower arrangements, all mixed up with Mr Randolph's revolting new scent *Noblesse* which had been sprayed around with something like a flit-gun. The tweed suit was horribly hot, her new roll-on was pinching like hell and she could feel beads of sweat breaking out under the panstick – any more and her false eyelashes would come unstuck.

She paused halfway down and, with one hand on her hips, rotated smoothly as they had been taught at modelling school, remembering to smile brilliantly all the while. The faces, with their devouring, critical eyes, tracked her from each side. None of them smiled back, except for a silver-haired old man in a wing collar, leaning forward with gloved hands resting on a cane. As she passed him he gave her a huge and vulgar wink. On she sailed towards the far end of the salon where Mr Randoph stood watching, dwarfed by tiers of pink and blue hydrangeas. When the model agency had sent her as a freelance extra for his winter show, he had not quite known how to react.

'Lady Atalanta, such a surprise . . . Well, of course, I should be delighted to have you helping show my little collection . . . What a pity that Lady Gresham will not be able to attend . . .' The Cow, thank God, was safely down at Les Rosiers.

As she reached Mr Randolph he gave her a thin smile. The pre-show nerves had been appalling, with everyone running around in circles and Mr Randolph and his assistant, Mr Bernard, having a spectacular row followed by the sulks. He was making some sort of sign at her now, hands fluttering round his shoulders.

The senior house model, in by far the nicest suit, was waiting to follow on, and gave her a bitchy look as she swept by, which meant she must have done it quite well. Tally rushed to get changed into her next outfit. After the suits, it was the coats, then the dresses and jackets, and

141

then the cocktail dresses with fussy little hats, and then the evening gowns. Tally glided up and down, smile pinned in place. Every time she passed the old man he winked.

At the end of the show all the models went on again in their final evening gowns – hers had silver sequins sewn all over layers of white net, and all she needed was a wand and she could have gone on top of a Christmas tree. There was a ripple of applause and Mr Randolph with Mr Bernard beside him now, tantrums and sulks forgotten, spread his hands modestly. Later on, he slimed up to her.

'I congratulate you, Lady Atalanta. You did very well. Tell me, how long have you been modelling?'

She had no intention of revealing that this was only her second job. The first had been a lunchtime ready-to-wear fashion show at Harvey Nichols to a lot of old women shoppers up from the country.

'Oh, quite a while.'

He was looking at her speculatively. 'Well, if you should ever require a permanent post, as one of my house models, I would be prepared to consider you.

'I'll think about it.'

He raised his eyebrows. 'I should point out that there is a *great* deal of competition to model here, Lady Atalanta. I have very high standards, you understand. I only employ the best.' He paused. 'However, I might be persuaded to take you on if I thought that we should both benefit from the arrangement . . .'

She frowned down at him. 'How do you mean exactly?'

'Your friends, Lady Atalanta . . . You must move in the highest circles and I should like to acquire some younger clients. An insurance against the future, if you follow me.'

She did. She followed him perfectly. What a loathsome little worm he was, expecting her to tout for business. As though anyone of her friends would want to wear his ghastly creations. She was about to tell him so, when Mr Bernard rushed up in another of his panics.

'The Marchioness would like a word with you, Paul . . . about "Grousemoor". It seems the Marquis was especially

142

taken with it.' He glanced at Atlanta uncertainly. 'And
several others that this model was wearing.'

She watched the two of them hurry off. The Marchioness
had a long face, just like a horse, and looked as though she
had just got off one. The Marquis, leaning on his cane beside
her, was the silver-haired old man who had kept ogling her.
He looked across and gave her another big wink.

'Not you again, Charles.'

He raised his bowler. 'I thought you might like a lift.'

'I've got my car.'

'Come and have a drink then.'

'Too early.'

'Tea, then. The Ritz? Fortnums?'

'Neither. I'm going home.'

Tally started to walk down Burlington Street, but Charles
fell into step beside her, twirling his rolled umbrella. He
really was becoming a terrible bore – always lying in wait
for her outside places and phoning almost every day. She
stopped.

'Look, Charles, I keep telling you that I'm not going out
with you any more. Can't you understand that?'

'I'm hoping you'll change your mind.'

'I won't. It doesn't work because you won't play by
the rules.'

'I swear I will . . .'

'You've said that too many times. Anyway, how did you
know I was here?'

'I ran into Sophia – you told her about doing the show.
How did it go?'

In future, she thought, she'd keep her whereabouts to
herself if he was going to carry on like this. 'Alright.
Pretty bloody having to put on winter clothes in the middle
of July.'

'Wish I'd seen you. I bet you looked absolutely stunning.'

'Flattery will get you nowhere.' Tally found her car key
and unlocked the Morris Minor. 'Charles, can't you go

and pester some other girl? There's not a shortage in London.'

'There's only one you.'

'I suggest you look harder. Anyway, I'm going away for a bit, so it'll be no use ringing, or waiting around for me.'

'Where to?'

'I'm going down to the villa in France. Not that it's anything to do with you. Flora's coming with me. And her brother. We're driving down.'

'Her brother?'

'That's right. Humphrey. He's a medical student. And before you ask, Charles, no, I'm not in love with him. He happens to be an old friend who I've known since we were kids – not that that's anything to do with you, either.'

She opened the car door and slung her vanity box on to the passenger seat. Inside, the Morris was like an oven and she wound down the window. Charles bent down to peer at her through it.

'See you when you get back.'

'No, you won't.'

But he was smiling as he doffed his bowler again – the smile that told her he still didn't believe that she could really mean it.

Flora watched the lizard running along the stone wall. It stopped suddenly and remained completely motionless for a moment so that she could see it quite clearly – the scaly skin, the lidded eye, the tapering tail and little, splayed feet. Then it moved again and vanished down a crevice. There were lots of them all over the villa gardens, sunning themselves on the walls and stones, and making sudden rustling noises in the dry undergrowth.

She couldn't get over Les Rosiers. It was so beautiful that sometimes all she wanted to do was to sit and drink everything in – sunlight and shade, wood and stone, lichen and tile. And everywhere there were flowers – smothering roofs, cascading down walls, spilling out of urns and pots, creeping down steps.

Not only Les Rosiers, but France itself enchanted her. It smelled and sounded and looked so different from England. She liked hearing French spoken in its own country, not murdered in a school classroom, seeing the French people waving their hands and shrugging their shoulders and gabbling away. She loved the smell of Gauloise cigarettes, of garlic and cheese, and freshly baked baguettes and newly ground coffee.

They had driven all the way from Calais in Tally's Morris Minor and Tally and Humphrey had taken it in turns to drive and map read. Flora had had nothing to do but sit in the back, rather squashed, but content, watching the scenery go by. They had stopped for the night in Paris and spent a day sightseeing, doing all the tourist things. They had gone up the Eiffel Tower and to the Louvre and Notre-Dame cathedral and walked beside the Seine and down the Champs-Elysées and eaten at a pavement cafe. Tally had wanted to go to an expensive restaurant in the evening and pay for the whole dinner, but Humphrey had refused to allow it. The two of them had had quite an argument on the pavement outside the restaurant – or rather, Tally had argued, waving her wallet at Humphrey, while he had shaken his head stubbornly.

'Honestly, Humphrey, I can easily afford it. Why won't you let me?'

'I just won't.'

'Well, I think you're being a stuffy old spoilsport. We could have a super dinner here and you want us to go somewhere cheap and nasty.'

'We could find somewhere cheap and nice.'

Frenchmen, passing by, had cast admiring and amused glances but Tally, flushed with annoyance, had ignored them. 'I can't be bothered. My feet are killing me. So are Flora's. And I'm getting a huge corn. So you're being incredibly selfish.'

'I'm sorry, Tally, but you're not paying for Flora and me, and that's all there is to be said.'

In the end, *she* had given in because it was clear that he wouldn't, and they had walked until they had found a much cheaper place. Tally hadn't sulked, though, and she had let Humphrey pay for the wine without a murmur.

From the terrace wall where she was sitting in the shade, Flora could see down to the swimming pool below. Tally was sunbathing beside it, stretched out on a lounger in a yellow two-piece swimsuit, and she had already gone a lovely golden-brown without burning anywhere. When Flora squinted sideways she could see the flakes peeling off her own burned nose, and her shoulders were still too red and painful to go out in the sun. As for her freckles, there were just hundreds of them all over her face and arms. If Nicholas came – and nobody seemed to know for sure if he would or he wouldn't – she'd be looking her very worst.

Nicholas arrived unexpectedly at the end of the first week, just as Flora had given up all hope. When she got up in the morning and went out on to the terrace he was there, sitting at the table under the fig tree, drinking coffee. He stood up, smiling, and pulled out a chair for her beside him.

'Come and sit down, Flora. And stop looking as though I'm a ghost.'

She sank into the chair, legs like jelly. 'I didn't know you were arriving.'

'I didn't know myself. I've been in Rome on business and finished earlier than I thought. It was hellishly hot there so I decided to get out. I've been driving through the night.'

'You must be awfully tired.'

'I'll sleep later. Have some coffee.'

He poured it for her. She loved the coffee in France; it never tasted the same in England. Nor did the bread or the butter or the wine, or practically anything else. Yvette, the maid, came slapping across the terrace in her sandals, bringing flaky croissants and pale butter and black cherry jam, setting them down on the table. The morning sun was filtering through the gaps between the fig tree's broad leaves, dappling the blue cloth. She watched all these things, trying to compose herself. It had been a shock seeing him so suddenly, like it had been in London. With warning, she could have prepared herself to be very calm and casual; without it, she needed time. She took some of the cherry jam and the spoon clattered against her plate. He didn't seem to notice anything, though. He wasn't even looking her way, but was intent on peeling the skin off a peach, pulling it away in thin strips with a small silver knife.

'Will you be staying long?' Her voice, at least, sounded casual enough.

'A day or two, that's all. As Atalanta will be relieved to hear. She's still fast asleep, I take it?'

'She doesn't usually get up till later.'

'Nothing's changed, has it? Is your brother here?'

'Yes. He'll be up soon. He reads awfully late at night. I'm usually the first up.'

He turned his head briefly to smile at her, still peeling away. 'I remember when I met you. You were first up then – a little girl in plaits, peeping to see what was in all the dishes. I gave you a fright then, too. I must try not to make a habit of it.'

Amazing that he remembered at all. But pathetic to think that it meant a thing.

'Does your mother know you're here?'

'No,' he said rather drily. 'I'm putting off the moment until I've had some sleep. You're not eating anything, Flora. Aren't you hungry?'

She started on a croissant while he ate his peach. She always loved breakfast out on the terrace. It was the best time of day to her – before the sun got too hot and when everything was fresh after the night. Yvette's husband, Georges, had been round watering the plants and the earth and stones were still wet, with little puddles left in hollows. There was always a lovely damp smell before the heat of the day scorched it away.

'Do you like it here?' he asked.

'I think it's one of the most beautiful places I've ever seen. I love France.'

'How's your French?'

'Not very good, but I'm trying. Tally's awfully good,

147

though. She did all the asking and ordering when we were driving down and people thought she was really French.'

'I was asking about you, not her. Are you staying long?'

'Until the end of next week. Humphrey has to go back and I'm supposed to be getting a job.'

'You finished your course, then?'

'Yes. I can do a hundred and forty words a minute in shorthand and sixty at typing.'

She wondered if he would say anything again about working for him, but he didn't. Instead he poured more coffee for her and then for himself. If we were married, she imagined stupidly, this is how it might be, the two of us at breakfast.

'Do you mind if I smoke?'

She shook her head and he found a case and lighter in the pocket of his linen jacket and lit a cigarette. He smiled at her again.

'You've got sunburned. Your nose is peeling.'

She rubbed at it with her fingers. 'I know. It looks awful. I stayed in the sun too long when we first got here. My shoulders are all burned, too.'

'It's much stronger than the English sun. You have to be careful. I like the freckles.'

'You couldn't possibly.'

'But I do. They suit you. I've always thought so. And now you've got more of them, which looks even better.' He drew on his cigarette, still studying her. 'Well, what are you going to do today?'

'Nothing much. Just swim and laze about. Sometimes we go down to the café in the village square and have a drink – that's quite fun, and it's cheap.'

'I know the one. Have you been into Cannes?'

'We went one evening in Tally's car. The trouble is it's a bit expensive and Humphrey and I can't really afford it. He won't let Tally pay, you see.' There had been another big argument outside a restaurant there.

'A man of principle. I admire that. I wonder if he'd let *me* pay?'

'I don't think so, I'm afraid.'

'He couldn't object to it if I just took you one evening, though, could he?'

'Me?'

'*You*. The freckled one. You ought to see something more of Cannes before you have to go back and sit typing in an office in London. Would you like that?'

'Well, yes. Very much. If you're sure—'

'That's settled then.' He stood up, stretching. 'Well, I think I'll go and get some kip. See you later.'

She sat there, finishing her croissant and her coffee, and wondering if he'd really meant it.

'Nicky, darling, do let's go down to the casino at Cannes tonight. I adore gambling.'

'If you like, Mama.'

Tally made a face at Flora from across the dinner table but she pretended not to notice. Her own must be long with disappointment. She had been hoping all day that he would keep his promise and take her down to Cannes in the evening. He had never actually said *which* evening, but if he was only here for a day or two there wouldn't be many to choose from.

'Of course the others wouldn't be allowed in . . .' Lady Gresham was saying.

'Humphrey's over twenty-one, Mama. Would you like to join us, Humphrey?'

It was nice of him to ask, even though he must have known that Humphrey would have to refuse. If only she were two years older she could have gone, even if she didn't actually gamble a sou. Before Humphrey could answer, Lady Gresham had turned to him.

'Have you a dinner jacket here? You'd need to wear one.' Her tone assumed that he hadn't.

'I'm afraid not, Lady Gresham. And even if I had, I couldn't afford to gamble.' Humphrey looked across at Nicholas. 'But thanks for the invitation.'

'Personally,' Tally said very clearly, 'I think it's deadly boring anyway.'

'As you have never been, Atalanta, I don't think you can possibly say.'

Tally started to say something back to her stepmother and then stopped. Instead, she began picking at the skin round her nails.

The evening was all spoiled now, Flora thought miserably. It had been lovely before – sitting round the table on the terrace under the fig tree in the candlelight, eating Yvette's roast chicken and drinking red wine. She had washed her hair earlier and set it in pin curls, and she had put on her nicest dress and some lipstick and powder, and her white high-heeled sandals. The peeling and the freckles didn't show nearly so much after dark. Nicholas had smiled at her when she had come out on to the terrace before dinner and said how pretty she looked.

She watched him during the day. He had reappeared after lunch and swum in the pool and sunbathed beside it. Tally, of course, had more or less ignored him, pulling her sun lounger well away from his. Flora, lying in the shade on the other side of the pool and pretending to read *The Cruel Sea*, had kept sneaking looks at him from behind the book. She looked at him again now, sitting at the other end of the table beside his mother, drinking his wine. He was going away for the rest of the evening, and soon he would be going away completely. He had never meant what he said about taking her to Cannes, just as he'd never meant what he said about the punting and the picnic.

The three of them went off to the casino, dressed up in evening clothes, with Lady Gresham swathed in white mink. Tally gave an exaggerated sigh of relief.

'Well, let's go down to André's. And I don't care what you say, Humphrey, *I'm* paying – the first round at least.'

They bumped up the track in the Morris and down to the village. André, fat and garlicky in his greasy apron, came out to greet them, as he always did whenever he caught sight of Tally. As they sat down at a table under the brown and green awning, André jabbered away to Tally in his almost incomprehensible French. The only thing Flora understood was his 'Ooh la, la!' accompanied by a shocked look round at all three of them. This was followed by a smile that showed the several gaps his teeth, and by much nodding, before he went back inside the cafe.

'He's bringing us some pastis – on the house,' Tally told them. 'He's absolutely shocked we've never tried it.'

It tasted, and looked, like medicine to Flora – cloudy white liquorice stuff in a small glass, like something Matron had dished out in the old days and that you held your nose to drink.

'*La petite ne boit pas!*' André was looking hurt.

She was always *la petite* with him.

'Drink up, Flora, or you'll offend him.' Tally nudged her.

She tried another small sip and then, with André's eyes upon her, a larger, valiant one.

'*C'est bon, n'est-ce-pas?*' André beamed at her and splashed more into her glass. He poured one for himself. '*Santé!*'

They all drank again. Humphrey drank his slowly but Tally was tossing hers back, and André kept on filling her glass. Then he topped up Flora's again. She'd found a way of throwing it quickly down the back of her throat so that she hardly tasted it. Tally was giggling and drinking faster and faster and André kept on refilling her glass until Humphrey leaned forward and put his hand over it.

'*Non,*' he said clearly in his very English accent. '*Cela suffit, merci, André.*'

'What a spoilsport you are, Humphrey!' Tally said crossly, as André went away, shrugging his big shoulders and muttering. 'It was all free, you know.'

'And you'd had enough.'

'No, I hadn't . . . I liked it. It was absolutely su-per.' She was slurring her words and her hair was falling over her face. 'You're an old killjoy. A stuffy, stick-in-the-mud, old killjoy. That's what you are, Humphrey. Humphrey-dumpty, sat on a wall. Humphrey-dumpty had a great fall . . . Stuffy old Humphrey, isn't he, Flora?'

'Not really.'

'Yes, he is. I want some more pastis.' She waved her empty glass. *'André!'*

But when André reappeared Humphrey ordered three coffees, very firmly, and though Tally slid down in her chair and sulked, she didn't argue with him.

There was nobody at the table in the morning and Flora started breakfast alone as usual. Humphrey was either still asleep or reading, Lord and Lady Gresham never appeared before mid-morning, and Tally certainly wouldn't do so for ages. She had felt ill on the way back from the cafe and Humphrey had had to stop the car very quickly so she could get out and be sick on the verge. Then she had gone cold and shivery so he had made her put on his sweater. She had flapped the too-long sleeves at him and called him an old fusspot.

It was another beautiful morning. A ray of sun felt hot on her bare arm and she could tell that it was going to be another scorcher. Yvette had left the cherry jam out for her and as she picked up the spoon she saw that some ants had got there first. She began to eject them carefully with the corner of her napkin.

'What on earth are you doing?'

She looked up to see Nicholas standing there. 'It's the ants. I'm trying to get rid of them.'

'What a kind heart you have, Flora. The usual treatment is boiling water or poison. You're fighting a losing battle, though, I'm afraid. They've already sent for reinforcements.' He pointed to a column of ants marching across the cloth towards the bowl. 'The best strategy is diversion.'

He removed the jam from the table, setting it down on the terrace at a distance, and brushed the remaining ants away with a napkin.

'It seems an awful waste of jam.'

'There speaks a child of wartime. No more rationing now, though. We'll let them enjoy it in peace and I'll get Yvette to bring some more for you.'

When Yvette appeared he spoke to her in French. It wasn't as good as Tally's, but it was pretty fluent. Then he sat down opposite Flora and poured some orange juice into a glass.

'Did you win lots of money at the casino?' she asked.

'Some. Don't ever believe anyone who tells you they won a lot gambling. They're not counting the losses.'

'What did you play?'

'Roulette, mostly. Some baccarat. It was a good evening. What did you do?'

'Oh, nothing very much. We went down to the cafe in the square that I told you about. André – that's the proprietor – gave us pastis to drink. It was revolting.'

He smiled. 'I've never managed to like it either. Rather like medicine, I always think.'

'That's *exactly* what I thought. I can't imagine why they drink so much of it all the time.'

Yvette came back with a tray of fresh coffee, croissants and more cherry jam, and then went off again. Nicholas poured some coffee and stirred it.

'What time would you like to go tonight?'

'Tonight?'

'You're looking blank. Remember, we agreed I'd take you into Cannes? It has to be tonight because I leave tomorrow. Would you like to go to dinner there?' He reached for a croissant. 'Don't you want to go? I thought you did.'

'But what about the others?'

'Well, I can't take Humphrey because he won't let me pay, and Atalanta certainly won't want to come. And I did my filial duty last night. So, that leaves you tonight. You're not going to disappoint me, are you?'

'No, of course not.'

'That's settled, then. Would you pass me the jam before the ants rumble our tactics and regroup.'

The first problem was that she had nothing really nice to wear. The beautiful blue dress that Tally had given her had

153

been left in London and, in any case, it wouldn't have been right on a summer holiday. She'd worn her best dress the night before and that left two other frocks to choose from, both very dull cottons.

The second problem was how to tell Tally.

She looked quite worried. 'Do you seriously want to go with him, Flora?'

'I wouldn't mind seeing Cannes again.'

'Well, don't go and get hurt. He's bound to take lots of girls out – you know, pretty, glamorous, older ones. They'll all be after him because of his money.'

'Heavens, I know he'd never be interested in me.'

'Hum. Well, at least you'll get a good dinner. He's bound to take you somewhere expensive. What are you going to wear?'

'My flowered dress, I suppose. It's my best.'

'Not very glam, is it? Tell you what, I'll lend you something of mine, if you like.'

'Oh, Tally . . . Thanks.'

'Well, what would you like to eat?'

Flora looked at the long menu which, naturally, was all in French. She recognized several things – *filet mignon* she knew was steak, *côtelettes d'agneau* were lamb cutlets . . .

'How about some lobster?' Nicholas suggested.

'I've never tried it.'

'It's very good.'

'Don't they cook them alive?'

'You'll have to stop being so soft-hearted, Flora. First ants, now lobsters . . . Something else, then?'

As Tally had predicted, the restaurant was obviously very expensive. She would really have preferred to be in one of the little cafes they had walked past after he had parked the car – not nearly so daunting as this one, with its starched pink linen and bowing waiters.

'I'll have the lamb cutlets, please.'

'What about to start with?'

She had completely forgotten to look at the starters

154

and had to begin all over again, trying to find something she could understand. In the end she chose melon,
which was dull, but safe. The waiter bore the huge menus
away.

Now was the time for her to sparkle with witty conversation, like the ones that seemed to be going on all
around her. The trouble was, she couldn't think of a
single thing to say, let alone sparkle with. She gulped
at the gin and tonic he'd ordered and when he offered
her a cigarette she took one, although she hardly ever
smoked. It took three tries before she could get it to
light.

'Tell me more about yourself, Flora.'

'What sort of thing?'

'Where you were born and brought up, about your
parents.'

'It's not very interesting.'

'If I wasn't interested, I wouldn't have asked you.'

So she told him about the house in Almond Avenue and
about her father being killed in the war, and about her mother
bringing Humphrey and her up alone. It all sounded very dull
to her – except the bit about her father. She was proud of
that, and especially of his medal. He listened, smoking his
cigarette.

'My father was in the RAF too, as a matter of fact, but
he was a fighter pilot. And he was lucky enough to survive.
He started his first business with his demob payment after
the war. Making bricks.'

'He's very successful, isn't he? Tally told me he has made
an awful lot of money.'

He said drily, 'She once referred to it as the "brick money".
As far as she's concerned, it doesn't really count.'

'Still, it must be nice for you.'

'What isn't so nice is not knowing who likes me for the
money and who for myself. You've no idea how unpleasant
that can be. You wonder about it all the time, and the only
people whom you can really trust are those who are just as
rich, or richer.'

She fiddled unhappily with a fork, thinking that he was probably wondering about her, too.

But he went on: 'I trust *you* implicity, though, Flora. If I didn't, you wouldn't be here.'

They had finished the first course and a waiter had brought her lamb cutlets, prettily arranged with paper frills on the ends. As she cut into the meat, her knife slipped and some of the sauce splashed on to her lap. It missed the napkin and landed on her skirt. She dabbed at it hurriedly.

'That's Atalanta's dress, isn't it?' he said.

'How did you know?'

He smiled. 'Well, in the first place it's the sort of thing she wears. In the second, it doesn't quite fit you – it's for someone much taller. And in the third, you're obviously in a panic about spoiling it.'

She said, embarrassed, 'She lent it to me. Mine are old as the hills.'

'You should have worn one of them, though. Don't ever try to be anyone but yourself, Flora.'

Who am I, though? she thought. Nobody, really. And nothing to him.

After dinner, when she was afraid that the evening was already almost over, he drove her along the coast road to Juan-les-Pins.

'I know a place called Maxim's where we can go and dance,' he said as he started up the car. 'Would you like that?'

It was in the open air, among the pine trees and close to the beach. She could hear the dance band playing in the distance as they walked across the sandy soil with its rough carpeting of pine needles. It was a song she knew, about music and heaven and the moon being high.

And there *was* a moon like a beautiful silver barque sailing high on a diamond-studded ocean. Flora stopped and stared upwards.

Nicholas waited beside her. 'What are you looking at?'

'Oh, nothing special. Just everything. It's a magic night, isn't it? The sort of night when you could do anything you

156

wanted and it wouldn't count in the rest of your life . . . if that makes any sense.'

'Perfect sense.'

He was being kind, because he couldn't possibly understand. She wasn't sure quite what she meant herself. They walked on towards the music.

There were tables set around the small dance floor and fairy lights strung among the trees. When they sat down Nicholas asked her what she would have to drink.

'Can I try a liqueur? I've never had one.'

'You can have anything you like. It's your magic night, remember? Cointreau? Chartreuse? Brandy? Drambuie?'

'That lovely green one.'

The dance floor was made of opaque glass with coloured lights glimmering through from beneath and changed colour all the time. More magic. More make-believe. When they danced he held her close to him so that the top of her head rested against his chin. Flora closed her eyes. The band was playing 'La Mer'. Whenever she heard the song again she knew she would think of this moment, dancing under the stars with Nicholas.

It was late when they got back to the villa and everyone had gone to bed.

'I'm leaving very early in the morning,' he said. 'So I may not see you.'

'I suppose you have to go?'

'Yes, I must. I'm going to New York in a few days.'

'Will you be gone long?' she couldn't help asking.

'Several months, at least. Perhaps longer. We may be setting up an office there.'

'Oh, I see. How exciting for you!' Her voice sounded as though she really meant it. Inside she was crying.

'Yes, I'm looking forward to it. Good luck with the job-hunting, Flora. And thank you for this evening.'

'It's me that ought to be thanking you – for dinner and everything.'

'No. You gave me the pleasure of your company. It's been a long time since I've had such an enjoyable evening

157

with anyone. Stay as sweet as you are, Flora.' He leaned forward to kiss her, then drew back and smiled at her. 'Nothing counts tonight, remember?'

In the morning she got up very early, hoping to see him, but he had already gone.

Ten

T he smog was thick as pea soup. Tally rubbed at the windscreen of the Morris with a handkerchief, but it didn't make a bit of difference. She could hardly see beyond the end of the bonnet. The wipers, squeaking to and fro, didn't make any difference either, nor did the headlights. The smog had closed in around the car like a clammy shroud. Rather frightening, really, especially in this area. She'd already passed the Tower of London, looming out of the fog at her like something in a horror film, and by now she must be right by the docks, though she couldn't see them. Knife fights and murders, Fagin and Bill Sykes, opium-dealing Chinamen, bodies floating in the river, big black rats and all the rest of it . . . Tally shivered. Curious how the smog deadened all sound. She could hear nothing except the throb of the car engine and the squeak-squeak of the wipers. No hollow-sounding footsteps, thank God, or any sign of another person at all. Well, nothing for it but to go on.

This was the street now, she could just see the sign on a wall close by. She inched the car along the kerbside, trying to make out numbers beside doors. She groped for the scrap of paper on the passenger seat and had to stop and switch on the overhead light to read it. It was only three in the afternoon but it might as well have been the middle of the night. Thirty-five was the one she wanted. She crawled on.

Who in heaven's name would want to live down in this slummy part of London? By the look of them, the houses might have been rather nice once upon a time, but not any more. Not for years and years. Twenty-five, twenty-seven . . .

A big gap where a bomb must have flattened the houses. Thirty-one, thirty-three, thirty-five. Well, this was it and bloody awful it looked too – peeling paint, dark doorway, no curtains, an empty milk bottle on the step, not washed out. The agency must have got it wrong. Still, she'd better check.

She parked the Morris, locked it and hurried to the doorway, holding her handkerchief over her nose and mouth. There was no bell at number thirty-five so she hammered loudly on the door. Nothing happened, so she hammered again, and was about to do so for the third time when the door opened.

'Crikey, didn't think you'd turn up in this! Shouldn't 'ave bothered.'

He was shorter than her, swarthy as a gypsy, with thick, dark hair and a five o'clock shadow, wearing a leather jacket and blue jeans. A cigarette drooped from the corner of his mouth.

She lowered the handkerchief. 'Are you Mr Sutton?'

'Yeah. Larry. That's me.' He looked her over. 'And you're Atalanta. Better come in, since you're 'ere.'

She stepped over the threshold into a bare and dimly lit hallway without a stick of furniture, only an old bicycle propped against the wall. An uncarpeted staircase led upwards to God knew what. To the visions of Chinamen and rats and floating bodies, she added white-slave trafficking.

He saw her hesitation and grinned.

'Nothin' to panic about, darlin'. All above board, though it may not look like it. Not one of yer posh West End places, but 'oo needs 'em? It's the photos what count, not the decor.'

He had a dreadful Cockney accent and spoke through the cigarette that wagged up and down in his mouth. With a flowery flourish of his hand, like a Regency rake, he indicated the stairs. 'Studio's up there. After you, madam.'

She preceded him doubtfully, glancing back over her shoulder. He grinned again.

'Trust me, darlin'.'

At the top, she stopped in surprise.

'Not bad, eh?' he said behind her.

160

The floor above had been opened up to make one huge barn-like room, reaching to the old rafters. Studio lamps stood about, along with a strange assortment of furniture that looked as though it had all been picked out of a junkyard. On the far side, a curtainless window ran almost the width of the wall, though she couldn't see out for the smog. In one corner there was a sink, a kitchen cabinet and a gas stove; in another was a large divan bed – unmade – and hangers of clothes hooked on to a sort of wire washing line. Oddments were scattered over the floor – books, magazines, shoes, sweaters, tins of food, boxes of film, unwashed plates . . . A real pig-mess, worse than her own room. What little heat there was came from two smelly old oil heaters.

'Do you actually *live* here?'

He was watching her, arms folded across his chest, cigarette still dangling from his mouth. 'Sure. Darkroom downstairs. All mod cons. It was a sailmaker's loft once.'

'Is that the river out there?'

'Yeah. Lime'ouse Reach. You can spit in it out the window. We're right on the bend. Great view, when you can see it.' He stubbed out the cigarette in an empty sardine tin. 'Well, I guess we'd better get crackin'.'

Mixed in with the Cockney there were bits of American. And he seemed to have cowboy boots on under the jeans.

'What am I supposed to be wearing?'

'This.' From somewhere among the chaos he produced a peculiar-looking yellow pinafore dress. The bodice was cut into two points at the waist to make it look like a waistcoat over the skirt. 'Mate of mine designed them. Same sort of thing as Quant.'

'Quant?'

'Mary Quant. You know, Bazaar. New shop in the King's Road.'

'I don't often go down there, I'm afraid.'

He grinned. 'Yeah, well I guess Knightsbridge's more your line. Or the West End. Old-fashioned stuff. You want to get with it a bit, darlin'. The New Look's old. Dead as a dodo. Things are changin'.'

161

He handed her the dress and a cream-coloured blouse with a round, frilled neck to wear under it. 'There's a bathroom downstairs. You can change there and do your make-up. Not too much of it, though. You don't need it and I don't want it.'

The bathroom seemed to have been made out of a coal hole and there was some kind of gas heater over the sink, but as she didn't know how to work it she had to make do with cold water. She opened up her vanity case and got to work on her face. The mirror over the basin was a spotted horror and she kept hitting her head on the bare electric light bulb hanging from the ceiling. *A rising young photographer*, the agency had told her. *Going places.* Huh! She spat into her mascara and loaded the little brush.

When she had finished her make-up, she wriggled into the blouse and the yellow dress. It was different from anything else she had ever worn and the skirt looked skimpy and short. Rather fun, though, she thought, trying to see more of it in the mirror.

Upstairs, Larry had switched on the studio lights and was shunting them around. She had got used to the glare in other studios – civilized places in civilized parts of London, and with civilized photographers who spoke properly.

He looked at her critically. 'You done much photographic stuff before?'

'Plenty.'

'Only I've never seen your face around . . .'

'I've never seen yours either.'

Compared with the top models she was a complete beginner, as she well knew, but certainly wasn't going to admit. After Mr Randolph's, she'd done some more freelancing for couture shows, and then started to get photographic work, which was more amusing, as well as better paid.

'Soon see if you're any good,' he said, dragging another light across the floor. 'Park yourself there, darlin', will you.'

She took up her position where he'd pointed, hands on her waist, hips forward, chin lifted – a stance photographers seemed to like.

'You playin' statues or somethin'?'

He had come forward into the lighted circle, camera slung round his neck. She looked down her nose at him. He was at least two inches shorter than her, if not more.

'Perhaps you'd show me what you want, then, Mr Sutton?'

'In the first place, some of that muck off your face.' He took a grubby handkerchief from his jeans and rubbed at her cheeks. Then he flicked at her hair with a pocket comb from his back pocket. 'That a perm? You want to let that grow out. Perms're for dinosaurs.'

He took a step or two back, combing his own hair at each side, and considered her a moment. 'Bit better. Your name really Atalanta?'

'Why shouldn't it be?'

'Thought you might've made it up – sort of a stage name.'

'I'm Lady Atalanta, actually, since you ask.' He definitely needed taking down a peg or two.

'No kiddin'?' He appeared to find that killingly funny. 'Your dad a Lord or somethin' then?'

'An Earl or something.'

'Thought you had a classy look . . . The genuine article. My dad's a porter.'

'How fascinating,' she said coldly. 'Which station?'

'Not railway. Meat. Works at Smithfield.'

'*Really*?'

'Yeah, really.' He squinted at her through the camera's viewfinder. 'Got your nose in the air still. You're goin' to have to forget all that old stiff-as-a-poker, la-di-da routine. That's 'istory.'

For the next hour he prowled around her, clicking away from all angles, including the floor. She had to stand this way and that, walk about, twirl round, stand on a chair, jump off, sit on it, stand up again . . .

'Let yourself go, love. Loosen up. You're lookin' like there's a bad smell under your nose . . . Forget about *me*. Think of somethin' nice. Ah, that's better. Now we're gettin' somewhere.'

He hauled the old bicycle up from the hallway and she had to sit astride it, one foot on the pedal, skirt riding up. Click, click, click, click . . .

By the time he'd finished she was exhausted, but he seemed fresh as a daisy.

'Bung the kettle on, darlin', will you, soon as you've got out the togs. I'll just get this lot sorted then we'll 'ave a cuppa.'

The gas stove appeared to have come off a dump and took several matches to light. While the kettle was heating, she rinsed out two dirty cups from the sink and scraped old tea leaves out of the pot – a horrible job that she always left to Flora. The half-empty bottle of milk had gone sour and there was only a spoonful of sugar stuck to the bottom of a jam jar. Not a strainer in sight anywhere. Larry was sitting at a table, scribbling away in a notebook.

'Ta, love. You be mother,' he said.

She shoved a cup over to him. 'This tea's quite disgusting.'

'Co-op's finest.' He was looking at her, the Woodbine parked again between his lips. 'You weren't bad, you know. Considerin'.'

'Considering what?'

'You're an amateur. Just playin' at it, aren't you? No need to work. Not a real pro. But you're a beautiful girl – one of the best lookers I've done – an' you've got a great body. An' knockout legs. We'll see how it all comes out. I might use you again.'

'I might not want to come here again.'

'You will. If they turn out like I think they will, you'll love 'em. An' me. I'm on the up and up. Everybody's goin' to want me to take their picture.'

'Modest, aren't you?'

'What's the point in bein' that? I'm good, an' I know it. Soon everyone else'll know it. Larry Sutton's goin' to be an 'ousehold name, just you wait an' see.'

What a hope! Household names, when it came to photography, were people like Baron and Beaton and Bassano. She put down her cup.

164

'I must go.'

He cocked his head towards the window. 'In that lot?'

'I'll manage.'

He shrugged. 'Daft, if you ask me. You don't want to get lost round 'ere. That's askin' for trouble. We're not in jolly old Chelsea or Kensington, you know. An' it's got worse. You can't tell so easy, now it's dark, but go an' take a dekko out the front door if you don't believe me.'

She went downstairs and opened the door. The hall light reflected off an impenetrable grey wall; she couldn't even see the car, which could only be feet away.

'Told you so,' he said when she went back upstairs. 'Nobody's goin' nowhere this evenin'.'

'What am I supposed to do, then?'

'Can you cook?'

'As a matter of fact, I'm a cordon bleu.'

'Then you can do supper.'

'You'd better leave early tonight, Flora,' Tim said, putting his head round the door. 'The smog's bad. Don't try to get all the letters done. They can wait until tomorrow.'

He was nice to work for and didn't mind if she made mistakes. The Knightsbridge offices were brand new and everyone in the advertising agency was young. They all used their Christian names and breezed in and out of each other's offices – nothing like as stiff and formal as she had expected from her training.

She'd gone for an interview all dressed up in her suit, hat and gloves, and found him lounging behind his desk in shirtsleeves. He hadn't been very interested in her shorthand and typing speeds, and no one had bothered to test her. He had just chatted away for a bit, talking about all sorts of other things, and then said casually that as far as he was concerned she'd got the job. She was paid eight pounds and ten shillings a week, with luncheon vouchers, and the products she worked with were Blue Miracle washing powder and Pink Cameo soap. The pay had seemed riches at first but it soon melted away, what with food and living in London, and so she still worked two evenings a week at the Oasis coffee bar.

When she left the office the smog was so thick that she had to grope her way down towards the corner of Scotch House. A few cars and buses were creeping along, nearly invisible. Fuzzy headlight beams appeared out of the fog and red tail lights disappeared back into it.

She managed to cross Brompton Road by the traffic lights and made her way past the lighted windows of Harvey Nichols, trying to get her bearings. Was she walking towards Hyde Park Corner, or down Sloane Street? Fog did the weirdest things to you. It was like being blindfolded, turned round and round, and then having to work out which way you were facing.

She had reached Pont Street, so she was definitely going the right way. She'd walked this route back from the office every day for the past three months. So, how many turnings now to Chesham Street? Two or three? If she crossed over she could count them by the kerbs . . . if only she could remember how many there were.

How was Tally managing in all this? She'd been given a modelling job at some photographer's studio in the East End, but maybe she'd had the sense not to go.

If this really was Chesham Street then she must bear left very soon into Lyall Street and she'd almost be there. She crept on, groping her way by the railings until she reached the arched mews entrance and felt the cobblestones beneath her feet. Inside, she peeled off her scarf and coat and gloves; they were all wet and the handkerchief she had held over her mouth was black. She went upstairs, switching on lights. The house was empty.

When the phone rang she ran to it, hoping that it might be Tally, but it was Charles, asking for her.

'She's not back yet. I'll tell her you called.'

She put the receiver down and went to draw the curtains to shut out the smog and the night. She felt safe now, like an animal back in its burrow, but Tally was still out there – somewhere.

*　　*　　*

166

'It'll have to be cheese omelettes and baked beans. That's all I can find.'

'Suits me.'

'Don't you ever wash this frying pan?'

'I use it all the time, so why bother? Like some plonk?' Larry was waving a bottle of something cheap and nasty from Spain.

'Is that all you've got?'

'Yeah. Just run out of bubbly.' He uncorked it and poured some into two plastic tumblers. 'There you are. Cheers!'

She took a sip and shuddered. 'Ugh!'

'Chateau Lime'ouse. Keep drinkin' an' you'll soon get used to it.' He sat astride one of the chairs, back to front, tumbler in hand and smoking one of his filthy little Woodbines. She started grating the stale cheese.

'Where do you 'ang out, then?'

'Where do I what?'

'Where's your ladyship's residence?'

'Belgravia.'

He seemed to find that very funny. 'With your mum and dad?'

'No, I share a mews house with a friend.'

'Bloke?'

'Girl, actually.' She started whisking the eggs with a bent fork. 'An old schoolfriend.'

'She a model, too?'

'No, she's a secretary. She works in an advertising agency.'

'Nice, is she?'

'Very. She's got a very kind heart. She puts spiders out of the window and won't kill flies. And she's very romantic. She cried when Princess Margaret gave up Peter Townsend.'

'An' you didn't?'

'I didn't care that much.' She lit the gas and cut some lard into the frying pan. 'I don't really believe in love and romance.'

'Never fallen for anyone?'

'Never.'

'Still a virgin?'

'None of your damn business.'

'You'd be the first model I've met that is, if you are.'

'How would you know?'

'First-'and knowledge, darlin'. Every one. Every time.'

She tilted the pan, letting the fat run across it. 'Well, you're in for a big disappointment so far as I'm concerned.'

'You wouldn't be with me.'

She ignored him and turned her back to pour in the eggs. When the omelette was cooked she tipped it on to a plate with some of the baked beans. 'There you are. And I hope it chokes you.'

'Bung us the OK, will you.'

He whacked horrible bottled brown sauce all over the omelette and started eating where he was sitting, the plate balanced on the chair back.

'You can cook alright, I'll say that,' he mumbled through a mouthful. 'Didn't really believe you.'

'I don't generally tell lies.'

'Bet you do. All the time.'

She ignored him again, especially as it was true, and started cooking her own omelette. He waved his fork at her.

'You looked good in the frock, you know. I'd chuck out all your old togs, if I was you – borin' stuff like you've got on now. I mean, I ask you – a pencil skirt an' *twinset*? That's all finished now. Get with it. Nobody's goin' to be wearin' those things any more, 'cept your mum an' gran.'

She removed a pile of magazines from a stool. The top one had a cover picture of a naked girl cuddling a toy rabbit. *Playboy, Entertainment for Men*. She dropped them on the floor with a thud.

'Come from America, that lot,' he said blandly. 'Bloke I know brought them over with 'im. Good stuff.'

'They look filthy.'

'Depends 'ow you look at it, don' it? Me, I look at it to see what they're up to with the camera. What new tricks they're usin', see. They know what's what over there. Everythin's comin' from the Yanks these days. All the ideas.'

She perched on the rickety stool, holding her plate on her lap. 'Do your clothes come from America, too? I mean, what are you supposed to look like? Are you trying to be like Marlon Brando or something?'

'I'm *me*, darlin'. That's who I am. Larry Sutton.' He wiped his mouth with the back of his hand. 'That's the point, see?'

'No, I don't see.'

He waved his fork again. 'Everythin's changin', love. Clothes, art, photography, music . . . Speakin' of that, want to 'ear some records my mate brought back from America?'

'Not particularly.'

But he had already gone over to the record player and was pressing switches and twiddling knobs. 'Get an earful of this.'

The noise that suddenly blasted out nearly made her fall off the stool. It filled the room with a pounding, pulsating, ear-splitting racket. Some man was yelling – you couldn't call it singing – and Larry was dancing about like a madman, shaking and wriggling and thrusting his hips pretty suggestively. Tally, fork stopped halfway to her mouth, wondered if he'd gone mad. Finally, the record stopped. So did Larry.

'"Shake Rattle an' Roll",' he said. 'Bill 'Aley. Top of the charts over there.'

'What an absolutely *ghastly* row!'

'I s'pose you're still listenin' to the Squadronaires in Belgravia.' He took a few stiff and stately ballroom steps, arms extended as though he was holding a partner. 'An' foxtrottin' around.'

'I've never heard such a din.'

'You'll be 'earin' a lot more of it in the future, sweet 'eart. You can throw away your Sinatras an' your Perry Comos an' your Doris Days.'

He put the record away in its sleeve and took out another, blowing the dust off it carefully.

'Wait till you 'ear this one.'

'What is it?'

'Not what. *Who*.'

169

'*Who* is it, then?'

'*This*,' he said, pressing the start button ceremoniously, 'is Elvis.'

'I'm afraid she's not back yet, Charles.'

'Oh. Do you know where she is?'

'She was doing some studio photographic work. I expect she's got held up in the fog. It's terribly thick here.'

'Here too. I hope she's alright.'

'So do I.'

'Well, I suppose there's not much we can do if we don't know where she is. Would you tell her I called when she does get back? Perhaps she'd give me a buzz?'

'Yes, I'll do that.'

Flora put the phone down. Tally wouldn't, of course. She never returned Charles's calls. She went over to the window and tweaked back the curtain. The smog looked worse than ever. Where *was* Tally?

'You've got an incredible cheek! Give me one good reason why I should go to bed with you?'

'Me. I'm the good reason, darlin'. Bound to 'appen sooner or later, in it? You want to be a top model, you've got to know 'ow many beans make five. Oils the wheels, see. An' you don't want some fumblin' git first time out the gate, do you? One of your upper-class johnnies without a bloody clue. Enough to put you off for life. Now me . . . I'll turn you on.'

Larry was leaning against the table, feet crossed at the ankles, arms folded, cigarette hanging from his mouth. Dead casual. Amused. Watching her. Something fluttered about inside her as she met his eyes. Something quite new. She looked away.

'What about . . . precautions? You know.'

'I'll take care of that. No problems. You won't get knocked up by me.' He took a slow drag on his cigarette. 'Anythin' else worryin' you?'

'This is ridiculous. I don't even *know* you. Or anything about you . . .'

170

'All the better. It'll be fun findin' out.' He smiled at her and stubbed out the cigarette. 'Face it, love, you're stuck 'ere in the fog with me, an' what the 'ell else're we goin' to do all bloody night?'

'You've got your shocked face on, Flora.'

'Have I? Sorry. I'm not really shocked, Tally. Just a bit surprised.'

'You *are* shocked. I can tell.'

'Well, just a bit. I mean, you'd only just met him.'

'I know.'

'And you stayed with him for *three* days.'

'Well, the fog didn't lift properly till then, did it? I told you when I phoned that I'd be back when it did.'

She didn't look any different, Flora thought. Not on the surface. She was curled up on the sofa, smoking a cigarette, as though nothing had happened to her. If Tally had made up some other story, some sort of plausible excuse for her absence, Flora would never have guessed.

She *was* shocked, though she was trying hard not to be. It wasn't as though Tally was a bit in love with this Larry, whoever he was. When she'd asked her about that, she'd laughed and said 'Heaven's, no!' How could she have done it with someone she didn't love? Didn't even know? How *could* she? Yes, she was shocked. But she was curious too. She couldn't help it. Tally knew now. She *knew*.

'What was it like, Tally? I mean . . . did it hurt?'

Tally smiled. 'Just the opposite.'

'But supposing you have a baby?'

'I won't. He wore something. You know . . . one of those French things. Actually, I think I might get myself fixed up.'

'Fixed up?'

'With a Dutch cap.'

'A cap? You mean to wear on your head?'

Tally burst out laughing. 'Oh, Flora, you're so funny sometimes. No, you don't wear it on your head, it's a thing for women so they don't have babies. Larry told me about it. You go to a gynaecologist and get one fitted. He's given me the name of one who doesn't care if you're not married. Lots of the models go to him. You put it up inside you and it stops the sperm swimming up to the egg, you know . . . Remember biology? "Turn to page one hundred, please girls, and refer to the diagram there . . ."'

'You mean, you're going to do it with him *again*, this Larry person?'

'Probably. Or someone else.'

Now she was even more shocked. She was horrified. And frightened for Tally. 'I wish you wouldn't. Not if you don't love them. It's all wrong.'

'You're such a hopeless romantic, Flora. God, you still read Georgette Heyer and believe in all that . . . I'm not even sure I *could* love anybody. But I *like* Larry. He's fun and he's nice. Does that make you feel better?'

'Not really.' Flora said stubbornly. 'I still think you ought to love someone, and wait until you're married before you go to bed with them.'

'Well, *I* don't. I might not ever fall in love with anybody, and I'm not sure I ever want to get married anyway – not from what I've seen of it.'

'You don't really mean that, do you?'

'Yes I do.' Tally continued to smoke her cigarette calmly. 'I've said that before, haven't I?'

'Sort of. By the way, I forgot, Charles kept phoning while you were away. Several times. He wanted you to ring when you got back.'

'Oh, God . . . Well, he knows I won't.'

'I feel a bit sorry for him.'

'Well, don't be. He's an idiot. He should have got the message long ago. Next time he calls, you can tell him I said so.'

'I couldn't do that.'

'I honestly think you'd go out with some man just because you didn't like to hurt his feelings by saying no.'

Flora flushed and was silent. She'd already done that with someone at the office and had ended up offending him even more than if she had refused in the first place.

Tally stubbed her cigarette out and got to her feet, stretching. 'Well, I'm off to bed. Wake me when you get up, will you, Flora? Larry's got some more work for me. I didn't believe him at first, but I think he's really going places.' She started up the stairs and then turned back and stuck her head round the corner. 'I'll tell you another thing, too.'

'What?'

'I'm glad I'm not a virgin any more. *Really* glad.'

PART FOUR

Eleven

Dear Bob,
    I'm sorry there has been a delay in getting our proposal to you. We have been giving the whole matter some considerable thought and have come up with some new ideas that I think you will find very excitigg . . .

Oh, God, not again! At this rate she'd be here till midnight. Flora stuck a torn scrap of paper behind the carbon and rubbed at the mistake on the top copy. It left a smeary mark and when she tried to rub that out it made a hole in the paper. She wrenched everything out of the typewriter. She would have to type the whole blessed thing over again. It had to be done tonight.

The more tired she got, the more mistakes she made, and it took six more tries before she got the long letter finished. By the time Tim had signed it and she had cleared up and left the office it was nearly seven o'clock. The nice thing about the summer, though, was that there was still something left of the day after work. She walked down Sloane Street in the evening sunshine, thinking how hard it was now to imagine the winter smog. To save time – and her feet – she decided to hop on a bus down to Sloane Square and then walk round to the Antelope where she was supposed to be meeting Algy. A woman sitting opposite her on the bus was carrying a glossy magazine and she could see Tally's face on the front cover. Larry's picture. If she hadn't known it was Tally, she didn't think she would have recognized her. Half her face was in shadow and the other half all grainy. Tally's face, usually much more recognizable, was to be seen in advertisements

177

everywhere and on billboards all over London. She was really getting quite famous, and so was Larry. His photos were everywhere, too, and there had been articles about him and photos of him dressed in really weird clothes. *Larry Sutton, the brilliant young photographer: original, creative, toughly professional . . . A Smithfield porter's son and proud of his working-class origins. A rebel of our times.*

He quite often came to the mews, where he did more eating than rebelling. Flora had been all prepared to hate him for what he'd done to Tally, but instead she'd liked him. At first he'd made her nervous, because he was so different from anybody she had ever met, but that had soon passed. He was easy to talk to – much easier than a lot of Tally's previous men had been – and he made her laugh. He could do a wonderful imitation of Marlon Brando, mumbling away into the collar of his leather jacket, and a brilliant one of Elvis Presley. Sometimes he talked about his family – the father who carried great sides of meat about at Smithfield and could down ten pints of beer in a row; his mother who was a charwoman and cleaned offices in the City at night; his nine brothers and sisters.

She could see that Tally could never marry someone like Larry, but she had changed quite a lot since she'd met him. She hardly saw any of the ex-debs any more, and went out with people Larry knew instead – other photographers, directors, writers, actors, people in television, and often from backgrounds like Larry's, too. She looked different as well. She'd grown her perm out and bought her clothes in trendy boutiques along the King's Road, instead of in Harrods and Harvey Nichols and Woollands. And now that she could afford to pay herself, nothing was put on her father's account any more.

Algy was waiting in his usual place at the bar in the Antelope, with his usual pint in front of him. He was looking at the racing results in the *Evening Standard*, and she could tell by his expression that his latest attempt to make some money had failed, like most of the previous ones.

'Quicksilver came in fifth,' he said mournfully. 'Slow

Lead, more like. And I thought he was a dead cert. Lucky I only put five bob on. The usual?'

He always insisted on paying for her and was just as difficult about it as Humphrey when she tried to go Dutch. She drank half a bitter because it was cheap and she could make it last a long time, and she'd grown used to the taste.

'Sorry I'm late. I had to get a letter finished and I kept making mistakes.'

He put his hand on his heart. 'I'd wait for you for ever, you know that.'

Algy was always making jokes. He was almost never serious so she never took him seriously. She'd asked him once if he joked with the patients on the wards, now that he'd been let loose on them.

'Lord, yes,' he'd said. 'Cockneys'll have a laugh no matter what. Specially when there's nothing to laugh about. Salt of the earth. I love 'em.'

At the end of their third year, Humphrey had taken a year out to do a BSc in physiology and biochemistry, but Algy had gone straight on to the wards and joined one of the hospital consultant's 'firms' with eight other students. They were responsible for taking the patients' notes, he had explained to her, as well as doing other things that he couldn't talk about in polite company.

'How's the Big White Chief?' she asked. That was his name for the consultant.

'Terrifying as ever. We all shake in our shoes at the sound of his approach, and that includes the registrar and housemen. They're just as petrified, so what hope have we mere students?'

'He can't kill you.'

'Don't you believe it. We could easily die of fright. You should see him on his rounds. It's like a Royal Progress at top speed with us all scampering after him and him barking right and left. Even the ward sisters grovel, and that's saying something.'

'What about the patients? Does he scare them too?'

'Actually, they're the only people he's fairly decent to.

You know, a kindly word here and there – a bone thrown, as it were – in between lashing the rest of us with his tongue. Mostly, though, the patients are expected to remain silent, unless spoken to, and lie perfectly still while everyone talks about them over their heads. This is just my three months on a surgical firm, so usually they don't feel like saying much.'

'Then what?'

'Three months on a medical firm, then three months each with eyes, ENT – that's ear, nose and throat – and paediatrics – that's kids. All the departments, see. After that it's women – gynaecology and obstetrics. I'll know all about you by the end of that lot.'

She avoided his merry eye. It embarassed her sometimes to think how much he already knew.

'It takes ages, doesn't it?'

'I'll do my finals at the end of five years. Then it's Doctor Baxter, I presume, though I can't actually register until I've done two six-month house jobs, living in. Another two-and-a-half years' slog before I can go and be a humble assistant to a GP – if one will have me. Oh, and before that, National Service, of course. I can't escape that forever. Will you wait for me, too, Flora?'

He was always joking about that, and she smiled, as she always did. While he was leaning across to ask for a packet of crisps, she glanced idly round the crowded pub and froze in shock. Nicholas was standing at the other end of the bar, his back turned to her, talking to a blonde girl. She couldn't see his face, but she was sure it was him. That was the way his hair grew and how his shoulders looked. And that was the sort of suit he wore. Her heart was thumping fast. She knew he'd been in New York since the end of last summer, but that he came back sometimes – Tally had run into him at some restaurant – but maybe he was back permanently at last. Maybe he'd only just arrived and would get in touch. Maybe he'd take her out to dinner again. Maybe . . . Then he turned round and she saw that it wasn't him after all. It was a stranger, somebody quite different – and not even handsome.

180

'Have a crisp.' Algy thrust the open packet under her nose.

'Oh, thanks.'

'You alright? You look as though you've seen a ghost.'

Her heart was slowing down, and instead of excitement there was now bitter disappointment. 'I thought I saw someone I knew, but it wasn't him. That's all.'

She ate the crisp. A bit stuck in her throat and she started coughing. Algy thumped her on the back.

'Choke up, chicken,' he said. 'And cheer up.'

'Guess what,' Tally said casually. 'I think I'm preggers.' She was lying on the sofa, smoking and staring up at the ceiling.

Flora, who had just come in from work, sat down very slowly. 'Are you sure?'

'No, but the Curse is over a week late, and that's pretty unusual for me.'

'But I thought . . . I thought you always used that thing. So it was safe.'

'Probably didn't get it in right or something.'

The situation was so appalling, so terrifying, that Flora didn't know what to say. Tally went out with different men all the time, and was often away overnight. She no longer asked questions or made comments because Tally got furious if she did, but she had never been prepared for this.

'What'll you do?'

'Find some way of getting rid of it, I suppose. Drink gin in a hot bath or jump off the table, or find someone who'll do it for me. Larry probably knows somebody.'

'Tally, you can't do that!'

'Well, what do you suggest?' Tally's voice was flat. She went on smoking. 'You can't seriously mean I should have it? Be an unmarried mother, and walk round Eaton Square pushing a pram.'

'Surely he'll marry you – whoever he is.'

'For Christ's sake, Flora! I wouldn't marry the man if he were the last one on earth. He's a bastard.'

181

'Then why . . . ?'

'Oh, I don't *know* . . .' Tally waved her cigarette impatiently. 'He was quite attractive and I'd probably drunk too much. Does it matter? It's done and now I'll have to get it undone. Do you think Humphrey would help?'

'*Humphrey?*'

'I didn't mean himself, but he might know somebody . . . No, on second thoughts, I don't suppose he would. Oh well, I'll give Larry a ring later and ask him.'

In the end, though, it was all a false alarm. Tally started the curse that evening and came out of the bathroom crying with relief. It was only then that Flora realized how frightened and upset she had been. It wasn't long, though, before she stayed away overnight once again.

'I don't suppose you're going to let me pay for my share of this, Humphrey? Just for once.'

'Sorry, Tally. Not even once. I asked you out, so, *I'm* paying.'

'Why did you, anyway? There was no need. I could have cooked something at home.'

'That's just the point. I owe you a great many suppers. It's time I repaid one at least.'

They had a table right by the window of the restaurant, and passers-by kept glancing in at Tally – sometimes even stopping to gawp. She was used to it now and scarcely noticed. Sometimes they would come up, thinking they knew her, or that she was an actress whose name they couldn't place. A few remembered that they had seen her in a particular advertisement. 'You're the girl in that ad for those cigarettes!' they'd say brightly. Or, 'Weren't you on the cover of *Vogue* the other week?' Both were true but she always said, with a smile, that they were mistaken.

She scanned the menu, ready to choose something low-priced. Not the cheapest, or Humphrey would know she'd done it on purpose, but something in the middle. Nothing looked that cheap, and she wished he'd chosen somewhere else. This was one of Charles's haunts. How long had it taken Humphrey to scrape together enough for this evening? How many evenings working in some pub, or whatever he did? Probably for a pittance. She must earn as much in an hour, standing around, as he could pulling pints and washing glasses for a week. An uncomfortable thought. Still, it was no use arguing with him – she'd learned that long ago. He was stubborn as hell.

She watched him ordering from the waiter – and actually rather impressively, considering he had probably never done it before. Afterwards he smiled at her.

'Did I do alright?'

'Brilliantly. Snooty type, that waiter. I never know why they've got to be so condescending.'

'I expect he was wondering what on earth a girl like you was doing having dinner with a chap like me.'

'Don't be silly.'

'Actually, I think half the restaurant is wondering the same thing. People keep staring. They obviously recognize you. Does it happen all the time?'

'Quite a lot. Mostly they can't remember where they've seen the face, though. It just looks vaguely familiar. I don't look quite the same in real life, do I?'

'You look even better, as a matter of fact. *I* think so, anyway.'

'You don't really approve of my being a model, do you, Humphrey? Come on now, admit it.'

He smiled again. 'It's not my business what you do, Tally, but it does seem a bit of a waste of you, in a way.'

'You mean I should have gone and been a nurse or something?'

The smile broadened. 'No, I can't exactly see you doing that. I don't know what I mean, really . . . Perhaps something that would give you more satisfaction in the end, as well as being more lasting.'

'That's where *you're* lucky, Humphrey. That's what you'll have with your work. Oodles of satisfaction.'

'Well, I certainly hope so. If I pass all the exams.'

'Oh, you'll do that easily. Flora's always saying how brilliant you are. You keep winning prizes – just like you did at school. And look at all the studying you do.'

'A stuffy old swot?'

'Well, you must admit, you are. You've always got your nose buried in some revolting medical book.'

'I have a lot to learn. Everything about the human body, and a lot more besides.'

'Well, shut up about it now, Humphrey, they're bringing our food.'

At the end of the meal – all three courses, or she knew he would have suspected her of deliberately hanging back – she suggested that they went and had coffee back at the mews. At least that would save something on the bill. She'd been adding up the grand total on her fingers under the table and it came to a lot.

'If you'd prefer.'

She sneaked a peek at the bill when it came and it was even worse than she'd expected. Humphrey looked at it without flinching, though. Watching him dealing with the snooty waiter again, she suddenly saw how he might be in the future, when he was no longer a poor medical student but a successful surgeon. Even the waiter seemed to see it too and changed his tune.

Humphrey's godfather had given him money for his twenty-first birthday and he had put most of it towards a car – some kind of second-hand Ford that she'd never been in before. He always drove carefully – she had found out that in France. Most men drove at breakneck speed – presumably to impress, when it actually did the reverse – and her foot was always on an imaginary brake. With Humphrey she could relax. She wound down the window on her side and let the wind blow her hair.

'Mmm. My favourite time of year – the summer just beginning and all of it to come.'

'Are you going down to Les Rosiers this year?'

'Doubt it. My stepmother will be there. A big put-off.'

Larry had asked her to go to Italy with him, but she

didn't think she'd mention that to Humphrey. Rome, Venice, Capri . . . Rather bliss.

Flora had gone home for the weekend and the mews house was empty and silent. She'd have gone away herself if it hadn't been for Humphrey's invitation. Tally went into the kitchen to make the coffee.

'Be an angel and put a record on, Humph. Something nice.'

She could hear him shuffling through the tottering pile as she spooned instant coffee into mugs, and then the faint click of the gramophone. He'd chosen one of her favourites – 'La Mer'. In spite of Larry, she still liked the old ones. She carried the coffee into the sitting room.

'Brilliant choice.'

'I knew you liked it. You used to play it in France.'

'It's Flora's big favourite too. She always goes into a trance when she puts it on.'

She handed him his mug, kicked her shoes off and curled up on the sofa, lighting a cigarette. Humphrey sat down in an armchair and they listened to the song in silence, drinking their coffee. When it had finished, he said suddenly: 'When I've done my FRCS, I'm hoping I might be able to get a Rockefeller Travelling Fellowship and go to America.'

'For ever, you mean?'

'No. Just for a while. I could learn such a lot over there – their techniques, discoveries, ideas . . . If I manage to get a fellowship, of course.' He had taken off his wire glasses and was polishing them distractedly.

'You will. You're going to be rich and famous one day.'

He looked up at her suddenly. He looked much better without the specs, she thought. Really quite dishy, in a quiet way, and he had nice eyes when you could see them properly.

'I honestly don't care much about being either of those things. It's the patients that really matter to me – making them well, giving them back their lives, restoring their hopes. I watch that happen at the hospital and that's what makes all the work worthwhile – to think that I'll be able to do the same

185

myself one day. And I want to do it for the poor just as much as for the rich. I suppose that sounds horribly priggish.'

'No, it doesn't. It sounds nice. I'm glad you think like that, Humphrey. I'm proud of you and I think you're absolutely terrific.' Compared with the men she knew, he was a complete saint.

'Do you really, Tally? Do you mean that? Even though I may never have golden apples to strew in your path . . .'

'Apples?' What on earth was he talking about?

'Like your namesake. You must know the story.'

'Oh, *that* old one.' She laughed. 'People are always making stupid jokes about it. I wish I'd been called something else.'

'I wasn't joking, and I think it suits you perfectly.'

'Well, Humphrey's a nice name, too. And it suits *you*.'

'Humphrey-dumpty . . . I remember you calling me that once when we were in France,' he said wryly.

'Did I? God, sorry. I promise not to again. I expect it'll be *Sir* Humphrey one day.'

'I doubt that.'

'*I* don't. Not for a minute.' The record had come to a stop and clicked off. 'Put it on again, will you? It's so dreamy.'

He got up and went over to the gramophone. Presently Charles Trenet's gorgeous, sexy voice started off again. It gave her goose flesh to hear it.

'How's your dancing, Humphrey?'

'Still pretty hopeless, I'm afraid.'

'I'll teach you some steps, if you like.'

He followed what she showed him quite well and they circled sedately round the room. When 'La Mer' had finished, she put on another record – a nice, quiet Sinatra. He was definitely improving, bless him, though he'd never exactly be Fred Astaire.

'Hold me more firmly. I won't break.'

'Sorry. Is that better?'

'You're doing fine.'

'You're a good teacher.'

The record stopped. 'We could put several on,' she said. 'They change automatically.'

They went on dancing, closely now, round and round the room. It was restful with him. Comfortable. Safe. No fighting off some lech. Peaceful. She rested her cheek against his, leaning on him a little, and he held her tighter. Dear old Humphrey . . . She could have given him a lot more than dancing lessons – God knew she'd had enough practice – but he was out of bounds. When the last record had ended she pushed him gently away.

'You'd better go now. It's late.'

He looked down at her for a moment. 'Must I?'

'I'm afraid you must.'

Oh hell, she should have twigged sooner, realized how he felt. It was written all over his face. All her fault, of course. She should never have gone out with him in the first place. Never have danced with him like this. She didn't care about men like Charles, but Humphrey was different. She didn't want to hurt him. *Damn, blast and bloody hell*!

He went quietly, like the lamb he was. There was none of the usual advances that she often couldn't be bothered to fight off. She heard the Ford start up tinnily in the mews below and drive slowly away.

Twelve

Letters from Los Angeles were few and far between. Usually Tally's mother scrawled a few words on a card when she sent a birthday or Christmas present. *For darling Atalanta, from your ever-loving Mama.* The presents were all stuffed away at the bottom of a cupboard – a cashmere cardigan embroidered with little pearls, earrings of silver dollars, a jewelled brooch in the shape of a Scottie dog with a bow round its neck, a powder compact made to look like a flying saucer . . . They all lay, unused, in their wrapping paper and boxes.

'What does she say?' Flora asked.

'She's coming over for Christmas, and bringing Milton, with her. The third husband, you know, for as long as he lasts. They're staying at the Savoy. Listen to this.' Tally put on a breathless American accent. '"I want to see my little girl again . . . to be with her for her twenty-first birthday . . . It's time we got re-acquainted and made up for the lost years . . . You've always been in my heart and I have been with you in spirit every day of your life . . . Your ever-loving Mama."'

Tally leaned over the side of the sofa and made a loud being-sick noise. She tossed the letter on to the floor.

'You'll have to see her, won't you?'

'I don't see why.'

'She's coming all that way . . .'

'She should have asked me if I wanted to see *her* first.'

'She is your mother, Tally.'

'Not as far as I'm concerned. I don't have one.' Tally was lighting a cigarette. She smoked a lot now.

'Well, perhaps you could just see her once. For a while. I think you should.'

'I'm not having her here.'

'You could go to the Savoy. Meet her there.'

'Hmm. If you come with me, Flora.'

'But she won't want to see *me*.'

'I don't care about that. If she wants to see me she'll have to see you, too. Promise you'll come? *Promise*?'

The Morris had a flat battery because Tally had left the lights on by mistake, so they took a taxi to the Savoy. Tally had put on a shocking-pink angora coat from one of her King's Road haunts, black stockings, very high heels and a great deal of make-up – on purpose, Flora suspected. Heads swivelled as they crossed the hotel lobby and the man behind reception rushed to attend to her.

'Would you please tell Mrs Brogan that her daughter is here.'

'Certainly, madam.'

They sat down. Tally slumped in her chair and picked at her nail polish, frowning; it clashed violently with the pink coat. Flora, on the edge of hers, watched people coming into the lobby.

'Will you know which one she is?'

'How can I? I haven't seen her since I was one. We'll just sit here until something happens. Let her find me.'

'What about the husband? Will he be with her?'

Tally shrugged. 'I suppose so. He's some sort of film producer, apparently. Milton D. Brogan. I don't know why Americans always put their middle initial in.' She stripped a long piece of red off her thumbnail and dropped it on the carpet.

'Are they going to spend Christmas here?'

'Haven't a clue. I'm not spending it with them, anyway. I absolutely refuse.'

'I wish you'd come and stay with us, Tally. Humphrey'll be there this year.'

'Thanks, Flora. It's nice of you, but I think I'll stay in

London. The Cow actually rang up the other day, you know. You should have heard her cooing down the phone. "*Do* come and spend Christmas Day with us, we'd simply *love* to have you." She wouldn't, of course, but I expect Papa got her to do it. She even suggested some sort of ghastly cocktail do for my birthday, but I couldn't face the sort of thing she'd arrange, so I said we were having something at the mews.'

'Are we?'

'Not sure I can be bothered. I don't much care about being twenty-one . . . It's not such a big thing, really.'

'Don't you come into that money your grandfather left?'

'Mmm. It's quite a lot, actually. Grandmama was talking about it last time I went to see her. Issuing dire warnings. I think she's worried I'll go and run off with a penniless actor or something. I told her she'd no need to worry. I've no intention of running off with anybody.'

Tally went on picking at her nails and Flora went on watching the people coming and going. How on earth were they going to know which was Tally's mother?

Actually it was easy, because she looked so like Tally. Flora knew it was her at once. She had the same pale gold hair, the same long legs, even the same way of walking, with her head held high. And she was walking straight towards them.

'Atalanta, darling!' She held out her arms, smiling. 'I'd know you anywhere . . .'

Tally, who had got to her feet, retreated, repelling the advance with an outstretched arm, stiff and straight as a broomstick. 'How do you do,' she said.

Her mother hesitated, then clasped the end of the broomstick with both hands. 'You're exactly how I always thought you'd be. She's just like me, isn't she, Milt?'

She turned to the man behind her. He was tall and broad-shouldered with rather long silvery-grey hair and a suntan the colour of brown boot polish; it looked very odd on a foggy day in London.

'Sure is, honey.'

'This is my husband, Milton.'

Tally swung the broomstick sideways. 'How do you do.'

'Hi there. Call me Milt.'

He'll be lucky if she calls him anything at all, Flora thought, watching apprehensively. This wasn't going well. Somehow Tally's mother had got off on completely the wrong foot. She was too effusive, too presuming, too *much*. If only she'd played it another way, it might have been alright.

'This is my friend, Flora Middleton.'

She shook hands and they both eyed her uncertainly. She could see that they were wondering why she was there at all.

She followed at a discreet distance as they moved to the lounge bar, Mrs Brogan leading the way, sweeping along. Milt must be worth a bit; her clothes looked fearfully expensive and she was carrying a mink wrap over her arm. There was a lot of gold glinting at her neck and wrists, and big, glittering rings on her fingers. She had a suntan, too, but it was pale by comparison to her husband's.

They sat down round a low table. Tally lit a cigarette immediately. She slouched back in the armchair and crossed her legs, swinging one foot to and fro, staring at her shoe. Drinks were ordered, a dish of nuts placed on the table. Tally's mother got a cigarette case out of her crocodile handbag and Milt leaned forward and snapped a lighter into flame. He was wearing a gold watch, with a thick gold strap like a bracelet, clasped round a hairy wrist.

Mrs Brogan blew out smoke and looked round at them all. 'Isn't this just wonderful . . .' She had a slight American accent, so there was no 'd' in wonderful.

'Great,' Milt agreed. He sat back, his eyes wandering to Tally's legs. Her skirt was up to her knees.

Mrs Brogan fished again in the bag and brought out a small and beautifully wrapped package. 'Atalanta, darling, I've brought you a present for your twenty-first birthday. I hope you'll like it.'

'Thank you.'

The present lay untouched on the table between them.

'Tell me, darling, what are you doing now?'

'I'm a model.' Tally was still swinging her leg.

'Really? How fascinating. Well, you certainly have the looks for it, doesn't she, Milt?'

'Sure does, honey. Takes after you.'

'I don't think I do, actually,' Tally said coldly. 'I certainly hope not.'

Fortunately the waiter brought their drinks at that moment, and when he had set them down, Flora spoke up bravely.

'Are you staying in England long, Mrs Brogan?'

'Well, we were planning on spending three weeks, but I guess it depends how long we can stand the weather. My husband can't bear this cold and damp, so we may take off for the south of France. I'd quite forgotten how dreadful English winters are. This appalling fog . . .'

'I expect it's lovely in California now.'

She gave a short laugh, tapping ash off her cigarette. 'It's always lovely. Sunshine all the year round. Always warm. I really don't know how people in England put up with this climate. I could never live here again.'

Perhaps that was just as well, Flora thought. She couldn't imagine that this beautiful but insensitive woman could ever be a mother to Tally. They acted like two strangers together, because that's what they were. The lost years that she had written of in her letter could never be made up. They were never going to get 're-acquainted'.

Things went from bad to worse. Tally chain-smoked and answered in monosyllables. She refused to stay for dinner, making some feeble excuse, and did her broomstick hand-shake again when they left.

'We'll call you,' her mother said. 'Won't we, Milton? So we can get together over Christmas.'

'Sure.'

She had left the present on the table and Milt had to run after them with it.

In the taxi, Tally lit yet another cigarette. 'Thank Christ that's over!' She stared out of the window. 'I know I was rude, Flora. I couldn't help it. The way she came at me, all smiles and open arms, as though everything was perfectly normal. As though she hadn't walked off and left me when I was a baby. *Deserted* me. She thought she could just walk into my life again after all this time and I'd fall into her arms . . . Well, she was wrong. I don't want to see her ever again.'

'That seems a shame, Tally. She *is* your mother.'

Tally turned on her fiercely. Unshed tears were glittering in her eyes. 'You keep on saying that, Flora. You don't have a clue what it's like. Your mother would never have done such a thing – not in a million years. You've never understood how lucky you are.'

When they got out of the taxi she left the present behind on the seat. Flora retrieved it.

'You forgot this again, Tally.'

'No, I didn't.' She thrust the package at the driver. 'Here, this is for you. Happy Christmas!'

Tally skirted a group of carol singers who were warbling away raggedly on the pavement and rang the front door bell. She still had her own key to the house somewhere but hadn't bothered to find it. Carver would let her in, with his bad-smell face – especially bad as she was late and probably the last to arrive for The Cow's Christmas Eve dinner party. It was going to be the usual no-expense-spared extravaganza.

'Good evening, Lady Atalanta.'

'Good evening, Carver.'

One of the carol singers had moved forward quickly in her wake, rattling a collection tin, but Carver, equally swift, shut the door smartly behind her.

Carver bore her fur coat away and Tally stood for a moment in the hall. She had had lunch with Papa a week or two ago, as she did from time to time, but it was months since she had last set foot in this house, and then only on the briefest visit. The Prodigal Daughter returned, she thought drily. Invited to come home and eat the fatted calf, or whatever it was, that The Cow and the new Italian chef had cooked up between them. The Cow always had a colour and a theme, and Tally could see by the Christmas tree that this year's colour was silver and, judging by the number of them twinkling away on the branches, the theme was stars. They would be stuck everywhere.

As she climbed the stairs to the drawing room she could hear the voices and laughter. From the sound of it, it was going to be a full table of sixteen. There was a *psst!* from above and she looked up to see Thomas hanging over the bannister on the next floor, waving and grinning. He was in his dressing gown and had obviously been banished upstairs for the evening. She waved back and went into the drawing room. Yes, she must be the last to arrive – they were all there, standing around and knocking back champagne cocktails. God, the room had been done over again, all in off-white this time, new curtains, covers, carpets, the lot. Thomas would be lucky if there was a penny left for him to inherit. Papa saw her.

'Tally . . . I'm so glad you're here. You look lovely.'

She'd made a special effort, it was true, and the black dress had been hellishly expensive.

'Atalanta! How charming!' The Cow oozed graciousness, baring her gums and taking her by the arm, drawing her into the gathering. 'Come and meet everyone . . .'

The men were portly penguins and the women variations on The Cow with stiff, dyed hair and camouflaged faces. There was absolutely nobody near her own age . . . This was going to be absolutely deadly. When she caught sight of Nicholas, standing by the fireplace, she was almost pleased to see him.

Predictably, the dining room looked like the Milky Way. A galaxy of silver stars hung over the table, sparkling by the light of silver candles in silver candlesticks. Everyone ooohed and aaahed. Nicholas had been placed next to her.

'I thought you were in New York,' she said as he held out her chair.

'I was until yesterday.'

'You must have flown back, unless it was a very fast boat. How long does it take?'

'About twelve hours, that's all.' He sat down beside her.

'And when I looked out of the taxi window coming into London, one of the first faces I saw was yours.'

'Where was I?'

'You were up on a huge billboard beside the Cromwell Road, telling me to buy vodka.'

'Oh, *that* one.'

He smiled. 'I thought it was very persuasive. You're a very successful model, I gather.'

She felt quite charitable towards him – after all, it *was* Christmas. She could even feel a bit of goodwill towards The Cow since she was being so friendly. And it was nice to be back home and feel part of it all again. The man on her other side started talking about hunting, reliving a recent day out with the Quorn. They went over every fence until the kill. It was years since she had gone hunting. Flame had been sold long ago and Thomas now had a different pony. They were on to the fish course before she resumed her conversation with Nicholas.

'Are you going back to New York after Christmas?'

'For about another year, I think. The company's expanding pretty fast over there.'

'Don't you get bored, expanding all the time?'

'Not at all. There are always risks and I enjoy that. How's Flora, by the way?'

'She's fine. She's gone home for Christmas.'

Flora had kept repeating the invitation to spend Christmas in Reading, but there was the problem of Humphrey – not that Tally had said a word about that. And in any case, she'd wanted to be at home.

'And you're coming tomorrow, too, I gather?' Nicholas said.

She smiled. 'That's the idea. Special invitation. Hatchets buried. Season of goodwill and all that. Are you staying in the house?'

He shook his head. 'In my flat.'

The woman opposite leaned across to speak to her. 'My dear, I saw you on the cover of *Vogue* . . .'

Papa was smiling at her down the table. The Cow was being

195

amazingly charming, as though she really meant it. Tally felt a nice, warm little glow of belonging.

After dinner, she slipped upstairs to say hello to Thomas, who was reading in bed. His room was an interior decorator's fantasy of what boys liked, with nautical touches everywhere: a bed like a cabin bunk with a compass at its head and a ship's wheel at its foot; false portholes; fake rigging; port and starboard lights. She sat on the end of the bunk and handed him a petit four that she'd saved.

He crammed it in his mouth. 'Thanks. I'm starving.'

'How are things?'

'OK.'

'How do you like your new room?'

'It's alright.'

He was reading *Swallows and Amazons*, so presumably the shipboard touches were OK by him. She patted the empty stocking hanging from the ship's wheel. 'Waiting up for Father Christmas?'

He grinned. 'Papa still does that stuff. I've asked for a new watch this year. Hope I get it. And a new fountain pen.'

He'd get them. He always got whatever he asked for, but she no longer begrudged it. 'I'll bring my present for you tomorrow.'

'Thanks. I've got something for you, too.'

She smiled at him. 'How's school been?'

He pulled a face. 'Pretty foul. I don't like it much.'

'You'll soon be going to Eton. I expect you'll like that better.'

'Hope so.'

'Well, see you tomorrow.'

She ruffled his hair and said goodnight. The men were still downstairs, lingering over their port, the other women were in The Cow's bedroom, titivating. She went to her old bedroom, opened the door and switched on the lights.

It had vanished. The blue and white had gone, and so had the four-poster bed and the rest of her furniture. It was all Chinese now – pagodas and writhing dragons over the walls, bamboo chairs and tables, paper lamp shades, a bed like an

Eastern pavilion, black lacquer, scarlet silk curtains . . . Every last trace of her had been obliterated.

'What's the matter?' Nicholas asked.

'Nothing.'

'There very obviously is. You were looking perfectly happy before, at dinner. Suddenly you're not. What's happened in between?'

He had come to sit beside her in the drawing room when the men reappeared.

'I've just been to see my old room. It's gone.'

'Gone?'

'Disappeared. Wiped out. Your mother's made sure there's nothing of me left. It's all been redone in fake Chinese.'

'I'm sorry,' he said. 'You know how she loves redecorating.'

'This was *my* home, for God's sake – long before *she* ever came on the scene. I was *born* here. I've a right to have a room here. To belong here still.'

'I can understand you feeling upset,' he went on, 'but would you really want to live here any more? You're twenty-one in a few days. You'll come into your inheritance, won't you? Be completely independent – if you aren't already with what you earn. Speaking personally, I've found I enjoy it. I'd never want to go back.'

'You weren't thrown out.'

'But I did suffer as well, you know,' he said mildly. 'You weren't alone. I hated my parents getting divorced and my home being broken up. I was utterly wretched about it.'

'You never looked it. And you never said anything.'

'To you? How could I? You'd scarcely speak to me. You've loathed the sight of me since the first day I walked into the house. You took one look and ran up the stairs to your room, slammed the door and refused to come out. I remember it well.'

She remembered it, too. He had stood in the hall, looking round with his nose in the air. 'Well, you were so bloody supercilious.'

'I wasn't. You just thought I was. Actually, I was bloody

197

miserable. Just like you. And I thought you were the rudest and most unpleasant little girl I'd ever had the misfortune to meet. I went on thinking that for a very long time.'

'I probably was. But I thought you were the complete dregs, too. For a very long time, as well.'

He smiled slowly. 'Apparently we were both mistaken about each other.'

'It's hardly worth it,' she said when he insisted on driving her round to the mews at the end of the evening. 'I walked here.'

'It's late and I'm going that way.'

He waited by the car in the mews as she unlocked her front door. She hesitated.

'Do you want to come in for a drink?'

'Is that a peace offering?'

'It's a Christmas Day offering. It's after midnight.'

She switched on the lamps in the sitting room, chucked her fur coat and bag on the sofa, and fetched glasses. He poured brandy for them.

'Well,' he said, raising his glass to her, 'happy Christmas, Tally.'

She clinked hers against his.

'Happy Christmas, Nicholas.'

Thirteen

The summer sunshine caught the diamond tiara on Tally's head as she stepped out of the Rolls. It flashed brilliantly and the crowd gathered on the pavement outside St Peter's gasped at the sight of her.

Flora hurried forward to straighten the long train of the beautiful white dress and to arrange the veil once more. Behind it, Tally's face was as luminous as a wax doll's. She turned to take her father's arm and they moved up the steps towards the open doors. As the procession entered the church, there was a burst of sound from the organ and the triumphal music began.

Four little bridesmaids and two page boys walked in careful pairs before Flora, and behind her were four more grown-up bridesmaids. Heads turned as they moved slowly towards the altar, faces smiled, and one woman in a big yellow hat was crying.

Flora kept her eyes straight ahead. *Don't look at him, whatever you do. Don't look. Don't look.* But she couldn't help it. He was there at the chancel steps, with Charles by his side, and as they drew nearer he turned towards them, watching Tally come to him. *Oh, Nicholas, if only it were me. If only, if only.* She stepped forward to take Tally's bouquet; the white lilies quivered in her hands.

'Dearly beloved, we are gathered together here in the sight of God, and in the face of this congregation, to join together this man and this woman in holy matrimony . . .'

Don't listen. And don't look at him. Look at the flowers, or the floor, or Tally's train – anywhere but at him.

*   *   *

199

'Hallo, Flora.'

'Oh, hallo, Algy.'

'You look jolly nice.'

'Thanks.' He was quite a stranger, all dressed up in a morning suit with a rose in his buttonhole. She raised her voice against the din of four hundred people talking in one room.

'How are you?'

'Alive, if not exactly kicking. I'm living in for six months, on call night and day, but I managed to sneak off for this. Knotted my sheets together and climbed out of the window. Couldn't miss out on all the bubbly. Jolly good wedding this. Decent of Tally to ask me. I've never darkened the doors of Claridges before.' He glanced round. 'Bit like the Chelsea Flower Shower in here.'

'Tally's stepmother organized it.'

Lady Gresham had taken over, in fact, and Tally had given way meekly as part of her new leaf. 'I've promised Nicholas I'll try really hard, Flora.'

She'd put her foot down over the photographer, though, and insisted on having Larry. 'Gave up doin' weddings years ago, darlin',' he'd told her. 'But anythin' for you.' It was Larry, too, who had taken the engagement photo that had appeared at the start of *Country Life* – not Bassano or Baron or Wilding, as the Countess had wanted. Flora thought that it was the best picture he'd ever taken of Tally.

Taking the group photographs after the church service, he had fired away very fast and very casually, walking about in front of them, dressed in a sort of blue denim boiler suit.

'Who on earth's that man?' the bridesmaid standing next to Flora had asked. 'He looks as though he's come to unblock the sink.'

'That's Larry Sutton.'

The girl's eyes widened. She was a young cousin of Tally's and very pretty. 'You mean, *the* Larry Sutton. Gosh!' She turned her head to smile brilliantly towards the camera lens. 'Do you think I could meet him?'

I ought to warn her, Flora had thought, but I don't think

she'd take any notice. Larry now had an Aston Martin and a house in Hampstead, as well as a never-ending stream of stunning girlfriends. She'd tried to smile herself. Larry, clicking the Leica in her direction, had winked at her.

The speeches began. A duke proposed the toast, Nicholas replied and proposed another toast to the bridesmaids, singling her out by name, and seeking her out in the crowd so that everyone looked at her and she had to smile and smile again. Charles replied and gave his best man's speech, making valiant jokes. Poor Charles, who was in just the same boat as herself. Telegrams were read out, one after the other. Would it never end? Would the torture never be over? In the general commotion after the speeches, she came face to face with Nicholas.

'I've been looking for you, Flora. I wanted to thank you again personally – not just in a speech.'

'Heavens . . .'

'Not just for being a wonderful chief bridesmaid today, but for everything you've done for Tally for years as her loyal friend. It's meant such a lot to her.'

'Oh, goodness . . .'

He smiled at her, but she wished he wouldn't. It made things even worse – harder still to bear.

'I wanted you to know that. And how much I appreciate it, too.'

She lifted the wrist wearing the gold bangle, the same as he had given to all the bridesmaids. 'Well, thank *you* for the lovely present. It's super.'

'I'm glad you like it. I'm sorry Humphrey couldn't come today.'

'He is too. He had to work, though.'

He started to say something else to her, but an elegant-looking woman came up and interrupted rudely, taking him by the arm and pulling him away.

'Shall I tell you where we're going for our honeymoon, Flora? It was supposed to be a big secret, but who cares?'

She was helping Tally to change into her going-away

201

clothes. The blue of the silk suit and hat matched the enormous sapphire engagement ring that Nicholas had given her.

'New York! We're going down to Southampton tonight and then we're sailing on the Queen Mary tomorrow.'

'Oh, Tally . . . How wonderful.'

'I know. It was a big thing to get a visa. I had to go to the American embassy and have my fingerprints taken and swear I wasn't Communist – can you imagine? We'll be away for about two months but I'll write all the news.' Tally tugged on her long kid gloves. 'Flora, you're sure you want to move out of the mews so soon? You can stay there as long as you like, you know. Papa insists there's no rush. We could get someone to share with you, if you like.'

Flora shook her head. 'It's awfully kind of him, but I'd sooner not.'

'It's not rent you're worried about is it? Because you wouldn't have to pay a bean.'

'I couldn't accept that any more, Tally. Not now you've gone. Besides, I've just been given a raise, so I can afford to get somewhere else. And I've seen a flat in Earl's Court that'll do fine, sharing with two other girls.'

'Well, let me have the address. You must come round to the Boltons when I'm back.' Tally bent to look in the dressing-table mirror and straightened the big hat. 'I want you to help me choose curtain material and wallpaper and things. I'm not letting The Cow get her hands on the place. Promise you will?'

'If you like.' When would she stop promising Tally to do things she didn't want to do at all? She gathered up the wedding dress from the floor where Tally had stepped out of it. The folds of silk billowed in her arms.

Tally turned round. 'You're looking awfully miserable, Flora. I could see you in the mirror. Are you alright?'

'Perfectly.' She summoned up yet another smile.

'It's not because of Nicholas, is it? You swore you'd got over him . . . Were you telling me the truth?'

'Of course I was. That was years ago. Just a silly schoolgirl crush – you know, like I used to get on Lord Vidal and people. Remember?'

Tally laughed. 'And Mr Darcy, and Mr Rochester, and Heathcliffe, and Dirk Bogarde and James Dean – God, you wept buckets when he was killed – and all the rest. You'll find your real-life hero one day, Flora. And he probably won't be in the least like any of them.' She picked up her bouquet from the dressing table. 'I'm going to make damn sure you catch this when I leave, so get ready.'

'I suppose there's no chance of you coming out this evening?' Algy asked when Tally and Nicholas had been driven away in the Rolls and it was all over at long last. She was standing on the pavement outside Claridges, clutching the bouquet that Tally had so carefully aimed at her.

'Sorry. I've got to go out with the best man and ushers and the other bridesmaids. You know, the usual sort of thing.'

He nodded. 'Oh, well.' He leaned forward and flicked lightly at her hair. 'Confetti . . .'

'Oh, thanks.'

Charles came up, his face flushed. He looked as though he'd been drowning his sorrows. 'Pick you up later, OK? We're all going to the Jacaranda.'

We're stuck with each other for the evening, she thought bleakly, and we'll both have to pretend that we're enjoying it. Back in the silent mews house at last, she sank down on the sofa, still holding the lilies, and started to cry.

Tally could see the back of Morecambe's head through the glass partition of the Rolls and she was glad that it was him driving them down to Southampton. He was part of her life, after all, had been around for as long as she could remember – back to the days when her feet couldn't touch the floor and she used to be sick on the carpet. His hair was completely white now and he must be about a hundred, but The Cow still couldn't get rid of him because he could still drive perfectly well.

God, she must try not to think of The Cow as *The Cow*

any longer or she might say it out aloud by mistake one day, in front of Nicholas. He'd no idea that she'd always called his mother that. Of course, he knew there wasn't much love lost on either side, but he thought it would work out, in time, once they were married. She wasn't sure that it ever would, but she hadn't told him so. Stepmother *and* mother-in-law, all rolled into one . . . Christ!

Larry wasn't sure it would either. '*Once a cow, always a cow, darlin'*,' he'd said. She talked to him about things more than she talked to anybody – even Flora. He was unshockable and unfazeable. He hadn't thought much of her marrying Nicholas.

'Bit sudden, innit? Thought you couldn't stand the bloke.'

'I changed my mind.'

'Just like that?'

'We saw a lot of each other over Christmas.'

He'd given her an old-fashioned look. 'Must've done, darlin'. An '*ell* of a lot.'

He hadn't believed it when she'd said she hadn't yet slept with Nicholas.

'Come off it, love. Who're you tryin' to kid? Pull the other one.'

'It's true! I swear.'

'Somethin' wrong with him? He a woofter?'

'Certainly not. He just wants us to wait.'

'Blimey . . . He know *you* 'aven't been waitin' exactly?'

Nicholas did know perfectly well, because when he'd asked she'd told him, though not the total score.

'I want us to wait till we're married. I want it to mean something,' he had said.

It was the sort of romantic thing that Flora would have loved, but she hadn't told her about it. She wasn't sure that Flora had completely got over Nicholas, however much she had protested that she had. When she'd broken the news that she was engaged to him, Flora had gone as white as a sheet and looked completely stunned. Well, it must have been a bit of a surprise, considering how much Tally had always said she loathed Nicholas. She was still pretty surprised herself,

204

come to that. She'd never expected to fall for anyone, let alone him. A *coup de foudre*, the French called it, which described it rather well. A bolt from the blue. A stroke of lightning. That's just what it had been like, and it had struck on Christmas Day. Over the turkey and the cranberry sauce and all the rest of it, she'd caught him watching her across the table and, instead of turning away, he'd gone on looking and looking. And she'd gone on looking back because she couldn't drag her eyes from his. The lightning had struck, and that had been that. She'd been amazed when Nicholas had confessed later that he'd been in love with her for a long time – even in France.

'Why on earth didn't you tell me?'

He'd laughed. 'I didn't exactly expect a sympathetic ear. And I hardly knew it myself, anyway.'

'You took Flora out, not me.'

'You wouldn't have come. And I was sorry for her – she never seems to have much fun. Besides, I always enjoy her company.'

'She was dotty about you in those days, did you realize that? So, it wasn't very fair of you.'

'I don't think I ever gave her any encouragement. I certainly hope not. I wouldn't want to hurt Flora for anything.'

'Nor would I. And I hope we don't.'

They were coming into Southampton now and heading down towards the docks. When they drew up outside the Cunard Hotel, the doorman, seeing all the confetti inside the Rolls, started grinning. Poor Morecambe, it would take him hours to clear it all out. She turned back to wave goodbye to him as she went into the hotel, and he touched his cap to her and gave her a grin and a thumbs up.

People turned to stare at them, but then she was used to it – used to the stares and the whispered asides. She knew they must make a good-looking couple and that her face was well known. In the dining room later, she smiled at the waiter who held her chair; he was dark and smouldering – Italian, probably. She liked Italian men. Giorgio, for instance, had been fantastic-looking, though vain as a peacock. The head waiter asked what she wanted to eat, but she wasn't really very hungry. Maybe some melon and then some fish; nothing else.

'Are you alright, darling?' Nicholas put his hand on hers.

'Fine, thanks. A bit tired, that's all.'

She smiled at him. God, he was attractive! How on earth hadn't she seen it before? Or perhaps she had, deep down inside her, but had refused to admit it to herself. Just to look at him now made her go weak at the knees, like one of Flora's book heroines.

She wondered how many women *he*'d slept with. She should have asked him that. Sauce for the gander as well as the goose. There'd been lots of girlfriends, of course. She'd known plenty of men in much the same situation – stinking rich, good-looking, and some titled as well, which gave them an even greater advantage. Not that that made them any better in bed, in her experience. Often the reverse. They could be brutally insensitive or hopelessly inadequate. Larry had been far better than any of them. It really ought to be part of the sixth-form curriculum for English public schoolboys: How to Make Love Decently. But they'd probably have to get the French master to teach it.

Going up in the lift after dinner, she felt panic rising within her. Supposing it was just the same disappointment as with the others? Supposing she didn't feel anything special at all? God, supposing she really *was* frigid, like one man had once yelled at her? Supposing this had all been a ghastly mistake?

Nicholas shut the bedroom door behind them. Without saying a word, he took her in his arms and, gradually, the panic ebbed away. It's going to be alright, she thought, swamped with relief. It's going to be quite different with him . . .

The Statue of Liberty appeared through the early-morning mist, her torched raised high. Beyond lay the hazy skyline of Manhattan. Tally leaned on the ship's rail and gazed at her first view of New York.

Nicholas pointed. 'The tall building over there's the Empire

State Building. I'll take you right up to the top. There's a wonderful view from there, especially at night.'

'How many stories?'

'A hundred and two.'

'Wow! Where else will you take me?'

He put his arm round her shoulders. 'Everywhere. We'll see it all. And do anything you want.'

'What about work?'

'You come first. This is our honeymoon, remember?'

She couldn't exactly forget. They'd spent a large part of the five-day voyage in bed. In between they'd emerged from their stateroom to knock back cocktails and eat amazing meals at the captain's table. They'd swum in the pool, gone to the cinema, strolled round the decks, or just lounged on chairs, watching the Atlantic go by. In the evenings they'd dressed to the nines for dinner and then danced in the ballroom to the ship's orchestra and, later, gone on dancing in the nightclub at the stern where they could wander out on to the open deck and stand at the rail, watching the wake of the liner stretching back like a luminous pathway across the ocean towards faraway Europe.

They stayed on deck as the *Queen Mary* steamed slowly up the Hudson River, escorted by tugs. The skyscrapers came nearer and nearer, packed tightly together, and she could see the rows and rows of windows, rising up into the blue. The liner docked almost in the city itself – it was like tying up at the end of Piccadilly. She hung over the rail, watching the men moving about on the quayside, manoeuvring the gangways into position – real, live Americans, and lots of them with black skins. When they eventually disembarked, the heat in the customs sheds on the quayside was terrific. She took her hat off and fanned herself.

'Is it always this hot, Nicholas?'

'In summer, usually, yes. But don't worry, the hotel has air conditioning.'

They took a yellow taxi, like the ones she'd seen in films, and the driver drove at breakneck speed on the wrong side of the road through streets like deep canyons.

'Fifth Avenue,' Nicholas said as they turned into another street that stretched ahead, straight as an arrow.

She made a mental note of the mouth-watering shops as they flashed by. Lord and Taylor, Saks, Bonwit Teller, Cartier, Tiffany and Co . . .

'Central Park on our left.' Nicholas said. 'Not as nice as the London parks, but it's pleasant enough.'

'What are those poor old horses doing waiting there?'

'Tourists hire the carriages to be driven round, sightseeing.'

'Don't let's do that. I feel sorry for them. They're like bags of bones.'

He smiled. 'You must have caught that from Flora. Don't worry, we won't. Here's the hotel now. I think you'll like it.'

She did. Their suite was on the thirty-sixth floor and overlooked Central Park. There was a silken bedroom with the biggest bed she'd ever seen, and a luxurious sitting room that looked like a Hollywood set. There were *three* telephones – one of them in the bathroom. She peered out of the window at the park far below and at the skyscrapers soaring dizzily above and thought that New York was the most exciting city she had ever seen.

'I think it's a jolly nice flat,' Humphrey insisted.

He sat down in one of the easy chairs and got up again when he encountered the broken spring.

'Sorry, I should have warned you,' Flora said. 'The other one's better.'

It was a pretty depressing place in all honesty, she knew – a poky little sitting room with ugly, uncomfortable chairs and sad prints of the Scottish Highlands shrouded in mist. There were two dark bedrooms at the back, furnished in fumed oak, a bathroom with a temperamental geyser and a string clothes line over the bath, and a kitchen not much bigger than a cupboard. And the street outside was Earl's Court at its drabbest – red-brick Victorian, dingy net curtains, paved front gardens, dustbins and dogs' mess . . . But it was affordable. I've been spoiled, she thought, that's the trouble with me. Spoiled rotten. It serves me right.

'How did you find it?'

'An ad in the *Evening Standard*. You know, "Third girl wanted to share . . ."'

'Where are the other two?'

'They're both out this evening. They'll be back later.'

'What are they like?'

'Well, Alison's very nice. I share a bedroom with her. She works as a secretary. Rhonda's a bit grim, though. She's with the British Council and organizes tours or something. Rather thinks she's the cat's mother. She was here first, so she has the single room.'

Not only the single and best room, but everything else she could manage to grab for herself: all the hot water, the last of the milk, and the most of anything that they were supposed to share – cakes, biscuits, boxes of chocolates. She often reminded Flora of Fish Face at school.

'Do you miss the mews?'

'Like anything. But I couldn't stay on there – not now Tally's gone. I suppose I shouldn't have stayed as long as I did rent-free.'

'Tally wanted you. She *needed* you, in fact. It worked both ways, you know.'

'Anyway, now she's married and she doesn't any more.'

'Oh, I think she always will.'

'She has Nicholas now.'

'She'll still need a good friend.'

'The thing is,' Flora said carefully, 'I'm going to find it a bit hard if I see much of them.'

'Because of Nicholas? You've never said anything to me about it, Flo, but I know you've carried a torch for him for years.'

'How did you know?'

He shrugged. 'I see. I observe. Actually, I guessed in France. It wasn't difficult. Are you still in love with him?'

''Fraid so.'

'The wedding must have been a bit of a strain for you. Having to watch it all from the front row.'

'It was.'

Humphrey smiled wryly. 'The funny thing is that I feel the same about Tally – that's really why I didn't come to the wedding. I couldn't face it, seeing her marry someone else. So I made an excuse about working. Pretty pathetic of me, considering you had to sweat it out. But there it is.'

She stared at him, astonished. 'I never realized, Humphrey. You never gave any sign. I mean, how long?'

He took his glasses off and began polishing them. 'Oh, years – rather like you with Nicholas. Almost ever since I first saw her, I think. Do you remember the first time you went off to boarding school, and Ma and I took you to Reading station? You got in the same carriage as her. I dumped your case in for you and there she was, sitting in the corner of the compartment, with her nose in the air – you know how she used to. She turned round and looked at me and I thought she was the most beautiful girl I'd ever seen. I still do.'

'Oh, Humphrey . . . Does she know? Did you ever say anything to her?'

'Not in so many words, but she knows. I kept it pretty well hidden until I took her out to dinner last year. We went back to the mews after and . . . well, she tumbled to it then. I could see she was dismayed. Wondering how on earth to turn me down without hurting my feelings. I knew then there wasn't a chance. I mean, the most hopelesss thing is if someone feels sorry for you . . . And, anyway, can you seriously imagine someone like Tally falling for me? I don't know how I ever thought it could possibly happen – complete lunacy on my part.' He put on his glasses again and smiled at her. 'All I've ever really been to her is stuffy old Humphrey.'

She smiled back. 'And all I've ever been to Nicholas is loyal little Flora. We've both been idiots, haven't we?'

He came and stood outside the cupboard-kitchen while she got their supper ready.

'Sorry, it's not very exciting. Nothing like the old days. Just spam and an egg salad. Is that OK?'

'I like spam. And it's a great deal better than I usually get, which is a stale cheese sandwich in a pub.'

She washed the lettuce and tomatoes under the cold tap. 'What are you doing now?'

'I'm with a surgical firm, clerking the patients, taking samples, running after the consultant on ward rounds.'

'Like Algy did?'

Humphrey nodded. 'Same ogre, but I don't mind. He's absolutely brilliant, so one learns a lot. I'm behind Algy at the moment because of taking that year out to do my BSc, but it was worth it. Only two years to go till finals now.'

'Then what?'

'Junior house jobs – surgical and medical for six months each, then a job as registrar – with the ogre, if I'm lucky. I want to study for my FRCS while I'm doing that.'

'Will you have time?'

'Not much to spare. It's a night-and-day job. Some people take time off for it and get paid work as an anatomy demonstrator or something while they study. But I want to get on as fast as I can. I've still got my National Service to do, as well as everything else.'

She looked up from slicing the spam. 'If it's any comfort, Humphrey, I'm not sure that Tally would have been very happy as a doctor's wife.'

He nodded. 'I know. She hated my even talking about anything medical – it made her feel sick. And I won't earn any decent money for years.'

'I don't think that would have worried her. She's got plenty of her own from modelling and she came into a fortune from her grandfather when she was twenty-one. Anyway, she's truly never cared about money.'

'I think that's probably because she's always had plenty, so she's never *had* to care about it. Or worry about the lack of it. You're quite right, though. I can't imagine her living with me in some grotty lodgings for the next few years, and I'd never have let *her* money keep us in her sort of style . . . Think of the rows we'd have had over that? Like with the restaurants in France, only far, far worse. But it's not just a question of money. Nicholas belongs in her kind of world, doesn't he? I don't. Simple as that.'

211

She arranged the lettuce and tomatoes on plates and began slicing the hard-boiled eggs. 'You said once that I didn't either. You warned me not to get too used to it.'

'I was a bit worried for you, that's all. The rich *are* different from you and me, just like the saying goes.'

'Well, I'm out of it now, so you needn't worry any more.'

They ate at the cramped little gatelegged table in the sitting room.

'Actually, I had a letter from Tally yesterday,' she told him. 'From New York.'

'She must be having a wonderful time.'

'Sounds like it.'

The envy had come flooding back again with a vengeance when she had read it, and so had the tears.

> Nicholas has taken me everywhere. We went over on a ferry to the Statue of Liberty and we've been up the Empire State Building at night. (102 storeys!) It's open on the top but there's a railing all the way round so you can't fall off. It's the most fantastic sight in the world, looking down at the city, and millions and millions of lights. Last night we went to see My Fair Lady on Broadway . . .

The letter, written on paper from the Sherry Netherland Hotel, had gone on for five pages in Tally's scrawly writing and Flora had scarcely been able to finish reading it. *It might have been me*, she kept on thinking, stupidly and pointlessly. *It might have been me.*

Alison returned before Humphrey left and they sat drinking mugs of coffee. She could tell that Alison liked him by the way she blushed when he spoke to her. Humphrey, though, hardly seemed to notice that she was there.

'That's Stirling Moss,' Algy shouted in her ear above the roar of the racing cars screaming past the stands. 'And that one, just behind him, is Mike Hawthorn. Could take him on the bend, if he doesn't look out.'

Flora watched the two dark-green cars tearing round the corner; the one behind suddenly flashed past the other.

'Told you so,' Algy yelled, looking pleased. 'Damn good driver, Hawthorn. Aren't you glad you came?'

Whether she actually wanted to go, or not, hadn't seemed to come into it. She simply found herself being driven down to Sussex one weekend in Algy's ramshackle old Morris. The switchback road took them over hill and down dale, puffing up the former and racing down the latter, and through a glorious countryside of fields and woods.

'Nicest track in England,' Algy had assured her. 'The others are OK, but Goodwood's the pick of the bunch. Before the war, of course, Brookland's was the place to go. Now *that* was racing! Bughattis, Mercedes, Alfas, Maseratis . . . All the old beauties. Sorry I missed out on that. Come on old girl, you can do it.'

This last was addressed to the Morris, struggling up another incline. As they drew near to the racetrack, joining a queue of other cars heading for the entrance, Algy sniffed the air ecstatically.

'Can you smell it?'

'Smell what?'

'Castrol.' He breathed in. 'Wonderful smell! Nothing like it.'

It was hard to share his enthusiasm for the acrid stink assaulting her nostrils, and the noise was appalling. But Flora could understand it for the sheer spectacle of the race. For the heart-stopping, risk-taking, terrifying speed of it all – the spins and crashes and near misses, and the final neck and neck finish as the leading two cars roared towards the chequered flag.

'Told you you'd enjoy it,' Algy said as they drove away after the race had ended. 'Wonderful day out.'

They stopped at a pub he knew on the way back to London and it was warm enough to sit out in the garden. Algy drank his beer and sighed contentedly.

'This makes a change from delivering babies.'

He came out with things like that in the most matter-of-fact

213

way. Flora looked into her glass and pretended to be fishing out an insect.

'Is that what you've been doing?'

'Yep. Sixteen so far. I have to do twenty deliveries before I'm certified. Truth to tell, it's the midwife who does most of it before I even get there. I just deliver the *coup de grâce*, so to speak. I ride rather slowly on my bike, hoping she'll be there long before me.'

'Bike?'

'Transport provided, courtesy of the hospital. I have to live in, see, and be on call, ready to leap on my trusty steed and pedal round the district to people's homes. You should see some of the places I've been in.' He shook his head. 'Grim! Not a mod con in sight. Water running down the walls. No heating. Rats and mice. Not the best places for coming into this world. Poor little blighters, I often think to myself, they won't stand much of a chance with a start like this.'

She was more intrigued than embarrassed now. 'It must be amazing . . . when a baby's born.'

'Oh, it is,' he said, quite seriously. 'There's always that moment of . . . well, *awe*, I suppose. You know, a new life just beginning. A miracle, really. The midwife says she's seen hundreds born, but she still feels like that, every time. Even the toughest fathers do. I had one dirty great docker with biceps like balloons and tattoos everywhere, who blubbed all over the baby. And it was his wife's sixth, so you'd think he'd've got used to the idea. Mind you, some of the fathers can't take being in the same room, or even the house. Most of them go off down to the boozer, out of harm's way. Better, really, if they get queasy. I was on my own without the midwife once and the mother needed stitching, so I hauled the husband in to hold my bicycle lamp so I could see what the hell I was doing. He went and crashed to the floor in a dead faint. *And* broke the bulb in the process. I had to revive him and do it by candlelight . . . Finals next year,' he remarked breezily as they drove back to London. 'The Big Swot. Then you can call me Doctor Baxter – if I pass, of course. Junior houseman for a year and I can register as

214

a fully fledged sawbones. The next thing will be to persuade some unsuspecting GP with a country practice to take me on. When I've done my National Service, that is.'

'Is that where you want to be – in the country?'

'I thought you'd prefer it.'

'Me?'

He turned his head briefly towards her. 'You've promised faithfully to wait for me, haven't you? As soon as I'm qualified we can get married.'

She smiled to show she knew that, as usual, he was joking.

The trees in Central Park looked dull and lifeless from the ghastly heat. Some of the leaves were already starting to turn yellow and fall off on to the scorched grass. It was nothing like as nice as the London parks, Tally thought, staring down from the hotel window. And the zoo was depressing. She'd felt sorry for the animals in their bare cages and, most of all, for the hippopotamus wallowing pathetically in a trough of filthy green water.

Come to that, New York itself wasn't as nice as London. More exciting, it was true. More slick and cosmopolitan and a lot more glitzy, but not really as *nice*. At first she'd thought it was wonderful, but now she was getting sick of it. Outside you died of heat and inside you froze to death. She'd caught a streaming cold from going in and out of the air conditioning.

The shopping had been fun, but she was tired of that, too. She'd spent hours wandering about the stores – she practically lived in Bloomingdales – and she'd bought more clothes than she'd ever really wear, and presents for everyone she could think of. Records of musicals for Flora, a button-down American shirt for Humphrey, cufflinks from Tiffany for Papa, earrings for The Cow, a portable transistor radio for Thomas, and Elvis records and an outrageous tie for Larry. She'd bought something for Nanny, too, and for Morecambe. Nothing for Carver, though: she couldn't bring herself to do that.

215

She watched the toy-size traffic moving along Fifth Avenue – the mustard-yellow taxis and the cars with jaws and fins like cruising sharks. They'd seemed pretty glamorous to begin with, but now she missed good old red buses and black taxis.

The trouble was, she was bored. Bored to death. Sick of being cooped up in the air-conditioned hotel suite, staring out of the window or reading magazines or flicking through umpteen channels on American television. Nicholas was spending more and more time working and she was spending more and more time on her own with nothing to do but shop and trail round museums. She'd wanted to go off exploring the whole city on her own but Nicholas had forbidden it. You couldn't go into the subway or wander off the main streets in case you were robbed or murdered.

She was tired of it all. Tired of being told how cute her accent was every time she opened her mouth – it was them that had the bloody accent, after all. And fed up with protesting to people that London wasn't *always* shrouded in dense fog, that there *were* refrigerators in England *and* central heating *and* television. Hadn't television been invented there, for God's sake? Nicholas always defended them, saying it was no different from the English always thinking of Americans as cowboys, millionaires or gangsters. Each side was just as ignorant as the other.

Flora had written, giving her new address, but hardly any other news.

> Nothing much has happened, really. Humphrey came to supper the other day . . . Algy took me motor racing at Goodwood . . . I went to the cinema with Alison, one of the girls I share with. The weather's been lovely lately, but I don't expect it will last . . .

She'd read the letter through several times, making the most of it, before she put it away. Long ago, she could remember her French governess, who suffered badly from *mal du pays*, doing exactly the same – reading and rereading her letters from home.

She stopped gazing downwards at the park and looked up instead. The late-afternoon sun was catching the tall steel pinnacle of an older skyscraper across the park, making it shimmer and glint like a towering, enchanted palace – like the wizard's in the Emerald City. Now, if she were Dorothy, all she would have to do would be to close her eyes, click her heels together and say the magic words: *There's no place like home, there's no place like home, there's no place like home* . . .

Fourteen

'Now, tell me which one you think would be best, Flora? Honestly.'

Flora looked at the lengths of curtain material draped all around the empty drawing room, over the painters' ladders and the trestle table and the radiators and the door.

'Gosh, I don't know.'

Tally waved her cigarette around. 'Come on, you must have *some* opinion.'

'What colour of carpet are you going to have?'

'Pale green, I think. Sort of grey-green. With plain white walls – I hate wallpaper, except in bedrooms.'

'Which one do *you* like best?'

'I'm not going to tell you till you say.'

'Well . . . I think that one over there, with the big flowers.'

'Mmm, it's not bad. But I've decided I don't want to be chintzy. I think I'll go for the yellow silk – floor-length, on poles, looped up. Rather dramatic, don't you think?'

'What about Nicholas? What would *he* think?'

'Oh, he won't care as long as it gets done by the time he comes back.'

Tally had flown home alone from New York, leaving Nicholas behind to finish with some business deal. She had phoned from a suite at Claridges, where she was staying until the house in the Boltons was ready.

'You can keep New York, actually,' she'd said. 'It was fun for a while but I couldn't stand another month or more, so I thought of the perfect excuse for coming back – to get on with doing up the house.'

218

I'd never have left him, Flora thought. Wild horses wouldn't have dragged me away, no matter how I felt about New York.

They went from the drawing room to the dining room to look at more materials, and from the dining room to the bedrooms and bathrooms on the floors above. It was a beautiful house, even with nothing in it, and Flora could see that by the time Tally had finished, it was going to be fabulous.

'The Cow came round and tried to get me to use her tame decorator but I absolutely refused.'

'Do you get on better with her now?'

'Oh, we're frightfully, frightfully polite to each other, but nothing's changed really. We still hate each other's guts. We just hide it better.'

Flora looked out of a back bedroom window. The light was fading fast but she could see a long, walled garden with a lawn and flower beds, well screened from the neighbours by trees and climbers and shrubs. The flowers were over, the leaves fallen, but in summer it must be lovely; almost as good as being out in the country.

'There's a terrace outside the dining room,' Tally said over her shoulder. 'But you can't see it from up here. Some man comes and does the garden, so I don't have to worry about that. We'll have to have some indoor staff, I suppose. A couple living in, or something like that.'

'Is there room for them?'

'Lord, yes. There are two more floors above this. Attics and nurseries. And, by the way, I've got a ghastly, sinking feeling that we might be needing the nurseries pretty soon.'

'You mean . . . ?'

'Worse luck, yes, I *do* mean . . . I'm two weeks late and I've been sick as a dog the last two mornings. Complete mistake on my part. I hadn't planned on having bloody kids for ages yet – if ever. Not being exactly the maternal type.'

Flora swallowed down her envy. 'Nicholas must be awfully pleased.'

219

'He doesn't know anything yet. I'll wait till I've been to see the doctor before I say anything. With any luck, it'll turn out to be a false alarm.' Tally dangled a piece of green and white glazed cotton against the window frame. 'Now, tell me what you think of this one.'

Flora spent Christmas at home with her mother in Reading. It wasn't a very happy one. Humphrey was on duty at the hospital and her mother went down with flu and had to spend most of the time in bed. Hercules was ill, too, lying listlessly beside the Aga. She carried him, protesting indignantly, off to the vet, who diagnosed kidney trouble for which there was no real cure. It was old age, he told her. Hercules was, after all, getting on. She returned, depressed, to the flat in Earl's Court after Christmas to find a postcard from Tally, who was in St Moritz with Nicholas

> Have stopped being sick, thank heavens. I'm going skiing whatever the doctor says. The snow's fantastic! Happy New Year!

London was grey and depressing in late December and the flat was drearier than ever. Alison had gone away on a skiing holiday, too, leaving her alone with Rhonda, who reminded her more and more of Fish Face. She knew she had read Tally's postcard, and probably her letters from New York, too. At work they had a new household cleaner account: *Green Tornado Will Whirl Through Your Home*. The television commercial showed a whirling green spiral transforming a filthy kitchen into pristine perfection in twenty seconds.

Algy phoned, inviting her to the Players' Theatre for New Year's Eve. He'd had a pretty grim Christmas, too, he told her when he arrived at the flat to pick her up. Most of it spent on duty at the hospital and the only light relief had been the ward show that some of the medical students had put on for the patients.

'What kind of show?'

'A mobile pantomime, you might call it. Only more for adults. Hospital tradition, you see. We wrote all our own words. Sort of limericks, really. We went round all the hospital wards, cheering up the patients, though actually one of them popped off right in the middle . . . Bit unfortunate that. They wouldn't let us into the children's ward when we got there. The sister was guarding the gates, breathing fire over us.'

'What part did you play?'

'Oh, I was Widow Twankey. You should have seen me. They're doing *Cinderella* at the Players' this year. They always put on a panto over Christmas and New Year. You'll enjoy it.'

Buttons, hands clasped coyly at his side, was singing to a ragged Cinderella in the Baron's kitchen. The words had been changed and the pantomime script was all in rythme, with dreadful puns that made the audience groan loudly.

'Absolute rubbish, really,' Algy said, downing his beer. 'Nobody cares, though.'

The performance finished to loud applause and whistles, mingled with booing and hissing for the Baron and the Ugly Sisters. Then the curtain went up again, the orchestra went on playing and the audience danced on the stage. As midnight approached, the music grew faster and louder, the stage more and more crowded. Algy, who had drunk a fair amount of beer, was doing some kind of wild Highland fling, leaping about in front of Flora. Just before midnight, everything went quiet.

The chimes of Big Ben sounded through loudspeakers and the first boom struck. Algy pulled Flora into his arms. Balloons were floating down from high up in the flies and landing all around them. It wasn't the first time he'd ever kissed her, but it was the first time he'd taken so long about it. All twelve booms were finished before he stopped.

Before she could get her breath back, another man, a total stranger, grabbed hold of her and kissed her too, and then another, and another. People were bursting the balloons with lighted cigarette ends. She put her hands over her ears.

> Should auld acquaintance be forgot,
> And never brought to mind,
> Should auld acquaintance be forgot,
> For the sake of auld lang syne . . .

Everyone surged wildly to and fro in ragged waves and she was dragged back and forth with them, faster and faster. Someone trod hard on her foot. She caught sight of Algy in the middle of the scrum, arms linked between two girls, charging forward.

> For auld lang syne, my dears,
> For auld lang syne,
> We'll take a cup of kindness yet,
> For the sake of auld lang syne.

1958, she thought. A new year. A new beginning.

'It's *twins*,' Tally said and pulled a long face. 'Peter told me yesterday.' She was sitting on one of the two white sofas in the drawing room, smoking a cigarette.

Peter, Flora remembered, was her Harley Street obstetrician.

'But that's rather exciting, isn't it?'

'No, it isn't, Flora. Not a bit. It's a bloody bore. I didn't even want *one*, let alone two. And I'm going to be *enormous*.' She patted her stomach, which was already a noticeable bump. 'Can you imagine, *two* of the things! Of all the stinking bad luck.'

'But it might be quite fun . . .'

'It won't be fun for me. I'm absolutely dreading it. It's bound to be hell.'

'He must be very good at delivering babies, isn't he – Peter?'

'Supposed to be. Everybody has him. They all fall madly in love with him. He's a real smoothie. Boring fusspot, though. I wanted to have it – *them* – at home here but he won't hear of it. He says I'll have to go into hospital, which I'll simply loathe.'

'It'll be a private room, won't it?'

'It'll still be horrible hospital, with that ghastly smell.' Tally held her nose.

Flora sat down on the sofa opposite her. She looked round the room – at the antique furniture, the paintings on the walls, the heavy yellow silk curtains draped at the windows, the looking glass over the mantlepiece, reflecting it all . . . 'Well, anyway, the house looks wonderful.'

The worm of envy was gnawing away inside her once again. Nicholas, the babies, and this beautiful house. Gnawing and gnawing, however much she tried to stop it.

Tally lit yet another cigarette.

'I've been interviewing nannies. What a drag! So far, I'd hate to have any of them. They're not a bit like real, old-fashioned ones any more. I wish I could get Nanny to come, but she says she's too old now. What did you think of Jose?'

'Who?'

'The bullfighter who opened the door to you? He's half of the Spanish couple we've got living in.'

'He seemed very nice.'

'He is. Hardly a word of English, but we manage. Carver would look down his nose, of course . . . The wife, Maria, cooks and Jose's our sort of butler-cum-dogsbody. I'm not sure how it'll work with dinner parties yet.'

'Will you have to give a lot of them?'

'Probably. Nicholas has to entertain boring business people all the time. A real fag. Still, I'm going to ask people *I* want, too – like you and Humphrey.'

'Would we fit in?'

'Of course you'd fit in! What a funny thing to say, Flora. How is Humphrey, by the way?'

'Working hard, as usual. He's doing eyes at the moment.'

'Yuk! Eyes, innards, blood and gore . . . What about Algy? Are you still seeing him?'

'Every so often.'

'He's crazy about you, you know. Hasn't the penny dropped with you yet?'

'He isn't at all. He's just a good friend.'

'To you, maybe, but you're much more than that to him. I've told you so before, but you always go all bolshie about it and put on your stubborn look. You've got it on now.'

'Well, I wish you wouldn't go on about it, Tally. He's a *friend*, that's all.'

'OK. OK. I'll shut up. He's a pretty super friend, though.'

Flora changed the subject firmly. 'I saw Fish Face the other day.'

'Poor you!'

'On the tube. The Piccadilly Line. I couldn't get away for six stops. She's married now and expecting, like you.'

'Her husband must be blind as a bat.'

'That's what I kept thinking. The baby's due in July, same as yours, but she's already fat as anything. Well, fatter, I should say. She was wearing a sort of spotted tent.'

'I refuse to wear those hideous smock things. I'm still doing my skirts up with safety pins, but I suppose I'll have to get some proper maternity clothes soon. I thought I might go tomorrow. Come and help me choose, Flora.'

'I can't. I've got to work.'

'Oh, lord, of course. Are you still with that ad agency?'

'Mmm. Actually, I've been promoted. Secretary to one of the directors.'

'Fantastic! Congratulations. Is he nice?'

'Pretty decent. He's American. They took over the company. It's like working on Madison Avenue now.'

'Lucky you're not. You'd hate it, I should think. How about one Saturday morning, then? Let's go to Harrods, like we used to.'

'Alright.' Flora looked at her watch. 'I'd better go now, Tally.'

'Not yet. You can't go yet. You must stay and have a drink. I always have a very large gin around this time. Ring the bell for Jose, will you? Nicholas will probably be back soon and he'd love to see you.'

Just as she had feared, she was still there when Nicholas returned.

'Lovely to see you, Flora,' he said and kissed her cheek.

Both his hands rested lightly on her shoulders for a moment and he smiled at her as though he really meant it.

She sat miserably with her gin and tonic in hand, watching the two of them together. Nicholas bent down to kiss Tally, and she put her hand up to stroke his face. As soon as she decently could, she escaped.

It was just like the old Saturday mornings, except that instead of driving them to Harrods in the Morris, Tally had a brand new car that Nicholas had given her – a pale-blue Sunbeam Rapier. They parked it in Hans Crescent and walked through to the back entrance of Harrods. Tally breezed through Menswear in exactly the same way that Flora remembered her doing when she was eleven – perfectly at home, knowing exactly where everything was and where she was going.

In the Maternity department, she picked out several things to be sent round to the Boltons on approval – none of them remotely like Fish Face's spotted tent. Then they went along to the Babies department, where she ordered two lots of everything – shawls, little Chilprufe vests, Turkish towelling nappies and fine muslin linings, Vyella nightgowns, white matinee jackets, tiny knitted bootees . . .

'What else will we need?'

'A perambulator, madam?'

'God, yes, I'd forgotten. It'll have to be a double one, I suppose.'

The pram was a very grand affair, sprung on big wheels, with dark-blue coachwork, a cream leather lining and a hood at each end. After that, at the assistant's prompting, came two wicker cots lined in white organdie, little satin eiderdowns, Lan Air Cel blankets, linen and rubber sheets, lace pillows for the pram . . . Everything was put on account and left to be delivered.

'Thank God that's over,' Tally said as they walked through to the zoo next door. 'The nanny can get the rest.'

As usual, they said hallo to the parrot on its stand, tapped at the fish tanks and went along the puppies' and kittens' cages. Tally stopped.

'Oh, Flora, do look at this one. Isn't he divine?'

The puppy, a King Charles spaniel, was up on its hind legs, front paws and a snub nose pressed against the wire mesh. It licked Tally's finger and wagged its tail furiously.

'Yes, he's sweet.' Flora poked her finger through the wire and tickled the long, silky ears. The puppy licked her too.

Tally was looking at the notice on the cage. 'How much is he? Thirty guineas? I'm going to get him.'

'Do you think you should? I mean, what will Nicholas say?'

'Nothing. So long as I'm happy. We'll take him with us now.'

'But . . .'

Tally was already on her way towards an assistant to buy a collar, a lead and a dog basket, as well as the puppy, which turned out to be a female. She carried her out in her arms and she sat quietly on Flora's lap in the car, still wagging her tail and licking her hand.

'I think I'll call her Minnie,' Tally decided. 'Isn't she heaven?'

She seemed a lot more enthusiastic about the puppy than about the babies.

Fifteen

'It's nice of you to come, Charles.'
He stood at the foot of the hospital bed, clutching a bunch of red roses to his canary-yellow waistcoat – the dark crimson, tight-budded kind that she hated. And, for Charles, he was looking quite embarrassed and awkward.

'I look like a beached whale, don't I? Don't bother to deny it, because I know I do. I'm simply huge. It's disgusting.'

He flushed. 'I'm awfully sorry you're stuck in here, Tally. Frightful bore for you.'

'It's worse than a bore, it's hell. I already feel as though I'm going to explode and there's another month to go.'

'Do you have to stay in here all that time?'

'Apparently. Doctor's bloody orders. I think I'll probably go mad.'

The private room had become a prison, and she felt just how a prisoner must feel, being visited by well-meaning, lucky people from the outside world.

The Cow had been in the day before, gushing away, with the sister sucking up like mad. *'She's doing very well, Lady Gresham. We're very pleased with her.'* She'd brought half of Moyses Stevens with her, a stack of glossy magazines and a huge box of Charbonnel & Walker chocolates that she couldn't possibly eat. The usual stink of *Ma Griffe* had nearly made her throw up and it had been a real effort to be polite – to play the silly game they both now played of pretending to like each other. Papa had come on his own one evening, and that had been easier. No need to pretend anything there. Larry had been, too, and brought more flowers, and a bottle of gin under his arm.

'Thought you might be in need of it, darlin'. If it's allowed,' he'd said.

She didn't care if it was or not, but in the end she couldn't drink it because it made her feel sick too. Most things made her feel sick, in fact, including the sight and smell of her prison.

She got rid of Charles as quickly as possible. Visitors were exhausting and she didn't want people like him to see her looking like this – the size of a house, with puffy hands and stringy hair. She didn't even like Nicholas to see her. Flora was the only one she didn't mind.

And Flora had been an absolute brick, coming in after work, sitting and keeping her company. She'd brought books for her, too, but it was hard to concentrate on reading for long. She'd flipped through some detective stories, not caring whodunnit, and cheating by looking at the last page.

The heat was getting worse, and there was a revolting fly buzzing away on the windowsill. The green walls seemed to be closing in on her like a trap and she could swear the ceiling had got lower. She felt as if she were suffocating. For two pins she'd have got up, dressed and walked out . . . if only she had the energy to do something more than just lie there like a great lump of lard.

The things kept moving about inside her, kicking and squirming. She always thought of them as *things*, never as babies, and the thought of them getting bigger and bigger, like two horrible growths, making her swell up like a balloon, revolted her. She refused to think of names for them. Nicholas kept suggesting them: Edward, Alexander, Charles, Henry. Or Victoria, Katherine, Louise, or, over her dead body, Frances, after The Cow. 'You'll feel differently when they're born,' he'd told her, but she thought she would probably hold this experience against them forever.

Flora, when she came to visit that evening after work, looked hot and tired. Her hair was sticking to her forehead, her office blouse and skirt were all creased. She flopped down wearily in the visitors' chair and eased her feet out of her shoes.

'I think there's going to be a thunderstorm. It feels like it. But at least it might help clear the air.'

Tally leaned back against her pillows and fanned herself with *Harper's Bazaar*. 'Just think, I could have been down at Les Rosiers now.'

Flora had brought some grapes and Tally forced herself to eat one or two, though she seemed to have no appetite left. It was the heat. At Les Rosiers she could have been lying by the pool, taking a cooling dip now and again, swimming lazily up and down. And later on there would have been dinner on the terrace under the fig tree with the candles flickering on the table in a gentle breeze. Yvette would have cooked something delicious – one of her cassoulets or a delicious fish dish – and there would be some nice *vin de pays* to go with it. The summer days would stretch ahead with nothing to do but loll about – if it weren't for the *things*.

She heaved herself up higher against the pillows, trying to get comfortable.

'I wish I could have Minnie in here. I wanted Nicholas to bring her to see me, but they wouldn't allow it. The sister's a real bitch and foul to all the nurses. She reminds me exactly of Grumpy Grainger. Do you remember her in Latin and how beastly she always was to you?'

'Don't remind me. I still have nightmares about her.'

'Oh, she was just an ugly old bitch. That's why she liked Fish Face, because she was ugly too.'

'She wasn't as bad to you.'

'She knew I wasn't afraid of her, that's why. But you used to cry, and she liked that.'

'I hated her.'

'I hated most things about that place. Except you. Do you remember when we first met on the train?'

'You were sitting in the corner of the compartment and there were some other girls being catty to you. I remember being terribly impressed by your title and very envious because you had braces on your teeth and no freckles.'

'I always envied *you*. You've always been the lucky one, you know.'

'*Me*? But Tally, you have so much. Now, especially.'

'Having *so much* isn't necessarily what counts. It's more *what* you have.' Tally flapped the magazine again. 'It's stifling in here. Could you open the windows wider, Flora?'

Flora got up. 'I don't think they'll go any further.' She looked out. 'It's a pity you haven't got a nicer view.'

'Instead of the tombstones?'

'Tombstones?'

'Can't you see them stacked up in that yard down there – all that awful pink and black marble? It's a tombstone-maker's yard, or whatever you call them. I suppose he thought it was a good place to set up shop – right by a hospital. Ready-made customers.'

'Don't . . .' Flora shivered. She sat down again. 'You'll soon be out of here, Tally. Back home again.'

'I bloody well hope so. Peter says he'll induce the *things* if nothing happens by the end of next week.'

'Not long, then.'

'It'll seem like forever. Every day's a week.'

Flora stayed for a while longer and then said she ought to go – the moment Tally always dreaded.

'Algy's coming to take me to a film.'

'How's it going with him?'

'I told you, it's not *going* anywhere.' Flora put on her shoes and stood up. 'I'll come and see you again soon.'

'Thanks. That'd be nice. And thanks for the grapes.' She smiled and waved the *Harper's.*

Flora was dithering at the door. 'Will you be alright?'

'Of course.'

'See you soon.'

'Yes. Go *on*, then.'

'Bye.'

'*Flora!*'

'Yes?' She popped her head round the door again.

Tally managed another smile. 'Oh, nothing. Bye . . .'

When Flora had gone, she flicked through the magazine, without any interest. Near the beginning, she came across the vodka advertisement she'd done and it was extremely depressing to be reminded of what she had looked like before turning into this bloated horror. She turned over the page quickly.

The *things* had started to squirm and kick again. She shut her eyes and tried to pretend she was somewhere else, free of them. For a while, she was at Les Rosiers, by the pool, sunning herself peacefully, and then, suddenly, she was back at school again. She was sitting in the hot marquee on Speech Day and Miss Walters was calling out: *French Prize. Atalanta Ashby.* Flora was nudging her hard. 'Go on, Tally. It's you. It's you!' She stood up slowly. Everybody was clapping as she walked up to receive the prize.

'Some man was trying to get hold of you,' Rhonda said. She made it sound immoral. 'He's rung three times already.'

Flora put her handbag down. It had been a long day at the office with a major panic over a big client who was threatening to go elsewhere. The heatwave was still on and she felt like a piece of chewed string.

'Who was it?'

'He refused to leave a message, or his name. I asked for it, of course, but he kept saying he'd ring again later.'

It was probably Algy, who couldn't stand Rhonda and called her the Valkyrie.

Rhonda followed her into the bedroom. 'He wanted to know when you'd be back. I said I couldn't tell him that if he wouldn't leave his name. You never know who he might have been.'

'Thanks anyway.'

The phone rang just as she'd changed out of her office clothes. She went into the sitting room and picked up the receiver. She recognized the voice at once.

'Flora? I've been trying to get you.'

'I'm sorry, Nicholas. I've only just got back. Is it news of Tally? Is everything alright?'

'No, it isn't.'

'The twins?' she asked, alarmed.

'One's alright – the girl. The boy was born dead.'

'Oh, Nicholas, I'm so sorry . . . So very sorry . . .' She stumbled on, trying to find the right words, but he cut her short.

'It's Tally,' he said. He stopped, trying to get his voice under control, and then started again. 'It's Tally . . .'

'I am the resurrection and the life, saith the Lord: he that believeth in me, though he were dead, yet shall he live . . .'

Tally couldn't possibly be lying in that wooden box in front of the altar. There was a single wreath of roses on the top – dark-crimson buds. She could hear Tally speaking quite clearly in her ear: *'Oh, God, not those ghastly things!'* Didn't Nicholas know how she hated them?

'. . . and whosoever liveth and believeth in me shall never die.'

The words didn't seem to make any sense at all. None of it did. Women didn't die in childbirth any more – that only happened in the bad old days. Toxaemia, Nicholas had said, and when they'd operated to deliver the babies, Tally had simply collapsed and died. They couldn't save her. They'd saved the girl but not the boy, who had been buried somewhere else. The girl had been named Victoria. Victoria Atalanta Frances. Tally would have been furious about that. She didn't know what names they'd given the boy.

'I know that my Redeemer liveth, and that he shall stand at the latter day upon the earth. And though after my skin worms destroy this body, yet in my flesh shall I see God . . .'

They followed the coffin out to the graveyard. Nicholas's face looked like stone. Lady Gresham, her arm tucked through his, was all in black. *What a hypocrite she is, Flora!* Tally whispered. *Under that veil she's simply delighted!* Lord Gresham supported Tally's grandmother on his arm and Thomas followed them, looking bewildered.

Humphrey and Algy were on each side of Flora, Larry and Charles were just ahead, and there were other faces that she knew from Tally's life – aunts and uncles, cousins, old flames, deb friends, models, photographers, dress designers, her hairdresser, a well-known actor.

232

'. . . *Forasmuch as it hath pleased Almighty God of his great mercy to take unto himself the soul of our dear sister here departed . . .*'

Tally's old nanny was here, too. And, oh my God, there was Fish Face, still pregnant and looking like a barrage balloon. That must be her husband next to her, with the sandy hair and glasses. What on earth had she come for? *To gloat, Flora.*

'. . . *who shall change our vile body that it may be like unto his glorious body, according to the mighty working . . .*'

None of it made any sense. And Tally couldn't possibly be in that box that they had lowered out of sight into the ground.

Humphrey put his arm round her as they walked away. She turned her head to look back and saw a grave digger already shovelling earth into the hole.

Sixteen

Flora let herself into the ground-floor flat and dumped her bag and evening paper on the table. Alison was already home and she could hear the bath running. She went through to the kitchen at the back and opened the French windows on to the little garden. The black cat from next door was lying along the top of the wall, and stretched out a lazy paw. He reminded her of Hercules, who had joined Desdemona under the apple tree long ago. He wasn't nearly so handsome, but he had the same take-it-or-leave-it attitude. He would pretend he hadn't seen her and start washing himself. If she waited and coaxed him humbly, he might saunter over, as though he had nothing better to do.

This evening, though, she hadn't enough patience to play the game. It had been a hot day and the flowers needed watering. She fetched the zinc can and filled it at the kitchen sink, thinking, as she often did, how pleasant the flat was to come back to and how glad she was that she and Alison had decided to leave Rhonda and Earl's Court. Putney was quite a bit further out, but you got more for less and it was worth it for the garden and for being so near the river.

She watered the plants, watched with apparent indifference by the cat, but when she had finished and was about to go back indoors he suddenly jumped down and stalked towards her, tail erect. She stroked him and tickled his ears and played with him for a bit, and then left him washing himself all over, as though he was tired of the game, too.

Alison was in the sitting room, dressed and ready to go out. She looks lovely, Flora thought. I'm so happy for her and Humphrey. They had been engaged for nearly six months now and were going to get married next year, when he had got his FRCS and done part of his National Service. After that, he wanted to go and do more training at a hospital in America, taking Alison with him. Then they would come back to London, to carve out his career as a thoracic surgeon. He'd got it all planned.

She didn't talk to him about Tally much any more, partly because of Alison and partly because it was better for both of them. She had been dead for three years now, but Flora often heard her quite clearly, saying just the sort of things that Tally would have said.

She hadn't seen Nicholas for a long time. Six weeks after the funeral he had taken the baby, Victoria, and a nanny off with him to New York. Minnie had been given to his mother – Tally would have hated that. Before he had left, Victoria had been christened and Nicholas had asked Flora to be godmother.

'Me?' she had said.

'I can't imagine anyone better suited. You were Tally's closest friend and she would have chosen you herself.'

'Wouldn't it be better to have someone who could do more for her?'

'You mean someone rich or titled or famous – or preferably all three? So they could send her big cheques or big presents every birthday and Christmas and invite her to stay on their yachts?' He smiled dryly. 'I want someone who will take a *real* interest in Victoria and help me make up for the fact that she's lost her mother.'

The christening was at St Peter's in Eaton Square, where Tally and Nicholas had been married. Charles was the godfather. (Tally wouldn't have liked that, either. She'd wanted Larry.) Holding the baby during the service, Flora had searched her face for a resemblance to Tally but, as she was fast asleep, it was hard to tell.

Humphrey came to collect Alison, and when they had gone she put on the long-playing record of *My Fair Lady* that Tally had brought back from New York. The phone rang halfway through.

'Flora?'

'Oh, hallo, Algy.'

'I've got a spot of leave. How about some grub out this evening?'

'Well, I was going to—'

'No you weren't. I'll be round in twenty minutes.'

He turned up in a dark suit and sober tie and looking most un-Algy.

'Proper togs for an interview,' he explained. 'I've been down to Devon to see a man about a job.'

'What job?'

'Assistant to a GP down there – as soon as I finish playing soldiers in six months' time.'

'How did you get on?'

'Must have done alright, because old Dr Tremayne offered me the job. On probation, as it were, with a view to being taken on as a partner in the practice if I'm a good boy.'

'That's wonderful, Algy.'

'Yes, it is, isn't it? I'm pretty chuffed about it, myself. We got on like a house on fire, right from the word go. Sealed the deal over an excellent glass of malt.'

'I'm awfully pleased for you.'

'Then come and help me celebrate. A drink at the Antelope first and then on to somewhere decent. No fish and chips or goulash tonight. We're going Italian.'

He couldn't have known that it was the same little Pimlico restaurant that Nicholas had taken her to long ago. It was even the same table. Instead of Algy opposite her, she saw Nicholas.

At the end of the meal he talked some more about the job and she could tell from his face how pleased he was.

'It's a real country practice, you see. Good Cornish folk, and all that. Penreath is just a village, but St Austell isn't too far. Wonderful sailing, of course. Have you ever been sailing?'

'Well, no.'

'You'd love it.' He twiddled his wine glass. 'And you'd like the old doctor. Charming chap. I think the partnership's

236

pretty much certain, if I don't make a total hash of things, and I don't plan on doing that.'

'I'm sure you won't. You'll be a marvellous GP.'

'There's a cottage, too, that sort of goes with the job,' he went on. 'Dr Tremayne showed me round. Lovely old stone place and a garden with a well with a piskie living in it.'

She smiled. 'It sounds lovely.'

He stopped twiddling and looked up at her. 'I'm glad you think so, because I want you to marry me and come and live there with me as soon as we can.'

'I'm a bit busy at the moment.'

He went on looking at her steadily. 'I'm not joking any more, Flora. I never was. I just used to pretend to be because you'd never have gone out with me otherwise. I love you like anything. Always have done, since I first saw you standing in the hall at old Mother Polomski's. I thought maybe you might finally have got used to the idea of having me around, permanently.'

Her smile had faded away as he spoke. *Told you so*, Tally whispered in her ear. *But you never listened.* He was looking so hopeful and she was going to have to hurt him.

'Algy, I don't know what to say . . .'

'Then don't say anything. Not now. Not yet. Think about it. And I'll keep on asking from time to time.' He raised his glass to her with a grin. 'Until you say yes.'

She hadn't been back to the house in the Boltons since Tally had died, but it was the same Jose who opened the door to her. The bullfighter, Tally had called him, and it made her smile to remember it. He did look very like one – slim-hipped and gaunt-faced. She always half expected him to flourish a red cape to entice her in.

Nicholas was at the top of the stairs and there was the old familiar lurch inside her at the sight of him.

'Flora . . . Thank you for coming.'

She went up towards him and he bent to kiss her cheek and kept his hands on her shoulders as he smiled at her. He looked quite a bit older, she thought, and rather tired.

She smiled back at him. 'Hallo, Nicholas. It's nice that you're back for Christmas.' She lifted the package in her hand. 'I've brought a present for Victoria.'

'How kind of you.' He took her arm. 'Come into the drawing room. I'll get Nanny to bring her down in a moment.'

The room was just the same – the yellow silk curtains, the paintings and the antiques, the sofa where Tally had spent so much time, lying with Minnie at her feet, the beautiful looking glass over the mantlepiece, reflecting the room. It seemed strange to her that it could all go on existing without Tally.

'You're looking lovely, Flora.'

'Thanks.' She wasn't really, of course, but she'd done her best, getting her hair set that morning and changing her outfit at least five times before she managed to get out of the flat.

'It must be ages since we saw each other.'

'Yes, it must be.' Three years and three months, to be precise.

'I haven't been back for a long time, of course, except for a few flying visits – strictly business ones. But this time I'm staying until at least the end of January. I thought it was time Victoria had an English Christmas and got to know her grandparents and her godparents.'

'I'd love to get to know her.'

He smiled. 'I'm sure you'll get on very well. She's very like Tally, as you'll see. You didn't mind coming this afternoon? I wanted you to see her well before bedtime. Nanny's fairly strict about that sort of thing.'

She shook her head. 'Saturday's are usually pretty free.'

'Are you still working at the advertising agency?'

'Actually, I left. I'm working for a PR company now, learning to be an account executive. It's rather fun.'

'More fun than being a secretary, I imagine. You were always rather wasted as that. Like Tally was rather wasted being a model.'

'She was a very good one.'

He smiled at her again. 'Loyal as ever, Flora. It's one of your nicest qualities. You know, I was afraid you'd be married by now.'

Afraid? 'Oh, no . . . But Humphrey's got engaged. To my flatmate, Alison. They're going to get married next year.'

'Humphrey? Yes, of course, your brother . . . I remember him. The medical student.'

'Well, doctor now, actually.'

'Congratulations to him on both counts, then.'

He rang the bell beside the mantlepiece and, when Jose appeared, spoke to him in rapid Spanish. In a moment or two the door opened again and the Norland nanny appeared, carrying a small, fair-haired girl in her arms. She set her down on the carpet.

'Here she is, sir. We're a bit grumpy as we've just woken up from our afternoon nap. Go and say hallo to Papa, Victoria.'

The child walked slowly over to her father, one finger in her mouth. Nicholas bent down and picked her up; she gazed at him doubtfully, the finger still in her mouth. She was the image of Tally.

'I've got tickets for *West Side Story* this evening, Flora. I know how much you like musicals, so I hope you'll let me take you.'

'That's awfully kind of you, Nicholas.'

'It isn't kind, it's selfish. I want your company and I knew that would lure you.'

They had seats in the front row of the stalls and she tingled with excitement as the lights dimmed and the overture began. *If I live to a hundred*, she thought, *I'll always feel the same.*

She cried at the sad ending, of course, wiping the tears away surreptitiously before the lights went up. Nicholas put an arm round her.

'Dinner now to cheer you up.'

He took her to a Chinese restaurant in Soho and teased her about her hopeless efforts with chopsticks. 'Last time I took you out I seem to remember you trying to eat spaghetti. I must be more considerate. Look, hold them like this . . .'

The car was a different one now – even more luxurious

than the one she remembered, with an impressive panel of
dials glowing and flickering away in the dark. He drove fast
down Knightsbridge, past all the Christmas shop windows,
past Harrods glittering like an ocean liner.

'Come back and have a drink with me, Flora. I want to
talk to you.'

Jose and Maria had gone to bed. The hall lights were on
but the rest of the house was in darkness. Nicholas switched
on the lamps in the drawing room and went to the cupboard
where Tally had kept her gin.

'Brandy? Will that suit you?'

'Lovely.'

He carried the glass over to her. 'We've known each other
a long time, haven't we? Since you were a little girl. You were
like one again tonight. I was watching you at the theatre; you
looked exactly the same as when we went to see *Oklahoma!*
I remember how thrilled you were then. You clapped and
clapped.'

'I'd never seen anything like it. Well, after the war,
and everything . . . It was wonderful tonight, too. I loved
the show.'

'Yes, Bernstein's marvellous. I saw his *Candide* in New
York. Pity it never got to London. You'd have liked that
as well.'

He sat down on the opposite sofa – the one where Tally
always lay. 'What did you think of Victoria?'

'She's beautiful. And very like Tally.'

'I know. Sometimes that's hard, and sometimes it makes
things easier.'

'I can understand that. She must remind you of her constantly, but it's a comfort that a part of Tally still lives on.'

'Exactly.' He paused. 'You're a part of Tally, too, in a
way, Flora. To me. You were very different, but you were
very close. She kept some of herself hidden from me, you
know. Victoria's rather like that. And it worries me. She
keeps most people at a distance. But she took to you at once.
I knew she would.'

The little girl had sat on her lap while she opened her

Christmas present for her. She had seemed pleased with the toy elephant and had pulled the long Dumbo ears and played with it until the nanny had come down to take her away.

'I don't see nearly enough of her, unfortunately,' Nicholas went on. 'I'm always home late, long after she's gone to bed, or away on business . . . Not much of a family life for a child, I'm afraid. It gets pretty lonely for me sometimes, as a matter of fact.'

She couldn't imagine him lonely. Surely he must be in huge demand. 'I pictured all the New York hostesses vying for you, like Mrs Van Hopper in *Rebecca*.'

He smiled faintly. 'Oh, I get plenty of invitations, but there's not a lot of time to socialize. Nor, frankly, the inclination on my part. I found out long ago that one of the drawbacks to my situation is never being quite sure if somebody really likes you for yourself.'

'You told me that once before.'

'Did I? I don't remember.'

'When we were in France – at the restaurant in Cannes.' He'd forgotten, of course, but she could remember almost every word that had ever passed between them. 'You said the only people you could trust were those who were as rich, or richer than you.'

'With a few exceptions, that's very true. You're one of my exceptions.'

'You said that before, too, or something like it.'

'Goodness, you do remember a lot, don't you? Well, I meant it.'

She stared into her glass of brandy for a moment. *I wish I could forget, though*, she thought. *I don't want to go through any more hell over him.*

'Will you stay there – in New York?'

'For the time being. After Tally died I just wanted to get away from London, but now I've really got things going . . . There's an immense future for our company in the States. It's expanding very fast. A heck of a lot to do.'

'The Americans seem awfully good at business.'

'They are. It's tremendously exciting in that respect . . .'

He was suddenly looking less tired. 'The apartment is convenient, but I'm buying a house out on Long Island as well. Somewhere to go for the weekends, and when it's too hot in New York. It's rather a beautiful old place and pretty big, with a swimming pool and tennis courts.'

'How lovely for you. And Victoria, too.'

'And I'm considering getting somewhere in the West Indies eventually – for holidays. Antigua perhaps. Or Barbados. Or maybe the south of France might be better. A place like Les Rosiers.'

'It sounds wonderful.' Like paradise, she thought to herself.

'I'll send Victoria to boarding school in England when she's old enough – at about eleven, I suppose.'

'Perhaps I could visit her and take her out?'

'I know she'd enjoy that.' He smiled at her. 'But as a matter of fact, I had a rather different idea.'

'Oh?'

He set down his glass on the low table between them. 'I thought you might like to come to New York and be with us.'

'Goodness! I'd love to, of course, but I don't have any holiday due until the summer. And, anyway, I couldn't possibly afford—'

'I didn't mean just for a holiday.'

'I don't quite see . . .'

'I thought you might consider being more than a godmother to Victoria.'

'What do you mean?'

'I mean that I'm asking you to marry me, Flora. And please don't look so shocked or I'll begin to think the whole idea horrifies you.'

She shut her mouth and swallowed hard. 'It's just that I'm so surprised.'

'I'm sorry. I thought you'd be pleased. You see, I always thought you had some feeling for me . . . but perhaps I was quite wrong?'

He'd known all along, then. All these years.

'I do.'

Was he going to say that he loved her, too – that the scales had suddenly fallen from his eyes, or something of the sort? That when he had seen her again this time he had realized how much she meant to him.

'Well then? It makes good sense for both of us, doesn't it? And for Victoria. Don't you agree?'

He was smiling at her with his wonderful smile, waiting for her to speak. Waiting for her answer.

Epilogue

1969

The tide must be going out, because the sea was getting further and further away. As she walked across the wet sand towards the water, the corrugated ridges left behind felt all bumpy beneath her bare feet. She skipped over a patch of stinky seaweed, skirted a disgusting-looking dead fish, and then paddled about in the shallows where the water wasn't too cold and she could see what was underneath it.

She wasn't used to beaches, of course; back home she always swam in the pool. She wasn't used to tides and sand and seaweed and rocks. The waves came crashing in frighteningly sometimes, and the foamy water rushed up and swirled round your feet, trying to suck you back with it.

It wasn't very rough today, and the waves were only smallish ones with hardly any white on top, but she could still feel the water tugging at her feet. And the wind was blowing her hair, lifting it right off her shoulders, as though it was playing with her too.

She paddled in a little bit deeper, almost up to her knees – daring herself to do it – and then stood watching a fishing boat chugging across the bay. There were lots of gulls flying along behind, making a lot of noise, and some men moving about on the deck. She watched it go out of sight, round the

244

corner of the bay, and then paddled slowly back towards the beach.

Her godmother was still sitting against her rock on a dry part of sand by the cliffs. She looked up from her book and waved to her, so she waved back a bit to show she was alright. She quite liked her godmother, even though she didn't know her very well. She never forgot her birthday, and often wrote letters. She liked her much better than her London grandmother, who'd dragged her round shopping all day. The California one just sent weird presents.

Of course, her godmother had known Mama, and they'd been at school together long ago. She'd like to ask her more about that one day, when she knew her better . . . now that Papa never said very much about her any more.

She hadn't wanted to come on this holiday in England, which was supposed to be some sort of treat before she went to boarding school. It was a foreign country to her, and everything was different – the weather, the houses, the cars, the people, the way they talked . . . She could talk just like them, too, if she wanted, but she didn't want to do it all the time.

And what she didn't want, most of all, was to go to boarding school – especially not in England.

She kicked at the sand, making it spurt up in wet blobs. Papa was sending her miles and miles away, as though he wanted to get rid of her. And, of course, Betsy thought it was a wonderful idea. She'd overheard them talking about it one evening. Papa had sounded a bit worried, but Betsy had gone on in that silly voice of hers about how it would be the best thing for her, especially with the baby coming. The baby! That's all they seemed to care about these days. Fuss, fuss, fuss . . . Everything had been perfectly alright before Betsy came along, before Papa had gone and married her.

If Mama had been alive, she wouldn't have sent her to boarding school – she was quite sure of that. She'd have wanted her to stay at home in America, not go far away. Of course, they'd never actually known each other, but she knew she looked quite a lot like Mama – Papa had always said so, and she could tell it from the photograph that he'd given her in a beautiful silver frame. She had to keep it hidden away in her bedroom now, though, because Papa said it upset Betsy to see it about the place.

She kicked at the sand several times and then picked up some shells and threw them as hard as she could towards the sea. The water had gone even further away now, so the tide was definitely going out. When it had gone as far as it could go it would turn round and come in again. And it would knock down the big sandcastle that the others were busy building.

She quite liked the other children, though she wasn't sure if any of them liked her much, except perhaps the eldest one, Ben. He was only six, but if her twin brother had lived she'd have wanted him to be something like Ben.

Dr Baxter was a sort of grown-up Ben – rather kind, and always making jokes. The whole family was always laughing about something. It made her feel envious, though she wasn't quite sure why because they didn't seem to have much to be envious of. Their house was alright but it wasn't very big and it only had one bathroom, and no swimming pool, or tennis court or anything like that. And the car was a funny old thing.

She could see Dr Baxter digging away with a spade, piling the sand up to make the battlements really high. He'd told her he'd proposed to her godmother about ten times before she finally said yes, but he must have been joking about that, too, because they were always so lovey-dovey together. Betsy was never like that with Papa. All she cared about was shopping. The others were busy filling buckets with sand. They'd build turrets and towers and make a big moat all round the castle, with a causeway across to the entrance. And when it was all finished, they'd stick a flag on the top – the English flag, of course – and it would flutter away in the wind.

Her godmother had put down her book and gone over to the sandcastle. She was helping the littlest one to fill a bucket and Dr Baxter had stopped digging to watch her.

Ben had headed off towards the rocks. He was climbing

across them much faster than she could manage, scrambling barefoot, like a monkey. She watched him bend down and look into one of the pools left behind by the tide. They had pretty little fish and weeds in them. In a moment, perhaps, she'd wander over and take a squint herself. That's if he didn't mind. After that, maybe she'd go and give a hand with the sandcastle, even though there wasn't much point.

Only a week left before she had to go to boarding school. The trunk was all ready, full of that horrible uniform that she'd have to wear. Papa had given her a Parker fountain pen and a red leather zip-up writing case with her initials across one corner: V.A.F.D. He'd kept saying how much she'd like boarding school and that it would be a wonderful chance to make friends with other English girls, but she didn't care about doing that. They wouldn't like her, anyway, because she wouldn't be like them.

She kicked another blob of sand into the air and trailed slowly across the beach in the direction of the rocks, aiming more kicks every few yards as she went.

As she got nearer, Ben looked up and saw her. He waved his hand, beckoning, and then stood up and shouted with his hands cupped round his mouth. His voice reached her faintly on the wind.

'Come on, Vicky . . . There's a *huge* crab in here. Come *on*!'

She walked a little bit faster towards him.